Also by Martin Booth

Fiction

Hiroshima Joe
The Jade Pavilion
Black Chameleon
Dreaming of Samarkand
A Very Private Gentleman
The Humble Disciple
The Iron Tree
Toys of Glass

Non-fiction

Carpet-Sahib — A life of Jim Corbett
The Triads
Rhino Road
The Dragon and the Pearl

Edited Books

The Book of Cats
(with George MacBeth)

Adrift in the Oceans of Mercy

Martin Booth

POCKET
BOOKS

LONDON · SYDNEY · NEW YORK · TOKYO · SINGAPORE · TORONTO

First published in Great Britain by Simon & Schuster, 1996
First published by Pocket Books, 1997
An imprint of Simon & Schuster Ltd
A Viacom Company

Simon & Schuster Ltd
West Garden Place
Kendal Street
London W2 2AQ

Simon & Schuster Australia
Sydney

A CIP catalogue record for this book is available from the British Library

ISBN 0 671 85466 6

Printed and bound in Great Britain by Cox & Wyman Ltd, Berkshire

for Alex and Emma

There is one spectacle grander than the sea, that is the sky; there is one spectacle grander than the sky, that is the interior of the soul.

Victor Hugo

Not a hundred metres away, across the paddock in front of Pyotr's wooden cabin, stood a copse of firs.

All around the trees were the allotments and vegetable beds of the villagers, the city families who visited only in the summer, and old Anikushin's wild patch which he rarely tended save to guard the thistles for the butterflies and make sure the heads of the rank grasses provided sufficient seed for the birds. He was the bane of Pyotr and the rest of the miniature agriculturists because once the butterflies had sipped his nectar, they flew over and laid their eggs on everyone else's cauliflowers or potatoes. The birds, having denuded the grasses, turned their attention to the beetroot and carrot tops when they had polished off those caterpillars they could find.

Why no one had ever felled the trees was one of life's ironic little mysteries. Their shadows cut the growing hours from the ground, their sharp needles were useless as mulch and their cones attracted squirrels out of the forest. They would have been better cut down and fed into the stove. Yet no one touched them.

That is Russia for you, Pyotr used to say. The idea is there but the will to do something about it is entirely lacking. I shall get my axe and level the lot.

He never did. He talked about it but he balked at the act as if, by making the decision, he would condemn not only the trees to fuel but himself in the eyes of the others who would say, look at him, that Pyotr always taking the initiative. And, by his decisive action, everyone would judge him to be a potentially dangerous man.

So the firs remained and, no doubt, they are there to this day.

In the winters, their boughs became heavy with snow which, when it got too deep or the trees grew too tired, slid to the drifts beneath with a hushing noise like an old woman placating an unhappy child. For a few minutes on a still day, each avalanche hung a mist of crystals in the air. The weak winter sun, struggling to rid itself of the horizon, would glisten in them as clearly and as magically as candle-light in chandeliers of Venetian crystal.

At the height of the summer, when the air was hot and the sun never died, the firs stood like a dark green phalanx of soft rockets, their narrow noses pointing to the sky as if awaiting the thumb on a distant red button and the turn of the Armageddon key.

Yet they could never be missiles. There was not one iota of threat in them. They were not aimed at New York, or Paris, or London; they were not intended for warheads. Instead, they were aimed at the moon, at Jupiter or the sun, at anonymous stars upon which, if they could reach them, they would bestow names.

Late summer and autumn, however, saw them at their best and it is how they were then I remember them.

In the evening, when I was through with my studies for the day, temporarily done with the intricacies of geometry and aerodynamics, formulae and equations, I used to sit on the porch Pyotr had built in front of his cabin. The earth, beaten hard and smoothed down with water to become as flat as floor tiles, was always cool underfoot and the roof of warping shingles above our heads kept the sky off. Hanging from one of the beams was a brass censer which he had acquired — *stolen* would be too strong a word — from a derelict church in some far-flung province where he had done his military service. In the censer smouldered a handful of fir cones and needles.

Those trees. They have their use, he would admit. If no one will drop them . . .

The sweet pungent smoke of the glowing embers hung beneath the shingles, giving the air an astringent tang of resin and holding the mosquitoes at bay.

We would sit with a bottle of vodka screwed down into a galvanized bucket of ice between us. There were no refrigerators or freezers in the village: indeed, there was no electricity. Yet there was ice throughout the summer.

Vitaly Menshikov, who claimed descent from the famous Alexander, Peter the Great's closest friend, adviser and aide-de-camp, and was therefore nicknamed Svetleishyi as his ancestor had been by Peter, owned the oldest cabin in the village. Beneath it was a deep cellar approached by a sloping tunnel at least ten metres long. The cellar, more of a cavern, had been cut by hand from solid rock. The walls were gouged with adze marks. No one knew its history nor cared about it. Like the firs no one bothered to bring down, it served its purpose and that was that.

Every February, Vitaly bundled himself into his winter clothing, shrugged on his coat of bear-skin which he had shot and cured and cut and sewn himself, bound his feet with rags inside his fur-lined boots and went to the river a kilometre away to cut one metre square blocks of ice from the banks using a rough-toothed saw. He dragged these to his cabin and slid them down the tunnel, packing them about with straw, dead leaves and sawdust he filched during July and August from the little timber mill in the forest near Lemovzha where they had a surplus which they dared not burn in the tinder-dry months.

Throughout the summer, he provided ice for those who requested it, selling it for a few kopecks or bartering for vegetables which he also stored in the cavern.

We used not to talk much. Instead, we sat and looked at the sky, the dark line of the forests our mothers had told us were never-ending, the vegetable plots laid out like a patchwork shawl spread over the earth, old Anikushin's insult to pastoral living, and Minarsky ploughing with a horse because he said a tractor was too quick and didn't fertilize the land as it went. And we drank.

When the sun got low, just before it dipped for an hour or two below the horizon, it cast an angled light over the land which struck the firs and seemed to penetrate their density. It hit the trunks, I used to think with my head still reeling with theorems and comfortably befuddled with alcohol, at an angle of eighty-seven degrees to the vertical.

The firs turned golden. It was not the sunlight, nor was it the sap in the bark. Nor was it, I am sure, a trick of the vodka.

The trunks seemed to be made of liquid gold with which they were not painted but ran as if, like an oil well, they were draining the metal from the earth and exuding it through their living derricks.

It never lasted long. Like a rainbow, the effect shifted as the sun travelled on.

Fill your glass, Pyotr would say, nodding at the bucket but never once commenting upon the wonder of the sunlight on the trees. Anna will be calling me soon.

She never did. She let us alone with a plate of *zakuski* — salted herrings, say, with a little oil, a small earthenware jar of pickled grapes or, if the air was chilly, some slav eggs — until the bottle was empty and the sky as dim as it was going to be.

It occurs to me now, knowing I shall never see those firs again, Pyotr did not put his axe to them because he relied upon them for the summer provision of pesticidal cones and needles, because he knew I was captured by the magic of their brief beauty and because, perhaps, he was afraid if he brought them down there would never again be any gold within our lives.

❦

I no longer count my life in months, weeks or days.

It is not practical, for my existence has ceased to be measured in sunrises and sunsets, but in the context of a time continuum starting from 00:00:00:00. It is as if I was born at zero and that creation began for me then.

To this moment, the digital counter reads +171:15:36:57 precisely. It indicates, since zero hour on launch date, I have spent 171 days and the stated number of hours, minutes and seconds in space.

From zero to +37 days, I was accompanied by Vladislav Cherkasov, Gavriil Asanov and Stepan Kukolnik. We had flown up together, four happy men who had smiled into the television cameras, chatted to the president, waved to the massed ranks of what had once been the Politburo, sent messages to our wives or sweethearts and generally put on a good show for the audiences. Gavriil had floated his pencil over the notepad, Stepan had turned a somersault and Vladislav had read a book suspended weightlessly before his face. I spun a pirouette about my long axis which would have been the envy of every dancer in the Bolshoi.

The plan had been we should replenish the space station with supplies and remain on board for fifty-one days, carrying out allotted tasks and experiments before returning to Earth, changing over with the next working party. However, at +36, it was announced the mission plans had been amended and three of us were to return immediately, one staying on to maintain the systems and make up the numbers of the next crew. Larionov, second in command of the relief team, had suffered a broken arm in a training exercise and there was no one else considered suitable to take his place.

Or so we were told.

We drew straws. More accurately, we drew self-tapping screws. I drew the one with the crossed thread.

So I have remained.

At first, I was informed by mission control at Baikonur it was only a matter of days before the relief trio would join me. I puzzled over this: a matter of days was a vague statement. Surely, I considered, they would have had an exact time already worked out to the minute if not the second, a specific window in time and space when they would press the button, launch the rocket, setting it on its trajectory to meet with my craft, as accurately as two hands coming together to pray. Yet I put this quandary out of my mind. The boffins knew what they were doing, I reasoned. I accepted there must have been contingency plans.

There were none. I know that now.

In the days after the others' departure, I was kept busy with hourly transmissions, wake-up calls, umpteen observations to take and report, endless batches of data to relay back to mission control but, gradually, these reduced.

It was not noticeable. I could not say, at +55:01:24:00, there was a change in mood, a marked slackening of orders, a sudden abatement in tasks to perform or data to record. They are not such fools, those little faceless men squatting in front of their monitors, watching orbital projections, checking telemetrical read-outs and crunching numbers; nor are their superiors, their breasts heavy with medals, their shoulders bedecked with stars.

No: for certain, it was all planned. I must have been, for days, the sole subject of discussion at a thousand meetings in a hundred offices where cigarette smoke marbled the air and the samovars were kept on the simmer in the corridors.

They did not want me panicked into doing something rash, acting out of emotion rather than logic, out of self-interest rather than preserving the national dignity. It was always impressed upon us there were others listening to our transmissions, assessing and learning, eavesdropping and understanding, spying and prying.

Gradually, excuses came to be made. The launch vehicle

had developed a malfunction; the weather was inclement; the window on catching the orbit was lost; there were spots on the sun likely to disrupt radio communication; the re-entry window was closed. Initially, every one of them was feasible but, little by little, they became less tenable, more technically orientated, further from my field of knowledge so I was unable to verify in my own mind the veracity of each claim.

Underlying every excuse, every bit of information, every technical apology, was a fading of hope. I could tell they were, bit by bit, giving up on me. Over fourteen days, I discerned an infinitesimal change of tone in the voice of the radio communications officer. He was usually ebullient, following on his orders or instructions with a jokey phrase, a passing comment about the recent success of Dynamo Moscow or his local ice hockey team.

And, bit by bit, there was a shift of tone. It started off filled with hope and assurance, went through phases of hope and reassurance, promises and confidence until it wound up as matter-of-fact. For a time, one of the communications officers was a woman. Unlike the others, who always gave me their names, I never knew hers. She did not last long. Perhaps the launch control superiors were afraid her voice might give more away. There again, perhaps she was just temporary because her male counterpart had broken a bone, or caught the flu or been bitten by a rabid monkey outside Archangel and sent to Tashkent to recuperate.

I would have accepted their excuses. I was no longer fooled. The reality had dawned upon me long before the woman was replaced by a gruff, efficient-voiced male whom I imagined to have crew-cut hair. He, too, was anonymous.

How little they knew me. A glance at my psychiatric records, my psychoanalytical dossier would have confirmed what I have known all along. I am not one to be shaken. I am at all times fully aware of what I am doing, conscious of my motives and alert to all the possibilities available to me.

At the start of the mission, we were in touch hourly, sometimes more frequently. As long as the other three were with me, it was at least every other hour, more often if we were conducting an experiment. Now, they contact me only when I call them.

They are hoping I am dead. Gone from the TV news, gone from the consciousness of men. Or, at least, waiting for me to die. To them, I am like a mad relative locked away in some asylum in a distant city, not forgotten yet not wanted, never visited but always remembered on birthdays or parties or anniversaries. I would bet a hundred roubles they speak of me in the past tense, always avoiding my name.

I am a state secret not to be released, not to be given to the media, to the public, to the Americans.

What was the phrase they used to apply to a criminal, a buffoon, an idealist or a man who was caught in the wrong place at the wrong time and sent to the labour camps in Siberia or tucked away above the Arctic Circle? A non-person. That was it. I am a non-person now, erased from the tomes of history, air-brushed from the fading photographs of the past.

As sure as hens lay eggs, I was in the wrong place at the wrong time.

Since +156, I have not bothered to communicate with ground control. They can offer me nothing and I am no longer inclined to speak to them. Let them think I am dead. It is what they want.

❧

Whilst I was sleeping, a tiny fault occurred in the AM/EVA cooling loop. It was not serious. A nylon washer had developed a minute crack, perhaps from being tightened just a little too firmly on installation, and was leaking. I addressed the problem by lowering the pressure of the nitrogen in the number 8 tank of the WMS, drawing the water into the tank, shutting down the loop, removing the washer and wrapping it around with a small spiral of foil torn from the edge of the aluminium honeycomb on the ECS fan muffler. With the washer replaced, I allowed the water to flow once more and carefully monitored it by tying a length of cloth around the site of the leak.

After an hour, the cloth is still quite dry so I assume the fault has been rectified.

For some time now, the spacecraft has been experiencing a number of minor faults none of which have been beyond my capability to patch up but which have been a cause of some frustration.

On occasion, I wake after a rest period to discover a screw or nut floating in the centre of the cabin. This necessitates a hunt – which can go on for an hour – to locate where it has come from and to replace it.

A fuse governing the lights in the top row of switches on the Attitude and Pointing Control System control panel kept blowing. I repeatedly removed it and checked it: it was the right fuse for the job — one and a half amps. Eventually, out of frustration rather than anything else, I removed the panel facing and studied the bulbs in the switches. The third from the left was too bright and was drawing too much current. I removed it and the fuse has not blown since.

One of the foot restraints in front of the urine collector has snapped. Made of nylon webbing, I have attempted to sew it up but the nylon mesh simply unravels further and the thing breaks again. This is awkward. In order to urinate, I need to have both feet anchored firmly to the deck so my hands are free to place my penis in the collector and operate the control. With only one foot anchored, I tend to drift a little and have to keep a tight hold on the switch to maintain position. This, in turn, is putting pressure on the switch mounting which is becoming loose. If it should break I shall be, as one might put it, considerably inconvenienced, being obliged to operate the switch with a pair of pliers or rig up some makeshift stopgap.

None of these petty malfunctions or disintegrations bothers me. When they first began to occur, not long into the mission, the ground staff were animated in their concern. The four of us were obliged to inform them of every single loose screw or stretched strap, every failed fuse and torn waste disposal bag. After the others left me, interest in these inconsequential nuisances waned and only drew a response if they were of a major variety.

The one event which did draw much attention was the bending of the starboard discone antenna. This item is a thin jointed arm which protrudes out from the exterior shell of the craft for some ten metres into space. At the tip is a small dish antenna about the size of a large dinner plate. It permits a clearer space-to-ground radio transmission by sending and receiving the signals at a distance from all the electronics of the spacecraft which can cause interference and static.

How it was bent is a mystery. No other part of the craft's exterior was damaged or missing so it could not have been hit by something else breaking off. There was no debris in the vicinity of the craft during the period when the damage occurred. I heard no sound of an impact, felt no jarring in flight: the onboard inertial guidance computers registered no shift of course, which would have been realized had the vessel been hit. The communications officer on duty — a man with a broader sense of humour than the one with sporting interests — suggested it might have been a bird strike.

Through one of the observation ports, I could see the arm. It was bent at right angles suggesting some not inconsiderable force had struck it, but I could not hazard a guess as to its source. A piece of space dust the size of a sugar cube, travelling at the speeds they do, could puncture each of the multi-layered skins of the spacecraft. A tiny fragment no larger than a grain of sand might easily be capable of snapping the DA.

I am not worried by what is going on, the loose screws and the unwinding nuts, the odd rattle and squeak. All ships creak as they sail. If they were too rigid they would fatigue and split asunder like an unyielding tree in a hurricane.

Now ground control has no knowledge of what is going on up here, they probably think I have broken up, that the image on their radar screens is not a solid spacecraft but a collection of disintegrated parts travelling together through space, waiting to burn up.

Major Artem Kozyrev, the senior project officer, sits in the garden outside his *dacha*, a glass of vodka by his side and a jar of pickled mushrooms next to his elbow, looking up into the night sky. Behind him, he can hear his wife humming as she kneads dough. His children are whispering in the darkness of their room and the sleeping dog across his feet twitches in some canine fantasy.

Knowing my orbit, he watches for me to go by, a pinprick of light moving in a straight line between Cassiopeia and Ursa Major, obeying the dictates of irreconcilable mathematics which he assimilated, approved and programmed into the system.

Yet, in his thoughts, no matter how guilty he may feel, he cannot recall a vision of my face in his memory and he has difficulty remembering if my given name was Alexei or Andrei. Or something.

He hopes perhaps, because he is a man and prone to sympathy, I am alive.

❧

Pyotr had a dog. It was a mongrel, half German Shepherd and half (possibly) Borzhoi. He was a most peculiar-looking animal, his tail feathered with straggling fur, his ears capable of being pricked up. Pyotr called him Bujan.

When he was not sleeping in a corner, looking rather like a sheepskin rug tossed aside during spring cleaning, he wandered about the forest chasing squirrels and being chased, on occasion, by wild boars. Rarely, he would return with a hare. Despite his ancestry, Bujan's mouth was as soft as a gun-dog's. Any prey he managed to get was unharmed but sopping with canine saliva when he delivered it to the cabin, dropping it in front of Pyotr where it remained frozen with fear, its wide eyes starting out of its skull with terror.

Whenever I think of Bujan, I am taken back to those idle summer days when the air was motionless and warm over the fields along the forest edge where Zoya Kuteeva, the farmer's widow, pastured her four cows and a bullock called Yedinorog which she kept out of sentimentality. It had only one horn, hence the name. She milked the cows, having one of them inseminated on a rota every spring. On the last occasion I visited the village, it was Milka's turn. She was fat with calf and spent half the night lowing mournfully in a lean-to far across the fields, up against the trees which were a thick black line drawn between the silver moonlit grass of the meadows and the silver-speckled, velvet sky.

One afternoon in the final year of my training, Pyotr and I were sitting outside his cabin. We were not talking. He was reading a much-thumbed and badly duplicated copy of the opening fifty pages of Solzhenitsyn's *One Day in the Life of Ivan Denisovitch*.

It was not a matter of the book being banned: Khrushchev himself, it was rumoured, had many years ago given his personal permission for publication. Besides, neither of us would have embarrassed the other by reading dubious literature in the other's company. The truth was, even though books were heavily subsidized and printed in large numbers, we could not find the whole volume in the bookshops so we were tapped into a reading circle. This was not so bad unless you received the last pages of a book before the first. The pleasure of reading was then removed but replaced by the enjoyment of teasing others who had received earlier material.

I was struggling with a particularly difficult exercise. I hated it, but the advanced navigation examinations were only a month off and I had to be up to form. Even Ilya Golubev, who spent his nights touring the bars and chasing elastic, as we used to say, had achieved a higher grade than I had. To direct my concentration and ease my torment, I looked up from my work but the fir trees caught my eye and imagination took over. I should have been a poet rather than a pilot.

Tell me, Pyotr suddenly said, seeing my mind was wandering, if you were in Shukhov's place, what would you chop up first for firewood?

I was dragged back from my reverie.

What? I asked.

Which would you burn first? The chair or the table?

I don't know what you mean.

If you were in a labour camp. In Siberia. In Kazakhstan. And it was snowing. And you were cold and the fire was going out and there was no kindling and you were feeling the ice move up your fingers and numb your toes, which would you burn first, the table or the chair?

For some minutes, I thought about it. The table was useful to eat off and you could sit on it. On the other hand, a chair eases the body after a day of labour. I was about to say the chair when I recalled my grandmother's words.

The table, I declared.

Why? Pyotr enquired.

Because, I replied, my grandmother said the chair was a sign of being civilized. She had not had one until she married and it was a signal to her of becoming more than a peasant. In the labour camp, it would be important to retain one's civilization.

The chair! Pyotr retorted with exasperation. Really! If it was me . . .

His words were halted by a distant thrashing of branches and leaves just inside the forest. We looked up, squinting in the sunlight. It was too early in the year for bears to be making sorties into the fields.

A low branch whipped aside and Bujan appeared with something dark, striped and larger than a hare in his mouth. He was running quite fast but only as fast as was necessary. He was a Russian dog.

What's he got now? Pyotr mused aloud.

Once he reached the open ground of the vegetable plots, Bujan slowed to a steady trot. Even from a distance, his step had a lazy pride about it. Once or twice, he cast a glance over his shoulder in the direction of the trees.

He was making his way past Anikushin's patch of rank weeds when I saw what the dog's burden was — a wild piglet. Its bristles were dark olive brown with black stripes, its ears pressed flat against its skull. The head and front feet hung down to the right of Bujan's jaws, the rump and little straight tail with its terminal tuft dropping to his left.

Bujan! Pyotr called, seeing at last what his dog had caught and putting down the duplicated pages. Bujan! Come here, boy! Come on, come on. Come here. Good boy!

The dog lolloped across to the cabin and stood before us,

unsure what to do next. His eyes were bright with canine accomplishment. The piglet was flecked with dog spit.

Drop it! Pyotr ordered but Bujan just stood there like a boy apprehended stealing apples and too stupid or surprised to rid himself of the evidence.

Pyotr pointed to the ground. Bujan finally got the idea and gently lowered the piglet to the beaten earth before our chairs.

Anna! Come and see this! Pyotr called out. Look what the daft mutt's found this time. He turned to me. You'll stay for supper? Anna's suckling pig . . . He pursed his finger and thumb and kissed the air between them.

The piglet lay on the ground. It was unmarked save by the white slaver. Its little Japanese eyes were open but blank with terror. Its mouth was slightly ajar, its ears still flat. The movement of its ribs as it breathed was barely discernible.

When Anna saw it, she raised her hands in exclamation then patted her apron.

Good boy, Bujan, she praised the dog. Good boy.

Bujan sidled up to her, his tail wagging and his lips drawn back in an ingratiating canine smile.

Is it dead? she asked Pyotr as she tousled the fur on the dog's nape.

Dead? With Bujan the hunter? Pyotr looked up at the heavens. Well-mouthed. Not dead.

There was a movement at the rim of the vegetable plots. The sow stood in full sunlight, her head raised in search for her infant. Her tusks caught the light, curving up from her lower jaw like an ivory sneer.

Anna! Gun! Pyotr ordered. He kept an old blunderbuss

which had belonged to his father, primarily to shoot squirrels for their fur and hares for the pot in winter.

Anna turned to go through the door. Pyotr stood up to judge the range of his shot. A breeze tickled Solzhenitsyn. I watched Bujan grinning. The piglet seized its moment.

In a split second it went from supine terror to full sprint. Its little legs were a blur under its body. It leapt clear over the shallow, metre-wide ditch which ran along the edge of Pyotr's allotment and sped through Knorozov's tangled barrier of hurdles and cucumber patch without so much as a missed step. It was so fast, my eyes could barely keep up with it.

Bujan carried on grinning. He seemed blissfully ignorant of his prey's escape.

Too late, Pyotr muttered.

The piglet reached the sow which flicked its head contemptuously at us and the pair disappeared into the forest.

That's fate, Pyotr declared. Russian fate, he added.

He squinted at the spot where the boar had vanished.

I am sure, he said after a moment, not taking his eye off the foliage, I would burn the chair.

❦

So what is this tiny spark upon which I sit between the galaxies, at which Major Kozyrev looks up to on a cold night? I am not a star-rider, one of those mythical creatures of Norse mythology. I am just a man: a special man, perhaps, but a man nevertheless.

At least for now.

This tiny spark I ride is known as *Mir IV*.

How ironic of our masters to choose that particular name!

The Americans called their spacecraft *Challenger*, *Endeavour* and *Columbus*. We called our first *Salyut*. And what does it mean? I will tell you. It means either *Hello there!* or *Firework display*. Hardly exercises in imaginative naming. Now we have *Mir*. *Peace* or *World*. What ingenuity!

The trouble is, it had to be banal. If they had called it *Glorious October* they might have got away with it but they had to avoid such names as *Leningrad* because the Muscovites would have complained; if they had christened it *Stalin* the Marxists would have complained and if they had called it *Trotsky* the Stalinists would have kicked up hell. Brezhnev is too recent and Gorbachev or Yeltsin — well, who was to know how long they would last? The space station is meant to survive ten years. A politician is lucky to make ten months.

From outside, it looks like a scrap metal yard held in order by a mad sculptor. At one end is the cone of the docking device followed by a cylinder three metres in diameter. This expands gradually to eleven metres. Next is a spherical body rather like a very large septic tank and at the other end is the cone of the booster rocket which allows for a major change of orbit and large-scale manoeuvres. Small adjustments, re-positionings and tiltings around a chosen axis are achieved by little thrusters and boosters dotted about the rear engine cluster.

In all, *Mir IV* is big. Including the rockets, it is over sixty metres long, has a volume approaching two hundred cubic metres and weighs over forty metric tons. On Earth. Up here, it is the weight of a sack of potatoes.

Sticking out from it are four wing-like structures, looking for all the world like a massive, immobile ceiling fan: these are solar panels. Two others, at right angles to the septic tank, provide more power. Various antennae and brackets project out here and there, hand-holds for ground engineering or mid-flight inspections and the like. In all, there are seven windows dotted about the central cylinder of the inhabitable quarters: this means there is always one pointing to Earth and one to the depths of space. I can, at all times, position myself between the devil and the deep blue planet.

The interior of the craft is a large cabin lined with control panels, lockers, scientific equipment, food storage, preservation and preparation areas, personal stowage cupboards, a table and seats with lap-straps, work benches, medical supply kits, bio-telemetric equipment, lighting modules, computer banks, switch arrays, television and VDU monitors, ranks of control lights and, towards the rear, screens which may be drawn around the waste management area and the cubicle containing the urine and faecal collection equipment. On one surface hang the sleep restraints, like sleeping bags but without the padding and foam. Within the In-flight Entertainment Activities Locker (IFEAL) is a shelf with restraint bars holding a small selection of books: most of them are operating or technical manuals but there is a copy of Dostoyevsky's *Crime and Punishment* and a collection of poems by Pushkin along with an assortment of what are considered uplifting, politically sound novels. In addition, there is a Bible, a copy of the Koran and a paperback of *From Russia With Love* by Ian Fleming. How these latter got on board I cannot imagine: certainly neither I nor my erstwhile companions brought them aboard. Presumably, some recidivist joker on the ground crew smuggled them in, believing our reading matter was insufficiently eclectic. Every book is bound in fireproof covers.

Reading apart, we are allowed a few other diversions to while away the time. A cassette recorder with earphones sits in the IFEAL accompanied by a number of tapes of martial marches, Russian folk songs, balalaika music and, possibly courtesy of the recidivist again, a pirated copy of a selection of Beatle songs including one entitled *Back in the USSR*. Packs of playing cards are provided, printed on fire-resistant paper and shot through, rather as a banknote is with silver foil, by a thin steel strip which allows them to be held in place on the card retention surface in which is laminated a magnetic surface. There is also a magnetized chessboard and pieces.

Our physical well-being and need to play, essential (so the psychology instructors told us) to all creatures, are catered for by a number of hand exercisers made of sponge rubber-coated, steel-sprung grips, a set of chest expanders, a spring-loaded device for placing behind the knee and flexing the leg with and three pyrell hand balls, each of a different size but all dipped in ammonium-dihydrogen phosphate and coated with a thin protection of supple laminate. Astonishingly, the final item is a dartboard and darts. Of course, these are not pointed but fitted with blunt ends covered in velcro hooks whilst the board is a painted square of pile on to which they stick.

Food is plentiful: there are three months of supplies for four men. Likewise the water, which is treated with silver to prevent it spoiling and, purportedly, to give it the taste of that on Earth. As I can no longer remember how water tastes in a mountain brook, or for that matter out of a tap, this nicety is of little import to me. Air is sufficient, too: the ECS controls carbon dioxide, nitrogen and oxygen levels and there is some capacity to recycle CO_2 by breaking it down. Odours, waste gas, unrecyclable liquids and waste solids are vented into space: rubbish goes out through the waste disposal airlock.

Everything is ordered. The air may be cooled or warmed, circulated by fan, regenerated by filters, cleaned by scrubbers, electrolysed or magnetized to remove metallic dust particles.

I eat when I choose and I sleep when I wish. I drink as I feel thirsty and I breathe as I will.

There will come a time, however, as there must for every man who ever walked upright, or struck a flint, or forged a blade, or raised a sail, or flew the skies, when I shall run out of water, or air, or food.

It will come.

If I were to measure the number of food trays, packs of dehydrated meat, salt, biscuits, silver water, litres of dry oxygen, I could assess when I will die, a luxury of which most men are robbed. Save, of course, determined suicides who are the most efficient of prophets.

Yet I do not. Who needs to know? Predictability removes the spice of life and the beautiful bite of death.

❧

There is no day and there is no night. There is only the wide canvas of space painted with time.

On occasion, I like to move to the centre of the cabin and hang perfectly still in weightless suspension. Then, touching nothing with my movement, driven only by the beating of my heart, I day-dream.

I do not dream of objects, or memories, or fantasies. No faces appear which were once friends or enemies, no familiar buildings or old haunts loom out of the dark mists swirling inside me.

Instead, I dream patterns.

Now and then, these are formless, swirling mists like cigarette smoke drifting on the hot, fetid air of a beer cellar or cordite smoke hanging over a gunnery range on a frosty, calm dawn, lingering after hours of night firing practice. They marble and mix, meld and commix without a pause. I may be a part of them, an integral, shapeless thing moving with them, breaking apart and joining with other strands which, no sooner have we coalesced, than we break up again: I may be a particle in one strand of smoke, an atom shifting under this force or that, ever travelling with the indecision of Brownian motion.

Or the patterns may have distinct interlocking shapes like the bizarre pictures of a painter whose name now escapes me. Squares gradually metamorphose into lizards, flower petals evolve into liver flukes, angels unfold into bats, or birds into horses *en route* to becoming fish, pelicans mutate into doves then devils.

One of the most common of these pattern dreams is the sight with the sky filled not with stars of varying magnitude but of clocks. Some are vast, the size of the sun, whilst others are microscopic although I can still see them as clearly as I do the solar ones. Their faces bear Roman numerals, some with IV and some with IIII, Arabic numbers, Chinese numbers and dots like the hour divisions on a Braille timepiece. Although the cases of the clocks are always absent, I know them to be from wrist-watches, pocket watches, upright clocks, carriage clocks and station clocks. A particular face is that of the clock in the main office of the KGB headquarters in Leningrad: although now it is St Petersburg and the KGB disbanded, the clock remains — according to my pattern spread across eternity.

Another day-dream which is quite common, and which frequently succeeds the clock face one, is what I call the colour journey.

First, I see colours. Rich, deep, satisfying colours. Pastel, delicate, ethereal colours. Powerful, masterful, cruel colours. Second, I feel them.

It is not necessarily their temperature I feel, red being hot with blue cool and white cold, but their personality, their mood or emotion. For example, red is not hot tempered as one would expect but scheming, devious, intensely selfish; blue is flippant, light headed and as petty as a girl pouting with disappointment at the poor quality of a suitor's gift; green, far from being jealous, is warm hearted and generous to a fault. It is not unknown, I have sensed, for green to give so much away it loses all its own possessions and splits into blue and yellow of which the latter is sad, always ill and, appropriately, jaundiced.

These colour dreams are not new to me. I experienced them first when smoking opium on a fighter base thirty kilometres north of Kabul in the years when the USSR — as it then was — was embroiled in a pointless effort to shore up a sympathetic but weak and corrupt regime.

My first pipe made me vomit but the second, taken half an hour later, calmed me. I lay back with my head on a parachute pack — we were on standby at the time, flying Mig-31s in air support to the infantry Mil MI-26 helicopters as they flew troops into what was euphemistically termed 'an unfriendly zone' — and closed my eyes. The folded nylon material under my head seemed to rise up and enshroud me in its soft tentacles. They fingered me better than any whore in Samarkand had ever done. Then, when they departed, I saw and met the colours.

When I travel with these hues shattered from the prism of my mind, I think of how I would be with them always if I could, journeying through a multi-tinctured eternity.

There is a hymn I tell myself on those voyages, a few lines of poetry picked up along the narrow lanes of education. It goes:

> The One remains, the many change and pass;
> Heaven's light forever shines, Earth's shadows fly;
> Life, like a dome of many-coloured glass,
> Stains the white radiance of Eternity,
> Until Death tramples it to fragments.

I do not recall who wrote those words. Not a Russian,

anyhow. Russian poetry, I find, is somehow less profound — *Young bull, best of Georgian stock, I love your strong charge, but why do you gore and pace the soil so? Your horns hold banners . . .* — that sort of thing. Obvious, irrecondite and generally boring.

Whoever the poet was, he could even have been a cosmonaut.

He knew a thing or two about infinity.

When I wake from my weightless trance, I swing myself towards whichever porthole is facing Earth. I gaze down on the planet where I was spawned, from whence I rose like a resurrection of fire from a gantry of iron, and consider how everything down there is finite.

The horizon is an irreconcilable line over which, unless the observer sets off on foot or takes to the wheel to satisfy his curiosity, remains unknown. Houses hold men in, streets govern their movement, politicians rule their business and wives their whims. They are retained against their wills, and content in their ignorance, by a set of finite parameters. Just as the copse of fir trees before Pyotr's cabin, which he would never fell, blocked off his view of the Moskalenko family's cauliflower patch, so did they restrict his imagination, his dreams, his world.

Up here, where there are no streets or houses or horizons or politicians or women or fir trees, all is immeasurably, exquisitely infinite.

❧

Mark!
+175:09:44:00.

I have just finished the last of the meals in the second crew member's food storage locker. This means I have consumed exactly fifty per cent of the provisions on board. From this, I am forced against my will to calculate I am half-way towards the boundary between being and not being. At least, around the half-way point: a man can survive a long time without food: it is water he must have in regular abundance.

No matter. I'm not interested in such exactitudes. It is just a vague way point, not so much an accurate ground beacon on the flight towards mortality but more a ragged mountain range which affords an ill-defined intimation of the distance travelled and the distance yet to go.

Each meal is pre-packed into an aluminium tray, not unlike the prepared meals one receives flying in the economy cabin on passenger aircraft, and a day's ration ensures a certain pre-assessed nutritional intake: 800mg of calcium, 5500mg of sodium, 1600mg of phosphorous, 375mg of magnesium and 125g of protein in addition to the average requirement of carbohydrates, vitamins, fats and minerals.

The meal — a breakfast — was not exceptional. I began with a can of rehydrated, reconstituted orange juice. It tasted weak, like orange cordial mixed by a miserly mess bar steward. The next course was sliced bacon in aspic.

Every meat dish, save the pâtés, is packed in either brine or jelly, partly to preserve its quality and partly to retain its moisture content. The result is a bland taste but it is a considerable improvement upon the freeze-dried cubes of jerky which was all we were issued with on my first space flight. That was atrocious. Preparation involved rehydrating it under pressure and heating it before swallowing it down with gulps of water. The meat invariably had a salty flavour and a slightly rubbery, striated texture. Petrenko, the commander of my first mission, said it was like eating shredded condoms.

After the bacon, I discovered the third and final course consisted of a tube of apple and rhubarb purée, not unlike the mush mothers feed to gurgling infants. This I followed, finally, with a rehydrated sugared black coffee. I have discovered if I only half depress the trigger of the hot water gun in the centre of the food table, and put in just a third of the suggested quantity of water, I am able to make a fair imitation of thick, sweet Turkish coffee.

I heated the bacon, which was accompanied by button mushrooms, in the microwave warmer. The cabin filled momentarily with the scent of the smoked meat: however, before I could become morbidly nostalgic, the detector on the ECS sensed the odour and turned the fan on high, sucking the smell into the activated charcoal filters, neutralizing it.

To feed, I have to sit at the food table, held in a seat by means of lap restraints. The meal is clipped into holes or slots on the table surface and each tin or dish has a fine plastic membrane over it to prevent the contents drifting off. Everything is consumed by use of a spoon and little pusher, rather like the trowel the *aficionados* of bonsai trees use to till their miniature arboreal plots. Drinks are sucked up through a straw.

There is little room for variation except in the case of the purée. With this, I pick up the tube but instead of squeezing the contents into a membraned container, I squirt them slowly into mid-air where they hang like a soft, flexible ribbon before my face. When the tube is empty, I release the lap restraints and allow myself to float slowly into the string of purée, letting it into my mouth as I go, like a length of fragile, coloured spaghetti.

So it is, by these tricks, a cosmonaut is reduced to little more than an infant in its high chair or a cat with a dead mouse.

He plays with his food.

Perhaps, if my one wish were fulfilled, if I was treated, like a man should be, to a tall glass (or tube: I am not fussy) of good Russian beer — a Baltyka, say — or even a western beer such as the Schlitz I was once served when a member of a delegation visited by American astronauts, I would abjure these infantile pastimes and regain a little of my masculinity.

❧

During my last leave before setting off on this — as it is turning out — last mission, I went one evening to St Petersburg to visit the grave of my parents.

One's motivation behind any such posthumous visit is

obscure. Nothing can be gained from it. The laying of flowers means little: the dead cannot appreciate the colours of the blossoms, the texture of the petals, the perfume. Indeed, they are utterly unaware of the presence of the blooms or, come to that, the one-time mourner. They are little more than an arrangement of calcium and trace elements in the remnants of a cheap pine box a metre or two under the ground.

In the summer Smolenskoye cemetery, on Vasilyevskiy Island between Maly Prospekt and Ulitsa Beringa, is a vast, unkempt wilderness of silver birch trees, dense undergrowth and forgotten headstones wreathed in ivy. Untended pathways cut through this urban forest, trodden no longer by weeping mourners and stiff-faced undertakers, sobbing children and bearded priests but by lovers looking for cover, old crippled women walking their dogs and people who prefer a long walk to a jam-packed tram taking a short cut to Birzhevaya Ploshchad and the Dvortsovy Bridge to the old city.

In winter, the place is barren, covered with a metre of grey, urban snow through which the tree trunks poke like silver-painted electric power poles blotched with rust or lichen. They say the fattest of St Petersburg's rats live here, plump on the provision of corpses which are interred in the cold months of darkness, buried deep in the ground and purportedly desiccated and preserved by the chill. I always considered this to be a legend of urban life, like the police dog said to have eaten two KGB officers on a stake-out in Kolomyagi, until I travelled into space. Those damned cubes of anonymous meat we were fed might well have been prepared in exactly the same manner as nature fixed the dead of St Petersburg.

To visit the graveyard in winter is pointless. Nothing can be found under the snow. In summer, it is easier. The graves, where they stick up above the foliage, serve as landmarks, the blotched marble or granite acting as guide-posts like those along the edge of snow-bound roads.

My parents are buried about two hundred metres north-east of the point on Ulitsa Beringa where some enterprising entrepreneur of the *glasnost* era has removed a five metre length of the iron railings, cutting them from their concrete base with an arc torch. Their grave is marked only by a low stone bearing their names but it is just a metre or two to the west of a distinctive tomb, the cross on which has lost one arm, the angel beneath it its nose. This damage is not due to vandalism but to the poor quality of the stonemason's materials and the bitter frosts of countless January nights which can split stone as easily as a spade cuts earth.

Finding the grave is the simple part. What is not so easy is getting to the place, for this is the largest part of the cemetery not to be served by pathways. To reach the spot, therefore, I have to hack my way through snatching briars, ferns, saplings, bushes and rank grasses. Silent birds flit ahead of me. Once, I saw a fox in there, nuzzling into a large bag it had almost certainly filched from the tourist hotel at the end of Ulitsa Nakhimova: the label on the bag read *Aeroporto di Roma — Duty Free* or somesuch.

If this was the forest near Pyotr's cabin, my clothes would be snagged and my skin nicked or stung by nettles but nothing more. Yet here, before I reach the approximate area of the grave, my cuffs are soiled, my trousers besmirched and my skin greyed by the filth clinging to the leaves, the grime of diesel fumes and smoke, industrial fall-out and the dust of a million people being swept out of apartments, stairwells, offices and shops. How sad it is, I always think as I struggle through the bushes, even in death the citizens of Russia's second city and one-time glorious capital cannot escape the common dirt of life.

On that last visit, I reached the grave after ten minutes of trampling and hacking away with a military issue sheath-knife, the sort handed out to the tactical attack units in Afghanistan. Finally discovering the stone, I cleared the weeds off it with swipes of the blade and sliced the tendrils of ivy off at the roots. I did not tear them free of the stone and, of course, no sooner had I cut them they were planning, in their slow vegetable subterranean way, to renew their assault on the meagre memorial.

My father's name is slightly darker than my mother's. She died several years before him so her name has weathered longer. He was called Pavel and she was Natalia. They have been dead a long time now.

With the grave cleared, I sat next to it on the soft humus of birch leaves and briar twigs. I did not speak to my parents as I sometimes saw others do at their family tombs. I did not whisper or even say a prayer inside my head. No one hears such things. I merely sat quietly, perhaps out of respect and perhaps out of a need in myself I could not identify and was afraid to address.

The sun went lower in the sky, the dappled beams moving higher up the birch stems. Squirrels skipped through the branches, keeping to some invisible highway of their own devising. A cat slouched into view, padding carefully through the dry arboreal debris: when it saw me, it halted, stared at me in the malevolent way felines have, then slunk off into the deep shadows of a fallen, ivy-strewn tree trunk.

It was well into twilight when I heard the voices. They were not preceded by any cutting or slashing sounds, just the gentle swish of branches, so their owners must have known of another route into this thicket of the long departed.

Judging from the conversation, there were three men. They drew to within ten metres of me then halted. Their voices were low but I could still eavesdrop upon them with impunity.

So, how much have you? one voice enquired.

Three, maybe four.

Deutschmarks? Dollars? Ks? What?

This third voice was impatient, annoyed.

Ks. Three Ks minimum, four maximum.

Let's see . . .

There followed two metallic clicks which I took to be the sound of a briefcase being opened.

Where did you get them?

There was no answer.

Come along, comrade, where did they come from?

It had been some time since I had heard anyone address his fellow as *comrade*. That is a habit which has died out. What was more, on this occasion, it was not said with any sense of solidarity: it reminded me of the way KGB officials spoke to a man whose collar they had felt. *Comrade* was not a title of fellowship but an ironic accusation.

Polyustrovo.

Polyustrovo! They still had some?

They still have. Maybe another six, seven Ks.

One of the men whistled quietly. A nondescript bird over my head responded then dipped away into the gathering darkness.

How much?

Three hundred per K. Dollars.

Three hundred! You crazy?

There was no reply.

Two twenty. That's our offer.

There followed a brief period of haggling but the man with the three or four Ks remained adamant, pleading he needed three hundred because of his hidden expenses.

No deal, then! the impatient voice finally cut in. Take them elsewhere.

There was a brief silence.

Go try your luck with the touts on Nevskiy Prospekt.

The briefcase catches snapped shut.

Don't waste our time again. Go on! Get the fuck out of here!

There was a shuffling of branches as, I assumed, the man left.

Then there was a sudden loud rustling as if a quick wind was momentarily sweeping through the trees. Mingled with it was a soft thump, followed by another, ending with a soft, prolonged hissing as if someone had punctured a tyre.

I waited. The shuffle of leaves returned then. Apart from the occasional snap of a twig or brief shuffle of leaves, there was silence.

After five minutes, when I deemed it safe to do so, I stood

up. A little way off, I could just make out in the twilight a depression in the bushes. I carefully made my way towards it, curious to see what had been going on. I made quite sure not to cut my path through: that would have made a passage to my parents' grave and, by proxy, to me. No Russian moves without a thought to the consequence: it is a training born of many years' caution.

In the little clearing which, judging by the litter of cigarette ends and packets, was obviously a frequent meeting place, lay a man dressed in black shoes, black trousers and a white shirt on which was pinned one of those dosimeter badges hospital staff or nuclear power workers wear to show the number of x-rays or roentgens to which they have been exposed.

He was on his back, his head turned slightly to his left. One hand was gripped firmly about a birch sapling the thickness of a broom handle. The fingers of the other twitched in decreasing spasms as if he was trying to make a fist. His eyes were open, and seeing, but that was all. He did not speak. His throat was cut right back through the oesophagus.

I did nothing. There was nothing possible. He was dying and I could not save him. I just looked down on him, avoided his last staring at the world he had known and made my way down the path his murderers had taken.

I left the cemetery by the entrance near the place where the tram lines turn round, not far from the petrol station. It was dark by the time I reached the street. The few street lights were on and the pumps in the petrol station were lit up like juke-boxes in a bar.

There were not many people about. Some office workers

walked by me, talking about their boss. A couple passed, arm in arm, the girl smiling at her lover and chewing hard on a piece of gum. When I reached Sredniy Prospekt, I came upon three sailors, very much the worse for drink, pissing in a doorway. They leered at me as I walked along, one of them shouting an obscenity at me which I did not catch in its entirety but it centred on what he thought of aviators. Quite how he knew I was a flier I could not tell for I was not in uniform.

By the time I reached the Vasileostrovskaya Metro station, I resented the dead man his death. I had gone to the cemetery to be with my parents, perhaps for the last time, and he had ruined my visit with his refusal to accept a deal which had cost him more than he had bargained for.

I wondered what he had been selling: heroin, possibly, or amphetamines, penicillin, barbiturates . . . Yet it was academic. I did not care. All that bothered me was that he had impinged his death upon my life.

Now, as my craft shifts slightly in space and the black liquid crystal index numbers behind their little perspex window on the navigation panel flick by, I consider him again. I cannot remember his face nor any detail of his moment of dying, except his fingers clenching and unclenching.

What does occur to me is this: one of the first books ever printed — certainly one of the first thousand or so — was made in southern Germany a year or two either side of 1465. It is a tiny block book with coloured illustrations. Its subject is the art of dying.

Five centuries on, we still study it and have learned little.

Yet what we are so refined at now is the exquisite artifice of killing.

❦

How great men do fall.

When the final trumpet blows, we are all equal, regardless of rank and wealth. Certainly, some of us may have a mighty tomb set up over our corpse, or have massive statues erected to our honour in city squares and parks, by which posterity may remember us, or judge us, or by the destruction of which eradicate us once and for all from the corporate memoirs of humanity: some of us may be preserved in our catafalque to provide an icon for devotees and entertain tourists whilst grabbing their dollars. Yet the fact remains we are all equal in death. The commoner and the king, the serf and the emperor, the citizen and the tsar, all reduced to dust and a hole in the ground, all returned to the primal function of all flesh — that is, to give succour to the new.

We may make requests to soothe our consciences or prepare us for death, but they are incidentals.

Leonid Brezhnev ordered, not long before he died, that he be buried face down in his mausoleum.

Great expense was made to try to get him to change his mind. Politburo members tried to dissuade him. Communist leaders tried to reason with him. The party propagandists sought to change his mind. Pains were taken to keep this death-wish secret. After all, Lenin lay face up in his glass case in the Kremlin wall. It set a standard for the others who stepped into his shoes. Even Stalin, who had done more to injure Russians than any other single man — including all the tsars — lay in state face up.

Lying in state, that's all right, Brezhnev declared when once again prevailed upon to think twice. But being buried is another.

I heard this from Anatoly Bakulin, a first secretary in the space programme who worked in the Kremlin offices as direct liaison between the space administration and the Central Committee, and who was unfortunate enough to be delegated on one occasion to broach the subject with the great man himself.

If you will allow your face to be seen at the lying in state, comrade, why insist on being face down when no one can, in fact, see you in the coffin? he was instructed to ask Brezhnev. Under the ground, he added.

Brezhnev would not be drawn.

Perhaps, Anatoly confided in me one day when visiting me in the village, Brezhnev had a terrible secret of which he was mortally guilty.

Perhaps, Pyotr butted in, he was simply sick and tired of looking at Russia and contemplating the next five-year plan.

The truth, when Anatoly discovered it and reported it to me, was even more bizarre.

He made one last reference, under orders, to the posthumous wish: if he failed to alter the leader's mind the responsibility was to pass on to another unfortunate.

Comrade, he said tentatively one afternoon, will you not reconsider your testamental request?

He was at a loss as to how to phrase the matter: everyone before him had gone through most of the vocabulary in an attempt to discuss it. There was a fear prevalent at the time that to keep on saying the same thing over and over would infuriate the great man.

No, Brezhnev replied bluntly.

Anatoly took his life in his hands.

May I ask, comrade, he enquired deferentially, why you are so . . . He searched for a word. . . . so adamant on this point?

Brezhnev turned slowly towards him. Anatoly reported his heart skipped a beat then raced as the man's bushy-browed eyes settled firmly on him.

Certainly, Brezhnev said, you may ask.

Then he paused. Anatoly had a brief picture in his mind of snow-covered plains and recalled a Muscovite taxi driver who, assuming he was an out-of-towner on a trip to the big city, had once pointed out the Lubianka to him and asked, Do you know what that is?

Anatoly had said he did not, just to see what the answer was: this was in the days when the KGB was all-powerful.

That is the Lubianka, the taxi driver had explained. They say, he added, from the basement there is a fine view of Siberia.

You may ask, Brezhnev repeated, and I will tell you. Whilst I am lying in state, the people filing past me will see my face and be in awe of it. But once I am buried, they will want to spit in my face. If I am facing downwards, they will not be able to do so.

Anatoly was at a loss for words. This was not some

petty bureaucrat speaking. It was the leader of the Supreme Soviet.

After five years, Brezhnev continued, they will no longer want to spit in my face. They will see what good I brought to our country and they will want to praise me. Good luck to them! The way I shall be lying they can spend the rest of eternity kissing my arse.

Anatoly did not know how to react. His response could be interpreted so many ways. Luckily for him, at that moment, an under-secretary entered the room and Brezhnev was called away to attend a committee.

What did you do afterwards? Pyotr enquired.

I went to a bar, Anatoly replied, removed my uniform jacket and drank myself into a stupor.

Ever since Anatoly recounted his tale, I have wondered about it. Brezhnev must have been deeply worried. As Anatoly suspected, he must have had a guilty secret he did not want let out, which the face-down request was intended to cover up: the best way to fight controversy is with controversy.

Maybe Brezhnev was aware of the rumour circulating in China after the death of Chairman Mao Tse-tung and he shared a similar trait of character.

The word on the street was that, in his later years, Mao had a penchant for young dancers.

Throughout his life, Mao was an enduring reader of erotica: he had a library of thousands of amatory volumes, everything from the classics of Chinese literature, collected for him by a secret police specialist in the art, one Kang Sheng. His favourite was, from all accounts, *Jin Ping Mei* or *The Golden Lotus*. Even Mao's private apartment, the

Study of Chrysanthemum Fragrance, had been the Quing emperors' library of naughty books and he maintained a substantial collection of erotic paintings, pictures and photographs there, too.

All this was told to me by Anatoly: he had seen KGB documents on the subject, received in the diplomatic bag from Beijing.

In his twilight years, Mao became randier than ever. He filled the heated swimming pool of Zhongnanhai, the senior party officials' compound, with coveys of naked young girls with whom he rutted *like an old stag that's lost its antlers*, as was stated in the report at which Anatoly sneaked a peek.

As the saying goes, nothing is new under the sun: Lavrenty Beria did the same thing for Stalin, lining up tarts to tickle his moustache for him and there were those who provided an identical service for John F. Kennedy.

Yet Mao was fond not only of wooing but also of waltzing. Every evening, or so gossip would have it, a dance band would turn up at Mao's palace near the Forbidden City and set up its instruments. These were not *pipas* and *ch'ins*, *yangqins* and *yuans* but trumpets and trombones, saxophones and xylophones and drum kits. At the appointed hour, the band struck up and Mao arrived. Young teenage girls were drafted in, filled with the idealism of serving their chairman. Serving, of course, was the name of the game. Mao waltzed and tangoed with them in the clumsy way of an old pederast itching to get his fingers on — or in — a bit of fluff then, as the evening wore on, he made it known he would like to spend a little more time, *ex musica*, with a select three or four of them. Kang Sheng singled them out and led them starry-eyed through the corridors of power where the pillars and the walls were painted yellow and red as they had been in the days when the real emperors had favoured ladies stripped naked, wrapped in silk like a New Year gift and delivered to the imperial bedchamber on the back of a muscular eunuch.

Once there, the fat old Patriarch of the People, Hero of the Long March, Master of Ten Thousand Years, dropped his pants and had them one by one. Or they had him. Who can tell?

And what is the real joke behind all this? The real irony? According to Anatoly, Kang Sheng was an agent, one of ours, recruited into the NKVD in 1932. So much for great men: as they used to say, look at a great man and find a greater servant.

So, perhaps, Brezhnev had just such a sordid appetite and wanted it suppressed with other talk. I simply do not know, no one does. Or they aren't talking. A man with such a macabre wish might be able to rise from the grave and get his own back.

What I do know is, when my time comes, and it will not be far off now with me already in the +170s, I shall not be like Brezhnev with his fear of spittle, or like Lenin with his ten thousand statues, or like Mao Tse-tung with his teenage dancing girls. I shall be different.

The details of my death may not emerge for generations, for aeons, even. It may remain secret until, five thousand years hence, an archaeologist or historian grubbing about in the dusty, sand-filled underground caverns of a northern Oceanian province stumbles upon the files of the twentieth century in lead-lined boxes.

When the time comes, and the Cyrillic is deciphered, men will wonder where my body lies buried, where the thoroughfares were named after me or the squares where my effigy was put up on plinths.

They will read on, the decoders of history, these time-spies, and it will gradually dawn on them I have no tomb, no orgulous sepulchre, no cities bearing my name.

In time, they will realize my monument is the vastness of space, the open fields of eternity.

It will be then that they shall see I have become not a man in death but a god whose spirit has mounted the stars to spur on the bastard Lords of Time.

◈

During the last four hours, I have had the strangest dream. Not a colourful, abstract day-dream but a real sleep-time fantasy.

When I became tired, I slid into my sleep restraint, zipped up the front and closed my eyes. I do not have a pillow: my head floated without gravity far more comfortably than it ever did in a terrestrial bed and I abjure blankets because the Atmosphere Control System maintains a cosy temperature in the craft. My going to sleep is registered by the computer through the biosensor I attach to my arm and, as I sleep, the ACS adjusts the environment accordingly. I can, when I wake, demand a read-out of my metabolism and bodily activities to check my health.

As a general rule, each sleep period lasts for about

four hours: on Earth, it was usual for me sleep the eight hours demanded by the average human but here in space my biological clock is disrupted by the change in diurnal/noctural time-span rhythms and I find I only need half that amount of complete rest every thirty-one hours.

According to the read-out, I experienced my dream 38.7 minutes before waking. My heart-rate and respiration increased significantly and my SEO, Singular Electrical Output, soared.

The dream was not, of course, captured by the equipment.

At first, I was aware only that I was a man. Walking along a well-lit corridor, people smiled at me. A few bowed as I reached a heavy door at the far end. The walls of the corridor were hung with paintings yet though I thought I knew them I recognised not one.

By the door were two guards. They wore uniforms but, once again, I paid them no more attention than I had the paintings. One of them, I think, saluted me but not in a military fashion. He used some other technique I cannot now recount.

Once the door was opened, I entered a long room. The floors were made of white marble flecked with gold, the walls were ornate and painted white with gold-leaf decoration, whilst overhead hung a massive chandelier shattered with the light of a thousand candles. Or they might have been microscopic suns: this image occurred to me as I walked slowly over the floor.

A flunky of some sort suddenly appeared to my left front, although whence he had materialized I could not tell. Certainly, there were no side doors to the long room which, I now appreciated, were lined with mirrors in which I could not see my own reflection, an omission which slightly panicked me.

Ahead, at the far end of the room, was a throne-like chair on a low dais covered with a vermilion carpet.

A hand reached out to me, wearing a white glove, flecked golden like the marble. The flunky flicked his fingers lightly against my chest. I looked down. He was brushing loose hairs from a rank of medals. I noticed, without really taking it in, I was wearing what appeared to be some sort of naval uniform. It was cut in dark blue serge with gold rings on the cuffs and gold epaulettes on each shoulder. My trousers had a gold stripe down the outside seams. My shoes made no noise as I stepped over the marble even though they were highly polished military-style boots.

Cats' hairs are a devil to remove, the flunky remarked. He picked one off my chest and I felt lighter for its loss, my step becoming suddenly sprightly.

On the throne sat a small man, his head out of proportion to the rest of his body, a peacock no larger than a parakeet perching on his right sleeve where his arm lay on the side of the throne. His upper lip bore a small, trim moustache no wider nor bushier than his eyebrows. His hair was wavy, verging on the unkempt.

Someone told me, or I might have informed myself, I was looking at Peter the Great.

As I was about to halt and bow to him, the chandelier caught my eye and I was that man sitting on the throne looking at someone who might have been me approaching across the marble floor.

Nothing was said. I smiled distantly and the man who

might have been me mouthed something I could not hear then vanished.

When I woke and unzipped the restraint I felt distinctly changed. For some reason, it was as if I had acquired a kind of power, a supernatural ability which made me particularly potent, although in what sphere of activity I could not tell.

There used to be a saying in Russia. There probably still is. It came to me as I looked at the biometric readings on the computer screen. If you want to understand a dream, or exorcise it, or make it come true, you should tell it to running water.

I was not able to stop myself. Reaching for the switch controlling the transfer of water from one tank to the other, I flicked it over. Water began to move from tank 2 into tank 4 which was all but empty. I could see it through a length of transparent inspection tube set in the pipe.

And I recapitulated my dream.

After a while, the tanks were equalized in pressure and the water flow halted. The switch automatically cut out. A green light came on.

I was no nearer an interpretation.

Suffice to say I was, perhaps, for a brief moment in space, the embodiment of Peter the Great.

It occurred to me I might be going mad. After all, no sane man dreams he is the architect of modern Russia, who westernized his country, studied ship-building in Holland, obliged all his courtiers to smoke tobacco and placed a tax on beards, not to mention building one of the greatest of the world's cities on a bog.

At least, he does not dream it then ask silver impregnated

water flowing through a titanium pipe 400 kilometres above the Sahara Desert to explain the implications to him.

❦

Why are we as we are? So doggedly rock-ribbed, so resilient, so resourceful and yet so resigned to our fate. We being the Russian people, of course.

I often think of this, as my tiny star moves inexorably along on its orbit, turning slowly, showing this window to the infinite and this to the fleck of dust whence I came.

In a St Petersburg suburb, not far from the Piskaryovka railway station, there is another cemetery called Piskaryovskoye Memorialnoye Kladbishche. It is quite unlike that in which my parents lie under a rampant forest of disregard. This place has a grand entrance swept clean by brooms as well as winter blasts, no one has sought to steal the railings, the expanses of lawns are well trimmed and, in summer, the flower beds are filled with annuals. Loudspeakers hidden in the trees crackle out a faint and sombre music. The pathways are paved and weeded, the bold monument at the far end of the cemetery never without its flags and blossoms: I have seen roses standing in deep snow there, frozen stiff in −26°C.

I say lawns when, to be accurate, I should say oblong banks of grass a few feet high, each about the size of a tennis court: before them stand granite blocks engraved with a star and a date − 1942, maybe. Under each lawn − there are over a hundred of the things in twenty-six hectares — lie what is left of 6000 people, a week's toll in the 900 days of the Nazi siege.

When the blockade began, people ate their food reserves, then their cats and dogs, then the rats and mice (the few which were left) inhabiting their walls, then they became inventive and scoured the city for other things — paste of nettle and sorrel picked in the parks and open spaces, fish-bone sauce from the canals and the Neva, goose-feet hamburgers from those birds stupid enough to risk flying through the artillery bombardment and landing in the city. A squirrel or a sparrow was a gourmet's delight. Finally, they boiled their belts and gloves and drank the soup. The only food ration was a lump of brick-like black bread issued every day. It weighed 125g. Some people ate the corpses of their relatives or the lost dead in the snowy streets and it was easy to tell who the cannibals were: their faces were as pink as a pork butcher's.

Once the coal had run out, they burned wood. When the *burzhuika* got hungry again and the room grew chilly and the wood ran out, they burned first books, then furniture, then the floorboards they stood on.

Yet the guides still showed visitors round the Hermitage, despite the fact the pictures had been removed. Before empty frames, they described what had been there, as best they could, and the visitors tried their best to envisage them.

We have always been a nation of magnificent dreamers.

In his bare apartment with a desk, two chairs, a grandfather clock and a piano, Shostakovich composed his *Seventh Symphony — the Leningrad.* In 1942, people queued to buy a ticket and hear it performed for the first time. And they cried.

Who needs a war to test the soul, Pyotr once remarked, when you have a government.

Men sent to labour camps survived years of penal servitude, years of abuse, years of summers a month long and filled with mosquitoes, and winters eight months long and filled with pain. Women trudged the snow of provinces they hadn't even heard of in geography lessons, carting timber and carrying bricks until their fingernails were split to the quick and their eyes stung with cement dust. Yet they carried on in the hope a husband or a wife or a child or a parent might be out there somewhere waiting for them with open arms at the railway station, waiting to hug them when they had paid off their debt for a crime which, even if they understood it, they could no longer remember or give a sod about.

If that were not enough — the privations of war and politicians — there is the inherent character of the land. Bleak tundra, black mountains, frozen wastes, plains so hot in summer you scorch the soles of your boots, rivers so dirty the fish flesh is grey. In some parts, the caviare is spurned because it is contaminated with nuclear waste. The air is filthy, the streets are dusty, the tram cars run but they need a coat of paint and the roads have pot-holes in them which are so big and deep they should have names.

It is this punishment that makes us hard, makes us survive.

Our crime is not that we steal from our neighbour, or sell him heroin, or cheat him out of his apartment, or rig the prices or the vote, or vandalize his car, or kick his dog, or fuck his wife, or piss on his doorstep. It is something more fundamental, more ingrained in us and therefore far more damning.

Pyotr told me a story once, from the days when he was conscripted. It was at the height of the Cold War with the Americans — well, with everyone really, except perhaps Cuba, and who gives a shit about a sugar plantation under the command of a bearded farmer — and the army was being readied for war.

His unit was at a basic training camp not far from Minsk. Their sergeant was a man of vicious tendencies, as Pyotr succinctly put it. One night, as the soldiers were milling about in their barrack, half undressed, jibing each other, flicking bare buttocks with wet towels, talking of home and boasting of non-existent sexual conquests, the sergeant appeared at the door. The room fell gradually silent as it was realized he was there. Nervous glances were exchanged. These young men were more afraid of him than a squad of KGB operatives looking to increase their arrest record.

Evening, boys, the sergeant greeted them.

No one spoke. Better to be hanged for a flock of sheep than for a lone lamb. United they stood, divided they fell. Safety in numbers.

The sergeant cast his eye from one to the next. The conscripts looked down, riddled with a guilt they admitted but of which they did not know the source or reason.

Nice night, the sergeant commented. Maybe your last, you ignorant rabble of turd-sucking wankers.

Such a comradely thing to say, Pyotr interjected. A good Communist addressing his fellow socialists.

At that point, the sergeant lobbed a grenade into the room and adroitly slammed the door.

No one moved. The little bomb rolled across the floor, rattling on the boards. The pin was out. The detonator handle was doing its own dance in a different direction towards the stove against which it chimed prettily.

Still no one moved.

There was a loud hiss. A thin smoke started to weep from the grenade, a spark flickering at a hole in its casing. Everyone stared. No one ran. There was a loud pop!

It's a dud, someone whispered.

That was all.

The door opened. The sergeant reappeared. He strolled through the ranks of immobile, semi-naked conscripts, picked the practice grenade up and juggled it from one hand to the other like a pioneer group leader cooling off a potato he had just removed from the camp-fire.

Got some guts, then, he said quietly and left the barrack.

What did you do? I asked Pyotr.

Same as the rest. Bugger all. And I've been ashamed ever since.

Because you didn't throw yourself on it to protect your mates?

No. Nothing like that. The sergeant was right. They — I mean we — were a load of wankers.

So, what then?

Because I accepted the situation, Pyotr admitted bitterly.

So what is the crime of the Russian people? It is this. We accept our punishment. Whatever fate tosses our way, we are stupid enough to reach out and catch it and, once we have it, be grateful to the tosser.

Nietzsche wrote punishment hardens and benumbs, produces concentration, sharpens the awareness of alienation and strengthens the powers to resist. What rot! In truth, it breeds uncomplainingness and fosters a compliant acceptance of circumstance.

The maxim is, punish the people long enough and they will grow to seek their punishment, enjoy or be anaesthetized by it: and what more can a government require than a population which is asleep to their machinations but still does a more or less adequate job and pays its taxes.

As the Chinese proverb says, beat your child once a day. If you don't know why, he does.

❧

Just an hour ago (it is now +177:15:34:54 precisely), my orbit took me directly overhead Livny, 350 kilometres south of Moscow.

The orbit the craft maintains has an apogee of 410 kilometres, a perigee of 375 kilometres, and I encircle the Earth once every 89 minutes: it follows a circular, non-sun-synchronous, near polar track. The groundtrack repeats on a 71-revolution, approximately 118-hour, roughly five-day cycle. For ten minutes, nine times a day, I pass through the South Atlantic Anomaly, a region of intense radiation trapped by the Earth's gravity. Two passes a day take me through the northern trapped electron belt where both electrons and protons are present in high numbers. Revolutions 25 to 27 are long, 28 to 30 comparatively short. Consecutive orbits are about 600 kilometres apart at the equator, to the east of the previous: I am not on a fixed orbit but, over the course of my cycle, cover the whole world.

I am, therefore, getting more than my fair share of radiation bombardment and, for certain, the craft is becoming positively and inexorably radioactive. And so am I.

There is still a very thin atmosphere outside the craft. I am not in deep space proper but it offers virtually no protection as it does to the planet below.

It is strange to think it is summer below me. At this moment. In another half an orbit, I'll be over winter. There are no seasons up here in space. Time has little consequence save as a linear progression ticking by on the counter.

Livny appears as a small, darkish blot near the River Sosna, which feeds into the Don just beside a flush rivet on the edge of the hatch glass which was painted red. I do not know why. Possibly, this was the first rivet to be gunned into place. Or the last. Or, and this thought is not to be considered long, it is thus marked out because it is faulty but no one replaced it.

The river looks like a hair drawn across the land which is, from this altitude, flat and slightly golden coloured. The coloration is not uniform but predominant. It is caused by thousands of square kilometres of wheat-fields. Hovering over the land are strands of white cumulus clouds which, from my vantage point, appear for all the world like a fine mould growing across the surface of a mellow cheese.

The only difference is the clouds cast a shadow beneath themselves.

On a few occasions passing overhead Livny, I have tried to get the craft repositioned so I might aim the telescope at the town. With it, I might just be able to make out a few of the main roads or identify a few major features like the football stadium.

If I could pump up the focus, zoom in with the lens, I might just be able to distinguish Shura's house.

Somewhere in my personal possessions locker near my sleeping restraint harnesses is a colour photograph of Alexandra Netulzhilova. In it, she is twenty-five years old with a round, smiling face but serious eyes, auburn hair cut quite short and long, thin, musician's fingers which are useful in her work for she is a dental technician. Her lips carry a half smile. In the background is a rowing boat tied to a river bank — the Sosna, as it happens, just east of Livny. She is leaning against a willow tree, one hand on the trunk with the other on her hip. There is a certain defiance in her stance.

At this very minute, she is below me, poking about in some old crone's mouth with a suction pipe, or handing a stainless steel instrument of torture to her employer, Dr Miroshnichenko. He is muttering some platitude about the weather or the state of the wheat harvest or the swifts which have nested in the eaves of his *dacha* and mess all over the flowers he has planted against the walls.

We met, Shura and me, at a winter party in Moscow when she was visiting her brother Kirill, a student in the Academy, a year below my own course. He introduced us and, for as long as she was in the city, we met to have a drink together in a bar, or walk in the streets or skate in Gorky Park. She was a very good skater, lithe and balanced, able to cut a perfect figure eight into the ice, capable of twisting round at full speed whilst moving her arms up and down as if she was the dying bird in the finale of *Swan Lake*.

When the early summer came, and my examinations were over, I travelled to Livny to stay with her. It was not her home town. She and her brother hailed from Br'ansk where their father was manager of a textile factory, their mother a teacher of physics in a high school.

Her apartment was tiny, typical of the Stalinist era constructions. The floors vibrated to passing lorries and the walls were so thin, Shura declared, if the couple living next door had a screw, she stood the risk of becoming pregnant.

During the day, she worked at the dental surgery and I stayed in her apartment with the warm, new sun cutting through the window, reading Pasternak and Akhmatova, Gumilev and Mandelstam, Tsvetayeva and Ratushinskaya.

Shura was a secret rebel. Her choice of authors proved it.

In the late afternoon she would return, smelling of antiseptic mouthwash and soap. After a coffee together, she would change out of her white coat into a short skirt and blouse with gathered sleeves and we would leave her apartment to cycle out into the wheat-fields towards the river, the young seed-heads blowing in a warm breeze which lulled all Russia into a sense of false security.

The tracks through the fields were dry. Little puffs of dust spurted up from our wheels, birds erupting from the wheat as we drew near. Grasshoppers sawed and flicked ahead of us and, from time to time, a mouse would appear to scuttle dryly into the wheat stems.

We always went to the same place, where a path petered out by a copse of willows leaning over the river bank. An old jetty projected from under the trees, five metres into the river, with a rowing boat tethered to it: yet we never saw anyone come to sail in it. She would take her shoes off and, pulling her short skirt even higher up her thighs, would sit on the end with her bare feet in the water. Small fish came to nibble at her toes.

Are you never afraid of sharks, Shura? I asked her once.

Sharks? she echoed, absent-mindedly. No. Sharks live only in the ocean. We are thousands of kilometres from sharks.

What about pike? I went on.

Pike? she repeated again. What would a pike want with my toes?

To eat them, I teased.

No pike's so foolish, she answered after a moment's thought. He might like a toe but it has a leg attached to it.

She was always practical, reasoned. I suppose it came from her training as a dentist's assistant. Do not question, just hand over the drill, the pick or the hypodermic and ask not why.

After dabbling her feet, we would sit in the shade of the trees as the sun went lower, the long shadows moving across her legs. When the dusk began to gather, I would lie her on her back, and push my hand slowly up the inside of her thighs until I felt the tight resistance of her knickers.

She would wriggle a little so I could hook my index finger round the elastic.

Shura always liked to be touched before her clothes came off. It was a ritual with her. After fifteen minutes of gently bringing her excitement on, I would remove her underwear and she would unbutton her skirt and blouse. She never wanted me totally naked, insisting I kept my shirt on, but she loved to lie under the willows with her skin free. When I entered her, she always gave a little mutter and a frisson of electricity ran through her skin. I could feel it twitch against me, even through the cotton of my shirt.

As if the little charge was a signal, or a shedding of some inhibition I was never to discover, she applied herself to making love, raising her buttocks slowly off the grass and dried willow leaves, tucking her legs under my bottom and pulling me into her. She did not like to kiss whilst making love but she slid her hands along her belly and rested them there, feeling us coming together and moving apart, coming together and moving apart.

When we were done, and if there was no one to see her, Shura would walk naked through the standing wheat, the ears brushing gently against her glistening thighs, her fingers teasing them as she passed them by as if they too were potential lovers.

Don't they prickle? I asked her the first time she did this.

No, not really.

But they must scratch.

A little.

Then why do it? I enquired.

She thought for a moment, tugging up her knickers,

buttoning her skirt about her waist and tucking her blouse into it.

It's like walking in an ocean, she replied.

An ocean?

The wheat is like water. After love-making, my skin is touchy, alert. Alive. Walking in the wheat is like walking in strange water.

An ocean of wheat, I remarked.

No, she answered, raising one leg to slip on her shoe, an ocean of mercy.

In the darkness, we cycled back to the town, no lights on our bicycles and riding slowly side by side. Sometimes, we stopped off for a coffee and a piece of walnut cake in a small café in the next street to her apartment. Once indoors, she showered, then I showered, and we slept together in her narrow bed, close against each other and yet, somehow, terribly apart.

For over a year, we corresponded but, as time went by, her letters became fewer and I was increasingly involved in training.

She was, I think, in love with me. She said so a few times, under the willow trees, in bed, in her earlier letters.

As for me, I might have been in love, for a short time. With her.

But the truth was always that I was in love not with Shura but with eternity.

Yet I still think of her, every now and then when overhead Livny. But not too often. After all, I pass by in the firmament at least once a week and no woman deserves so much attention from a man who might become a god.

❧

I have experienced a serious malfunction in the spacecraft. One of the three Control Moment Gyros is intermittently failing.

It is a complex piece of equipment for me to repair by myself and, worse, it is a vital one. It consists of a constant speed gyroscopic wheel driven by a pair of double squirrel cage, three-phase induction motors, gimbal supported to provide 3° of freedom. An electronics package attached to the side positions the gimbals and controls the gimbal rate whilst an inverter assembly provides the power. The actuator pivot contains a direct current torque motor, a gear system and a tachometer to measure rate-feedback and the output shaft. The sensor pivots contain ball-bearing races holding the pivot shaft and a resolver unit which gives gimbal positioning data for caging, momentum management and control law computations.

Their function, put in layman's terms, is to spin at high speed and provide the forces required to control the whole mass of *Mir* in space by altering the orientation of the spin axis of the wheel. They simultaneously pass information to the central computer so it knows the exact orientation of the craft to the Earth and the Sun, working out the relationship between the two in conjunction with the Sun Acquisition Sensor, the Fine Sun Sensor, the Rate Gyro Processors and the Star Track Sensor. In other words, the gyros tell the spacecraft where it is and at what angle to the other bodies in space around it, allowing for adjustment when this is unsatisfactory.

This operation is not just one of aesthetic use. If *Mir* does not automatically roll every so often during the time it is in direct sunlight, one side gets too hot and that is dangerous.

It is possible to manually over-ride the system, to physically control the gimbal rate commands by means of a computerized address system but to do this means staying awake for thirty minutes in every hour which is neither practical nor possible. I may be a part of this machine but I am a human part, made of flesh not silicon chips, heart and lungs, not valves and bellows and fans. It is no more possible for me as a circumnavigatory cosmonaut to take over piloting my spacecraft than it is for a circumnavigatory yachtsman to remain at the helm of his vessel all the time. He relies upon self-steering gear and satellite navigation; I rely upon the gravitational pull of Mother Earth and three double gimbal hard-mounted Control Moment Gyros fixed at 90° to each other.

The first I knew one of them was malfunctioning was when I was woken three hours into a sleep period by a curt if muted warning klaxon. I struggled out of my sleeping-bag-like restraint and kicked myself through the cabin to the central control panel. The red outer hull surface temperature warning light was flicking on, off, on, in time to the wail of the klaxon.

I killed the sound before it split my head asunder and tapped in a temperature reading: the outer skin was 78°C. It should never go beyond 60°.

It was immediately obvious to me the craft was not

adjusting to spin when in sunlight, indicating gyro failure.

The related systems — SAS, FSS, RGP, STS — seemed in working order. No errors appeared, the computer had no record of failure data. Using the manual pointing device, not unlike the miniature joystick to be found on radio-controlled model aircraft transmitters, I was able to manipulate the various pieces of equipment into an incorrect operating conjunction. Setting them back to automatic under the central computer, they instantly returned to the right condition.

As a precaution, I switched on a primary cooling loop. This functions as a radiator might in a car, running water through a series of pipes and heat exchangers just beneath the outer skin. The water heats quickly but dissipates at least fifty per cent of its thermal uptake when it reaches the cool side of the craft. It is just a stopgap. After ten minutes, it is no longer able to cool and starts to head towards boiling. Needless to say, that is to be avoided at all costs: a boiling radiator is one thing on a Zhiguli heading down a highway, quite another in *Mir* riding the highway to the stars.

At the first pass, the skin temperature dropped to 65°, affording me a breathing space.

I soon discovered one of the gyro readings was way out but that it had attempted to correct itself after about three minutes. When well on the way to behaving properly once more, the equipment failed again and triggered the alarm klaxon.

Very carefully, I removed the housing to the faulty gyro, positioning myself to look into every possible crevice. Floating weightlessly around it helped.

It was, I considered, conceivable a screw had come loose and jammed in the mechanism. Yet the motors seemed to be operating satisfactorily, humming quietly to themselves with the monotonic music of fine-tuned machinery. I studied every joint and surface I could for a missing screw or nut but discovered nothing untoward: there was not even a sign of undue dust collecting anywhere and, certainly, I could see no damage. The wheel was whirling at high speed and when I reached over and jiggled the little joystick, the gimbals moved smoothly.

The thought struck me then the cause was electrical, an occasional short circuit or failing transistor. If this was the case, I was in trouble, for such intermittent faults are all but impossible to trace. Unless one actually observes a failure occurrence, one has little chance of catching it, deducing its cause and rectifying it.

To cover my options, I carefully cleaned all the surfaces I could reach with the nozzle of the little suction device used for collecting loose debris and food crumbs which might have escaped the plastic safety covers. It was not a machine to use with impunity for, unlike the wife who accidentally sucks her wedding ring into the vacuum whilst cleaning the carpet and can retrieve it from the dust bag, once I have sucked something up it is gone forever. The rubbish is automatically vented into space by way of a flexible tube connected to a one-way valve on the waste management airlock.

Every *Mir* is equipped with a fat, ring-bound volume which is a complete in-flight technical manual. It duplicates what is in the computer help files if one knows what to ask for. I typed into the computer *Help: gyros failure electrical?*

and got back a screen full of data which scrolled for at least twenty seconds before demanding *More parameters/criteria*. So I reverted to the book.

Strapping myself into a seat restraint at the food table, I opened the book, letting it hover over the table surface as I worked through the index, poring over every page which bore a reference to the gyro systems and their interrelation with the SAS and the rest. Overhead, the bulkhead illumination unit shone coldly down, the neon light unflickering, casting dark shadows when I passed into the night section of my orbit.

When the sun rose again, after a night of half an hour or so, the light automatically dimmed but the craft did not adjust to commence its spin. I looked at the gyro wheel. It seemed perfectly in order.

There was nothing for it. For as long as I was in sunlight, I had no alternative but to take command and manually spin the vessel, making sure at the same time the computer was functioning properly and keeping the solar cell arrays facing the sun so the batteries were recharged.

The book offered little suggestion but one line caught my eye. It read, *If no apparent fault is traced, check induction motor input voltage — see XII-43*. I turned to page XII-43. The voltage input should be 16v DC. I rummaged in the locker where tools were kept in clips or racks or little polythene boxes with plastic zip-strips. At last, I found a simple voltmeter. Unravelling the probe wires, I floated across to the gyro over which I had not replaced the housing in the hope of maybe seeing a spark jump or hearing the hum change pitch. Wedging my feet into hand-holds on the bulkhead to give me a firm stance,

I tentatively put the probes on to the power cable. The ammeter drifted in front of my face.

16 volts.

I tried again, repositioning the probes.

16 volts.

Suddenly, the needle momentarily dipped to 8.5 volts before returning to 16. I felt as joyful as a boy who has just scored a goal between two coats on the grass or finally worked out a complicated and esoteric theorem set for homework.

The fault was not with the gyro but with the power supply to it which was momentarily slowing down the rate of spin. This in turn was confusing the other systems and fooling the central computer.

My elation was soon dampened. *Mir* has over 17,000 kilometres of electrical wiring. It could take hours, days even, to trace the cause of the failure. My only hope was to pray (even a good Communist prays at times: you only had to look into any orthodox church when the party machine was looking the other way) that the fault was not too far from the motor.

My grandmother, who I am sure in retrospect was in love with her local priest, once said, If you pray hard enough, you'll be answered. It's a way of calling for help. Keep it up and God will hear you.

I argued against this old wives' tale with the cold logic of a Communist youth studying hard at the certainties of mathematics, physics, chemistry.

It's true! she exploded after some minutes of rationalization on my part and mounting anger on hers. I've seen it.

You've seen it, *babushka*? I replied, feigning incredulity. With your own eyes?

With my very own eyes. These, she pointed to them to ensure I was not mixing them up with any others she might have had, in my head seeing you as clearly as a pig has a curly tail.

Deciding not to point out to her that most pigs had straight tails, I requested she tell me of this proof.

It was a miracle, she began, and I saw it with these, my very own eyes, when I was sixteen. It was while I was staying at my father's *dacha*. Not far from the house was a deep pool, an inlet in the river where all the children from the village gathered to swim and sometimes to fish.

Well, one day, I was there with my elder brother, Yvgeny. He was killed at Stalingrad, you know. Such a handsome, brave young man he was.

She glowered at me as if my looks, not being overtly handsome, and my demeanour, not being outwardly brave, were my fault. She never approved of me.

I wonder what she would think of me now, circling the Earth like an angel.

Anyway, she continued, he was fishing and I was watching him. Some children were in the pool, swimming about and diving. One boy, he must have been about eight, came near to us to dive in. My brother told him not to come so close to the point where the pool emptied into the river. Under the water, as all the fishermen knew, there was a sunken log, jammed across the narrow mouth of the pool. The boy, thinking my brother just wanted to protect his fishing, stuck his tongue out at us.

The log was oak, you know, she digressed. They pulled it out with a tractor after.

She fell silent.

After what? I prompted her. Her mind was beginning to go.

After the accident. The boy, unheedful of Yvgeny, dived in. His head hit the log and his body floated to the surface, face down. Eddies started to steal him out of the pool. My brother reeled his line and cast it at the boy. The hook caught in the boy's singlet. No one swam near naked in those days. Not like now.

She tutched and tutted at the thought of bikinis on the beaches of the Black Sea coast.

And?

And he pulled him in to the little mud bank just inside the pool. All the other children ran around. They started to come towards us shouting, but then they fell silent. Yvgeny rolled the boy on to his back. His face was pale. Blood oozed out of a nasty gash in his hair. Just then, there was a shout. Running across the field was Mr Glushko. His hat fell off. It was a straw one. Lots of farmers wore straw hats in those days. They wove them themselves. Or their wives did.

What about the boy, *babushka*? I asked.

Well, he was very still. Ashen faced. And the blood was running on to the mud, mixing with it.

What did you do? I enquired.

Do? Do? I prayed. I prayed the boy would wake up and stop bleeding. Then Mr Glushko reached us. Push his ribs, Yvgeny, he bawled at my brother even though he was standing right there. Up and down, up and down. Like a blacksmith's bellows. Yvgeny did as he was told.

Mr Glushko knelt down and started to suck and blow on the boy's mouth. In less than a minute, he was coughing and retching. The boy, you understand, not Mr Glushko. He was panting for breath. So! It was a miracle.

It was artificial respiration, I said. We were taught it at school.

She was thoughtful but only for a long moment.

It might be *artifiscal resprotion* now but when I was a girl, it was a miracle and God's answer to my prayers. Besides, she went on, what about the finder's glass?

I was almost prepared to give her the benefit of the doubt. Whenever we mislaid something — a pen, a bunch of keys, an object we had just put down — she used to make us take a glass from the cupboard and, putting it on the table, turn it upside-down. Within minutes, we would find what we had lost, even if we had already spent an hour looking for it.

Whatever the veracity or efficacy of prayer, I had not spent ten minutes on tracking the failure when — there it was. At one point 16 volts flowed, at the other 9. Between the two points was a side cable coming in from the Redundant Electronic Support Package (RESP) not fifty centimetres from the motor.

This is a duplicate of the circuitry operating the current to the motor. In theory, if the Primary ESP breaks down, the RESP cuts in and a warning goes to the computer to inform the systems management software — and the cosmonauts — what has happened so they may take restorative action to the PESP.

I looked hard at the RESP. It appeared to be in order. I compared it with the diagram and notes in the manual. The fault was obvious once one knew where it was. The

RESP is controlled by a dip switch not much larger than the head of a matchstick. It should have been placed in the down position before launch but it was in the up. Some arsehole of a ground technician had overlooked it.

With the end of the positive probe from the ammeter, I clicked it down.

The motor changed its tune. What it had been humming was a dirge compared to the merry hornpipe it now took up.

I put the ammeter away, replaced the gyro housing and lay down in mid-air. I felt my heart racing.

The orbit progressed. As *Mir* moved into sunlight once more, the whole craft began gently to roll.

I was saved but reminded that another similar fault or two and it will be the end.

Ten minutes later, I met a small self-tapping screw drifting along in front of the food lockers.

The sobering realization dawned on me. *Mir* was dying, just as I was dying. Screw by nut, bracket by circuit, cell by cell.

❦

What am I most afraid of?

What a question! Every man asks it of himself yet I would bet a shoe to a shallot not one in a million finds the answer. If he should stumble upon it I am certain he ignores or pooh-poohs it, or pretends it does not exist and rides it by in a quandary.

For some it is disease, the terrible fear of the joints seizing with arthritis, the fingers so gnarled and painful that gripping the spoon to eat mashed stew is a chore requiring courage and determination. Alternatively, it is being crept up upon by Alzheimer's disease, waking one morning to be unsure who it is leaning over to mop your brow or turning you over to wipe your arse. Or Parkinson's disease. It might be finding you can no longer have a woman after the surgeon has seen to your prostate, fixed your waterworks for you.

And what of love? There are those who dread losing love, for whom the worst fear is not having a friend, not having a woman who cares, not having a dog which wags its tail as soon as they enter the room, not having a face which smiles when they turn, not having a hand to hold when the roof of life leaks.

Bankruptcy scares all men, the dread of running out of money, of no longer having enough to purchase a packet of western cigarettes, or put petrol in the car or food in the family's mouths. Linked to this is the trepidation of losing the respect a fat wallet buys when the bar opens or it's time to buy presents for relatives at New Year.

Those who are thinkers or dreamers, optimists and kneelers, are most in awe of being robbed of the divine love of their god, to be cast into eternal damnation beyond the warming glow of the thrones of Heaven. And, conversely, they live in terror of the divine hatred of their god.

Be not fooled. Every god who preaches love has a hateful nature with which he keeps his deific balance. After all, what is the use of promising love if you do not threaten hate: consider the strict parent who offers a sweet to a child for doing good but guarantees a hiding if wrong is done.

If you want proof of the divine hatred, come with me. Glide across the cabin and press your nose to the window. Look down on the world and think of men wracked with malaria and children with famine-bloated bellies, of drug peddlers in playgrounds and whoremasters in alleyways, of kings in palaces and politicians in parliaments, of beggars in the gutters and murderers in the shadows, of the urban bomber and the soldiers with right on their side. Then you will know how hateful God is, how cruel He can be, how utterly blind He is to mercy.

Or, maybe, the greatest trepidity is simply one of losing control. Perhaps this is the nub of the matter, that what most men fear most is their individual inability to be in command of their own destiny, to steer their own vessel through the reefs and shallows, the hurricanoes and harbours of the seas of life.

Where I am concerned, no longer attached to the interstellar speck of rock from whence I came where God conducts His experiments in pain and hopelessness, and therefore divorced from the concerns of everyday planetary existence, madness is what engenders most alarm, most apprehension and brings me out in a cold sweat, for insanity makes you think you are in control when you are not.

And I wonder if, for a reason I cannot come to terms with, I may be going mad.

Over the last five orbits during which I have not slept I have, perhaps, been on the verge of madness. Not barking mad, not lunatically insane, gibbering and muttering and shitting myself. Nothing like that, nothing so obvious and, therefore, comprehending. Such a variety of insanity I can accept. This was something altogether different.

For those five orbits, I have had the intense feeling someone else has resided in me, owned me and run me.

My heart has beaten, my lungs have pumped air, my hands have obeyed my brain but, lurking deep within me, I sense there has been another who joined me during my last sleep period. This is, I know with all the logicality of a scientific mind, utter balderdash but it cannot dispel the feeling I am not always alone inside myself.

Whilst I was sleeping, I had no dreams: at least, none I could recall when I awoke. As I opened my eyes, I felt refreshed, alert, ready to go about the routine tasks of maintaining *Mir* in its orbit, of checking systems and observing the machinery which keeps me living. Yet, as soon as I started on my chores, I felt someone was watching me and that the someone was me.

The question is – who? For to be myself but also someone else is bizarre and puzzling, prompting a burning curiosity far greater than initial fear. Suspended in the sleeping restraint, I tried to work it out but came up with only one answer.

I was – or rather, a portion of me was – Napoleon Bonaparte.

This realization made me laugh aloud. I have no duodenal ulcer or chronic indigestion, no desire to unify Europe under the flag of France, no sexy Josephine to warm my bed, no stirring national anthem to hum in the bath.

The act of laughing aloud frightened me. I do not do that, not even to the most riotous, hilarious, bawdy barrack-room joke told to me when I'm in my cups. I smile, I grin, I laugh inside myself but I do not so much as chuckle audibly.

It was incredible. Once I accepted I was not physically

Napoleon, looking in the mirror by the personal hygiene facility situated beside the urine and faecal materials collection unit to check the fact and being instantly ashamed at the stupidity of the action, I began to feel a singular power swelling in me. It was like a charge of confidence, the feeling one gets on sitting down in a university hall, being handed the examination paper, opening it and knowing the detailed answer to every single question: or akin to the emotion one has the first time the wheels lift off the tarmac with the instructor in the conning tower, a pair of binoculars firmly pressed against his eyes.

I felt I was the master of everything, a mere flick of my wrist capable of eradicating — or exacerbating — every ill on the blue disc moving across the triangular window beside the left-hand experimentations console.

There was more than this, of which I was not a little afraid. Once I came to terms with the feeling, I thought I was beginning to enjoy it. Every man likes to be powerful and, if he could, rule with a fist of justice in the velvet glove of compassion. If I had enemies, I thought, they were doomed but my friends were safe and secure in the knowledge I had of playing fair by them.

A god might feel like this, a loving god capable of hatred when it was demanded of him.

The experience only lasted a few hours. As I entered the sixth orbit, I suddenly felt as if I was again alone, my face to the Earth and my back to the stars. I slipped back into the sleep restraint, dog-tired after so long without a moment's nap, yet I could not get to sleep. There was the utterly fallacious apprehension of dropping off only to wake a few more times round the world to discover I was wearing epaulettes and a hat like the gable end of a Ming dynasty house, my pants tight to the crotch and my hand pressing hard on my belly.

It is now +186:11:23:14. I am fighting to stay awake and losing. I know I shall not be able to avoid falling asleep soon. In another hour, I may cease to exist and cannot help thinking of Kafka and the man who woke to discover he was a cockroach.

Maybe this is the greatest fear a man can have, dozing off to find, when he awakes, he is a stranger.

❧

The communications equipment on board is understandably sophisticated. Apart from a short-distance intercom which connects the craft with the in-built spacesuit radios, there is a gamut of equipment for contact with the cosmodrome at Baikonur, the Co-ordinating Data-Processing Centre, the various relay stations around what was the USSR as well as the one positioned in Cuba, and another even installed in the Kremlin itself.

In all, there are six different systems: the primary equipment is a unified side band unit sending voice, television and telemetric data signals in either real or delayed time on 2265.6, 2198.4 and 2289.7MHz. Three VHF radios deal with voice and telemetry only while two UHF systems beam ground-to-space command or teleprinter signals at 450MHz. These are all military wavelengths but, that notwithstanding, any sensitive information is transmitted via a scrambler.

It has been some time now since the CDPC contacted me. At this moment, the digits register +190:07:18:31. My last transmission from them was logged at +156 and I have made no attempt to re-establish communication.

I may have been in a fit of pique these last thirty-four days, annoyed at their ignoring of me, a Hero of the Soviet Union (as it was), the cosmonaut riding the world like a jockey charging ten lengths ahead of the second-placed nag. Pissed off might be an adequate and more appropriate expression.

Yet I do not know, nor do I care. I no longer need them just as they no longer need me. True, I have been lonely but, after a while, solitude becomes not a burden but a luxury. Monks who cloister themselves away for years on end in Trappist monasteries know the feeling and I am in this respect no different from them save in that they meditate and mumble to their god whilst I speed around the Earth, a superman above all men.

Perhaps it was curiosity, therefore, which had me switch on the USB unit as I entered the northern hemisphere of my last orbit, where signal traffic is more easily picked up. It was not my intention to communicate but to eavesdrop.

Of course, I did not use the wavebands set on the machine. They would be filled with static or silence. Instead, I shifted the tuner to 2188.7MHz. This is the most commonly used communications frequency between Baikonur and other main space programme centres.

Below me, it was mid-afternoon. I could see the sun shining across the entire length of Italy, the peaks of the Appennines touched with the last vestiges of winter snow. There was hardly a cloud between me and the ground although Rome, Naples, Milan and Turin were hazy with pollution, as if someone had airbrushed them with a fine nozzle of grey.

At first, I picked up no signals at all but left the unit switched on, the speaker next to the flight control panel active. I hovered in the centre of the craft and settled myself to a session of day-dreaming.

The first colours were just commencing to swirl in my thoughts when the speaker came to life. The signal was quite clear, fading only once or twice as some anomaly in the atmosphere distorted it.

What I heard was a shocking surprise. They were talking about me.

I was listening in to a conference call between four people. They did not refer to their surnames but relied upon given names, except for one of them whom all the others addressed as *Sir*. Once it would have been *comrade* but times change.

The conversation went like this, the operator introducing the first speaker by stating, You're through, Pavel:

Pavel: Hello? Hello? Are we all now linked?

There followed a hubbub of affirmations.

Pavel: Might you like to start, Gherman?
Gherman: Thank you, Pavel. Well, to get straight to the point, we have a major problem with regards to Argonaut. Basically, we can't recover. Not in the immediate future.

It was at this point I came smartly out of my embryonic

reverie and pushed myself towards the speaker: Argonaut was my call sign.

There was an impatient cough, the deep and resonant sort a fat man in his late forties who smokes a lot makes when he's just got out of his mistress's bed, still breathless from unfamiliar exertion.

Gherman: It's like this, sir. We are operating under considerable fiscal restraint. The budget . . .
Sir: We may be able to find the necessary budgetary input. Don't let this deter you.
Gherman: Thank you, sir. However, we are experiencing other setbacks of a technical nature. Valya?

A woman's voice completed the quartet.

Valya: The last rocket we fired . . . It was carrying the earth resource package . . . It malfunctioned at 76,000 metres. The second stage afterburn cycle did not run its full course.
Sir: Use another.
Valya (after a long pause): There isn't another, sir.
Sir: Explain.

I could feel the tension between the four of them. Go back a decade or so and one of them was about to be invited to undertake a long vacation not a million kilometres from Zhigansk.

Valya: The rocket was the last, sir. Although we had planned to have two others available for the first of next month, this is no longer the case. The manufacturing complex has gone on to short-term production and the dismantling of missile systems. There is a shortage of spares and . . .

She paused. The air waves were pregnant with fear, anguish and suppressed anger. When she began again, she spoke quickly as if speed might somehow camouflage the truth of the situation.

Valya: . . . and the parts we have been receiving are sub-standard. The afterburn failure was caused by a seal breaking on a fuel injection vent on the left-hand thruster assembly. The ceramic ring was not manufactured to a sufficiently fine tolerance and caused a loss of pressure which in turn not only reduced fuel input but allowed seepage into the cavity between . . .
Sir: I know what happened. The damn thing exploded.
Gherman: Yes, sir. And this has left us with no reliable back-up.

There was a deep sigh from *Sir*.

Pavel: Another factor is we are under-manned in that we have insufficient cosmonauts trained to the standard necessary to take part in a relief mission.
Sir: What about Cherkasov or Kukolnik? They were returned from Mir.
Pavel: They . . . We have broached the subject, sir, but . . .
Sir: Hmm! I understand. So what you are telling me is Argonaut is expended.

I listened to this with a cool detachment. I have long ago considered this to be the case. Excuses, procrastinations, deviations, false heartiness — I have had them all and I have known what they have meant.

Pavel: In not so many words, sir . . .
Sir: Either he is or he isn't, man!
Pavel: Yes, sir, he is.
Sir: I see. Like that poor bloody bitch, Laika.

Charming, I thought, I have been reduced to the same status as a dog. Laika, which means *barker*, was a mongrel bitch sent into orbit on November 3, 1957 aboard *Sputnik-2:* she was the first living terrestrial to escape from Earth. The official report, which I read many years later, stated bluntly at the end, *It* (the dog) *continued in existence for 163 days.*

Gherman: There is another possibility, sir. We could ask the Americans for assistance.
Sir: This is not politically viable at present. Besides, despite the link-ups in the past, the docking mechanisms are not matched with the new Mir.
Valya: We might succeed in an EVA transfer, sir. If the craft were close enough . . .
Sir: Not politically viable.

There was a pause as this fact sunk in.

Pavel: We are also up against a time constraint, sir. We estimate Argonaut's LSS has . . .

Sir: It seems we are faced with an inevitable non-viable life situation. You cannot get a rocket together because the programme is short of money because the rouble has collapsed and the budget was overspent in any case. Even if I am able to raise a budgetary increase, you are unable to construct a rocket because the manufacturing standards of some key items have fallen due, no doubt, to trained technicians leaving the factories to earn more in private enterprise companies. And even if you could get a rocket together which worked, time conspires against you. As do the other cosmonauts. Am I correct?

Pavel and Gherman: That about sums it up, sir.

Sir: In that case, gentlemen — and lady — we are into a damage limitation scenario. Argonaut is lost but we cannot allow this information to leak out. The publicity would be extremely detrimental at a time when we are under intense public pressure to maintain . . .

The signal began to break up. I fiddled with the tuning dial but there was only static. I had passed over the horizon and could receive nothing more. Tapping on the keyboard, I tried a few more wavelengths but picked up nothing but teleprinter chatter and deep-space solar interference.

So that was it. I was to continue to circle the Earth on a non-sun-synchronous orbit until either the food, the water or the oxygen ran out, or the radiation got to me, or the spacecraft — to use the jargon — underwent a catastrophic malfunction.

The chain of socialism was broken. The louts in the factories had ignored their lathes, the state finance officials had fucked up, the politicians were listening to the public relations spivs and my erstwhile comrades-in-spacesuits had deserted me.

Well, I could hardly blame them, hearing that the last rocket had failed. Most of us have been cagey about flying with Aeroflot for the past few years: if a comfortable seat on an Ilyushin IL—96—300 from Moscow to Novosibirsk was cause for concern then a precarious perch on the pointed end of 800,000 litres of aviation kerosene, 1.7 million litres of liquid oxygen and 1.1 million litres of liquid hydrogen going from Baikonur to Eternity was not to be considered.

Well, what the hell! That's what I say. I shall face the future with impunity.

As Seneca advised us two millenia ago, and he knew more than a thing or two, fate guides the willing and drags along the reluctant.

So, take my hand, Seneca. Let's go. A waltz, I think.

I'll lead to the music of infinity playing its tuneless hymn.

❦

Pyotr has a keen, sometimes dry sense of humour and is always ready with a good joke or a fine story. He also hates Ukrainians.

On a number of occasions, when he has had it in for them, slagging them off and making quite crude comments about them, I have questioned him about his hatred. It is most uncharacteristic for he is not generally a prejudiced man, holds no racial views and can, at times, show a deep sympathy for those who are in trouble. He wept openly when seeing television news film of the thousands of people starving in Ethiopia and he becomes irate when he sees an injustice perpetrated against the innocent.

And yet, with Ukrainians, he has absolutely no sympathy at all. They were filthy, dirty-minded, ignorant, backward, uncultured, perverted, anti-social and (in the days before the Party had its wings clipped) anti-socialist. They stank of sweat, raw onions, coal dust and offal. They dressed in unlaundered and un-ironed clothes. Their women were obese, ugly, sluggish and frigid. Their men, he said with emphasis, were under-endowed in the trousers area, thick-skulled, dull-witted, lazy, obstinate and probably a mutation from a sub-species of man which had branched out from the tree of life carrying *Homo Erectus* in the days when evolution was shaping what humans are today.

Come on, I once remonstrated with him after he had finished venting his spleen and had a shot of ice-cold vodka from the bucket. You can't say they are mutated.

Oh! I can, Pyotr insisted. I can say or claim what I will.

This annoyed me. When Pyotr was this stubborn and unwilling to justify his words or deeds, I got riled. Without discussion there can be no assessment of reality.

Sensing I was cross, he refilled my glass and leaned back in his chair, balancing on the two rear legs, leaning against the rough logs of his cabin wall.

Let me tell you a story, my old friend, he began, one to perhaps sway your opinions.

I nodded and knocked back the freezing alcohol. The sun

was beginning to set and the fir trees were just thinking about turning to liquid gold.

There was this man, Pyotr said. His name was Nikiforov. The same surname as Privy Councillor Nikiforov. You know the one. In Dostoyevsky's novella. *A Nasty Story*. Except his name was Stepan Nikiforovich and our Nikiforov was called Ilya. And he was not a Privy Councillor or a writer. He was a ventriloquist. And it's a nasty story, all the same, too. About — no! Concerning a Ukrainian. Nikiforov was a true Russian. From Rybinsk.

A black and white dog with one ear torn wandered into view. Bujan growled but not ominously. It was more a clearing of his throat than a territorial statement. Pyotr reached down, almost tipping off his chair, and picked up a stone.

Go on, mutt! he shouted. Sod off from my carrots.

The dog ignored him. Instead, it started to angle to cock its leg on a taller than most clump of carrot tufts.

God damned Ukrainian dog! Pyotr muttered and he hurled the stone.

It was a flat missile, ideal for skimming off water. Pyotr's aim was faultless. It sailed smartly through the air like a small aircraft — a flying saucer, perhaps — and hit the dog squarely on its cranium, on the bump between its ears. The dog yelped, more with surprise than pain. Bujan, perhaps in admiration of his master's prowess but more likely because he saw he was being offered moral support by him, started to bark in a desultory fashion. The dog, looking peeved, sauntered off and, as if to prove a point and keep face, cocked his leg on the farthest corner marker post of Pyotr's vegetable patch.

Nikiforov, I prompted.

Yes, Nikiforov. He was a ventriloquist. He had performed all his life in the state circus, on television, in side booths at a hundred horse fairs and at a thousand Party officials' children's parties. Now aged fifty-five, he had had enough. It was time to retire. His wife was in support and together they decided they had enough money to purchase a house and a piece of land. There, they would raise hens and pigs, grow their vegetables and, with luck, become self-sufficient.

Buy a piece of land? A plot? I enquired. Surely you can't buy land? Anyway, would they not get an allotment from the state?

Pyotr looked hurt: he did not like his stories interrupted.

How do I know? Perhaps it was after *perestroika*. Perhaps the rules have changed. Perhaps it's wishful thinking. I only heard the story a few months ago. Anything can happen these days.

He cast a wary eye at the dog which was now at least a hundred metres off and sauntering along the path to the river.

Nikiforov started looking for a smallholding somewhere. After years of entertaining people, he wanted to get away from it all. But he and his wife could find nowhere which pleased or suited them. Until one Saturday. They were driving in their car over the hills north of Belgorod. You know the area? North of Kharkov. In the Ukraine, he added for emphasis.

By the roadside was a sign pointing up a narrow track. It read: *Small farm for sale*. He turned the car off the road and they followed the track for eight kilometres. At last, they arrived at a little house and stopped the car before it. It was idyllic. The front was lined by a deep veranda, the posts carved. The roof was made of shingles. The chimney leaned. A vine twisted over the door, hung with small grapes. Chrysanthemums and lupins grew against the walls. Several paddocks were enclosed by split log fences. Not a kilometre away was a wood. Not firs but deciduous trees.

They switched off the car engine. Peace. Not a sound of mankind. Birds twittered in the skies. The breeze was warm and sung a gentle melody. This is the place, Nikiforov's wife said. It's heaven.

The door to the house opened and a man of about their own age — say fifty — came out. Can I help you? he asked — in a Ukrainian accent. Is this the farm for sale? Nikiforov enquired. Yes, it is. May we look round it? asked Mrs Nikiforov. The farmer, who by his own admission lived there alone, set off with them on a tour of inspection.

At the rear of the house some hens scratched in the ground. Nikiforov winked at his wife — he had a fine sense of humour. Not unlike my own.

The rag-eared dog was returning in the direction of the carrot patch. Pyotr rattled the vodka bottle in the bucket. The dog took the hint.

What happened next? I asked.

Nikiforov turned to a hen and asked, What's it like here? And the hen replied — it was Nikiforov ventriloquizing, you understand — It's wonderful. We are allowed to keep some of our eggs and hatch them, none of us get our necks wrung and the cockerel perching over there on the plough is my great-great-great-grandfather. Well, the farmer —

the Ukrainian — gawped. I've kept hens for thirty years. They've never spoken to me. Well, said Nikiforov, I have a way with animals.

They moved on. In a sty was a pig. Nikiforov did the same thing again and the pig said, Marvellous! We get a boar come round once a year to mount us, we are allowed to keep all the female piglets and we are never slaughtered. That old sow in the paddock is my great-great-grandmother. Well, I'll be damned! the Ukrainian exclaimed. I've kept pigs for thirty years. They've never spoken to me. Well, replied Nikiforov, as I said, I have a way with animals.

In a byre stood a cow and Nikiforov did it again. The cow said, We are very happy here. We are milked every day and, once a year, a bull visits to tup us. We keep our calves although the bullocks go off to market. We get plenty of hay in the winter and wonderful pasture in the summer. The cow over there by the hayrick is my granddaughter.

Cows, too! the Ukrainian muttered. I've looked after a small dairy herd since I was fourteen. No cow's ever spoken to me. Well, replied Nikiforov, it's a gift I have with animals.

And so it was with the ducks which never had their wings clipped, and the cat which was given the cream in the pail to lick and was never hampered by mousetraps, and the doves cooing in the cote which were never prevented from taking their share of the pea harvest.

At last, Nikiforov and his wife were at the end of their tour of inspection. Or almost. Far across the fields, at least three hundred metres away, was a little log barn, close to the edge of the woods. What's over there? Nikiforov enquired. Oh, nothing, the Ukrainian farmer said dismissively. Nothing at all. Just a barn. Hay store. Firewood. Can we see it? Mrs Nikiforov asked. No, the farmer answered promptly, repeating, there's nothing over there. Just hay. Sacks of seed. Well, replied Nikiforov, if we are to buy your farm — and it is certainly exactly what we are looking for — we must see everything.

Pyotr paused, re-filling his glass, building up the suspense.

Well, all right, the Ukrainian farmer finally allowed, but whatever the ewe over there says, it's a bloody lie.

Pyotr downed his vodka in one and glowered at me to give emphasis to his opinion.

The firs trees were golden now, honeyed with the last rays of the sun.

So, you see? Ukrainians! he exclaimed.

Anna came out with a paraffin lantern and hung it from an old meat hook nailed to the roof over our heads.

You heard that story in a cabaret, I responded. Or in a bar.

No! As honest as that flame, it's a true story.

Yet he grinned.

You like Ukrainians really, don't you? I challenged. You just use them as butts for all you don't like in mankind.

Pyotr shrugged.

The Spanish hate the French, the French hate the Belgians, the Belgians hate the Dutch, he declared, and I don't like anybody very much.

You lie, I said.

Pyotr looked out across the vegetable patch at the firs. They were losing their gold fast.

Maybe, he admitted. Maybe not. That's your decision.

❧

Weightlessness in space gives a man a strange sense of invincibility.

It is not so much a matter of power because he is unable to exercise himself outside the confines of his spacecraft, save when indulging in extra-vehicular activity throughout which he is tethered to it like a foetus to its mother's womb. Indeed, the tether is referred to as the umbilical, carrying as it does a comms. link or oxygen line. It is more a matter of giving a man abilities about which ordinary mortals can merely dream.

When I was a child, I used to dream of flying. It was a simple matter. I stood quite still, erect as a lead soldier, took a deep breath, extended my arms in a crucifix, made a little jump with my legs, using my heels to push me up rather than bending my knees, and away I went. I could rise to an altitude of fifty metres. Beyond that, instinct informed me I would fall because there was insufficient air to swim in.

The action of flying was akin to swimming. I lay horizontal in the sky and, with my legs straight out behind me, moved forwards with a breast stroke motion of the arms, my hands working as paddles, the fingers close together. Unlike in the swimming pool at the gymnasium, however, one firm stroke could take me ten metres. By extending my arms, I could glide, whilst landing was merely a matter of swinging my legs under me and lowering them to the surface of whatever I wished to settle on – the ground, a branch, the roof of Leonov the tailor's house or Pyshnov the butcher's shop.

People below rarely saw me. Indeed, I can think of only a few instances in my many hundreds of nocturnal travels when someone looked up and exclaimed, Look! A flying boy! or whatever. They frequently raised their eyes — men study the clouds, judge the distance of the rainstorm, wonder when the sun will shine, catch a sight of a passing aircraft, look for the source of bird-song — but they hardly ever spied me.

That was mere fantasy. Now I do it for real. I am flying, in my metal tube, in the sky, in the weightless environment of the cabin and space beyond imagination or the ticking of clocks. What is more, people look up, millions upon millions of them, yet they never see me. Or, if they do, they do not recognize me.

Perhaps it has always been the case. They looked up but instead of seeing a flying boy they saw a bird.

Now, if they are lucky and the night sky is clear, they see a moving star.

Moving without weight is fascinating. I can do almost anything. Fly like a sparrow, cavort like a seal, twist like an otter, tumble like an acrobat, streak like a dart, spin like a dervish, twirl like a top or hang in mid-air like a swimmer waiting to drown.

There are dangers. I must take great care not to hit my head, damage some part of the complex instrumentation surrounding me, get carried away by the experience. I do not get dizzy. Partly, this is due to the athletics module of the cosmonaut training programme and partly to the fact there is no gravity to affect the inner ear which registers balance. I do get a headache on occasion, but it is caused not by the rush of blood to the brain but by the vision of metal walls and status lights flashing before my eyes.

Not only can I move with an incredible flexibility, but so too can I do other things an Earthbound human cannot.

Half-way through my penultimate orbit, I was obliged to go through the weekly house-cleaning routine.

Every time I use any part of the equipment which I might contaminate, I have to clean it: the urine and faecal materials collection unit, the waste processors and venting airlock, the food table, the cardiogram electrodes, the drinking water dispenser — all must be kept in pristine condition.

This is done with a series of wipes, moist pads impregnated with one of two disinfectants, zepherin or betadine. The former is used on items I might come into intimate or bodily invasive contact with, such as eating utensils or the electronic thermometer probe in the diagnostic evaluation kit. The latter cleans down surfaces.

Taking a pack of wipes, I started on the food table, leaving the door to the waste processing airlock open. As I worked, I crumpled each used wipe into a ball and tossed it into the airlock. It went in, unaffected by gravity, slammed against the back of the venting container and stayed there. The pack hovered next to my elbow. There was no need to even shift position to grab another. I was able to move to wipe the underside without any effort. How many Muscovite housewives, I suggest, would pull their own teeth to be able to have the dusters handy at all times, never bending to sweep under the bed, and never having to trot out to the dustbin five flights down in a grubby courtyard always infested with scabby cats and mangy curs except in the deepest of winters?

Apart from the convenience of always having what one wants in reach, I can play games with myself, too. When I change my clothes, I can actually position my overalls in mid-air then wriggle myself into them rather than tug them on. A game of solitaire is fun because the cards, with care, can be placed in suspension so the game, rather than being a two-dimensional activity on a table, becomes a three-dimensional positioning act.

Of course, I cannot juggle or balance anything on my nose. There being no gravity, the balls would not return and the ruler or book I might want to balance would simply drift off under the force of my breath.

There is, however, one weightless game I like beyond all others.

It is this: I take a spoon and, very carefully, place it under the nozzle of the drinking water dispenser. This equipment is devised in such a way that, in theory, one may drink without any liquid escaping: to have water, rather than vapour, moving about in an environment which is almost entirely dependent upon electrical power is asking for trouble. The dispenser, therefore, consists not of a tap but a miniature mouthpiece rather like that on a snorkel tube. To drink, the little oval guard is placed inside the lips but in front of the teeth: the plain drinking straw-type arrangement in earlier craft has been superseded after an accident. A switch is then depressed which delivers a predetermined amount of water into the mouth. The unit of measurement is presumably the metric gulp. Once this is swallowed, another may be obtained and so on until one's thirst is slaked.

The mouthpiece is detachable so it may be cleaned. Once removed, the end becomes a supple 4mm diameter nylon pipe. A flick of the switch delivers a small measure of water but at very low speed. If it was under pressure, it would make drinking difficult and unpleasant, like taking a draught from a hose turned full on.

By placing a spoon under the nozzle, I can collect a gulp. It sits on the spoon like a living creature.

As there is no gravity to affect the water, and as it has a surface tension holding it together, when I very slowly remove the spoon, the water remains in space forming a protean bubble, ever changing shape and colour as movements in the atmosphere or light coming from vents, the array of control panels or the windows, hit it.

When the sun strikes it, it explodes into shards of brilliance, more glorious than the biggest diamond or the grandest chandelier. Prisms of rainbow colours dance all round the cabin, a fantastic exposition of light ever shifting, ever seeking.

As they flitter and shatter, I sense a strange emotion, unlike any other I have ever known. It comes from somewhere very deep within me. My heart feels ready to burst as if with the most powerful love in the universe. My breath comes in bouts as if I had just been with Shura under the willow trees by the Sosna. My flesh tingles as if I had just dipped myself in ice from the middle of a boiling hot July day on the Kazakh plains. My soul is filled with a strange music the tune of which was written by God for his own orchestra.

In an absence of sunlight, the bubble of water seems to take on a coating of silver. This has nothing to do with the metallic content of the liquid but the way in which, if the sun is *in absentia*, the water rejects other light, reflecting it from its surface as if any other source was not good enough.

I can stay for hours and watch the glob of water as it lives its proud life waiting for the next orbit to bring it to its lover once again. Sometimes, I touch it, gently press my finger into it. It does not disintegrate but keeps its integrity, allowing my finger to move into it as if into the folds of a woman's body, softly enveloping it.

There is another aspect to this game which gives it an added edge.

If I lose my attention, if I let it drift too far from the centre of the cabin or, worse, if I allow it to fragment, I am doomed. It will strike a bulkhead, eke through a crack, squeeze through a cavity no thicker than a hair to seek out a bare wire, a circuit board, a fine array of relays, a naked fuse. Then, it will all be over. The sparks will prance, the wires will singe, the transistors will fume and the world will end.

But that moment is not about to come. Not yet.

When I have had enough of my little game, I swim through the air, like a flying boy, and manoeuvre my mouth round the bubble.

It is like consuming the heart of an atom, like swallowing a share of the sun.

❧

Whilst one of the VHF radios on board is capable only of tuning in to military wavelengths, the other two are able to pick up ordinary civilian transmissions. Admittedly, most of these are not clear and do not last for long. Anyone with a radio in their car knows VHF signals do not travel well above eighty to a hundred kilometres unless they have a relay or booster to recharge the signal. As there are no such beacons in space and I have an orbit, at its closest to the Earth, of 375 kilometres, it follows that anything I tune in to is transitional, usually not much over a few minutes long.

Ever since the others left me on +37, I have resisted the temptation to eavesdrop on the ether. It has been a conscious decision: just as the schoolboy away at boarding school does not telephone home for fear of prompting nostalgia, misery and homesickness, so have I left the machines on their Baikonur band settings.

Until recently, that is.

I am not homesick, have no desire to return to Earth now. I have accepted the *status quo* and resigned myself to my lot. Fate has shaken the liar dice cup and thrown five aces. I accepted the challenge and called his bluff. So here I am, circling the planet and waiting for the inevitable: but then isn't every man who was ever spawned of woman's belly? I circle in my spacecraft and he cycles round to the library or the cosy home-from-home of a smoke-filled, beer-smelling bar. There is, at the most common denominator, no distinction between us.

Assuring myself I would not become maudlin, I have re-tuned one of the radios. It has a seek facility by which it will search for and, once found, automatically log on to a signal in a pre-set waveband range until the signal loses strength when it will, once again, search and log on to another setting.

Over much of the surface of the world, it is a waste of my time to attempt to tune in. I do not speak Swahili, Japanese, Chinese or Hindi. My knowledge of Spanish is at best slight, my French only marginally better, my German adequate: however, not many radio stations transmit in German, except of course those in Germany but I pass over them in less than ten minutes. My best listening-in area is over North America. Bar the occasional French-Canadian or Latin-American programme, the continent gives me a good twenty-five minutes of English language broadcasting from which to choose and which I understand: I learnt it as a flier, for the international air traffic control language is English.

Inevitably, I only pick up snippets of broadcasts. Much of it consists of music, the bulk a blending of rock and roll or popular music. On occasion, I am fortunate enough to grab a minute of modern jazz but this frustrates me for, no sooner have I come to appreciate the saxophonist or the syncopation, the signal weakens and the equipment goes into seek mode again. The result can be a confusing cacophony of disjointed musical phrases, styles, beats and instruments as raucously jarring as a military band tuning up before a May Day parade. A regiment of clumsy flight mechanics emptying a thousand bags of spanners on to the tarmac has more musical aesthetics.

Understandably, I tend to ignore music channels, arbiters of a common taste with which I share little affinity and target voice transmissions which broadcast information and opinion. Over the USA, these can be staggering in their range and prosaicism, amazing in their catholicity of sentiment. In the two days since I have availed myself of the opportunity, I have listened to disembodied voices decrying or promoting abortion, virulently attacking or patronizingly commiserating with coloured people, libelling or praising politicians and offering views on the merits of existentialism, the justification of nuclear deterrence, the necessity to withhold foreign aid and the importance in everyday life of the media of publicity.

This latter was delivered in blank verse and brought to mind a name I had not considered for many years.

As a student in St Petersburg I had a friend, Viktor Asheshov, who fancied himself a poet.

In those days, it was forbidden for us to wear our hair long and 'artistically cut', as the instruction would have it. Only drama students and, curiously, architecture students seemed to get away with it – and, for some reason, Viktor, who was reading for a degree in chemical engineering: it was rumoured he had an uncle in high places. To extend his bohemian appearance, he wore a white leather jacket, tight black jeans and a shirt which, when he took his jacket off, was seen to have flared cuffs. Like Shelley's, as he would say, producing an illustrated volume of early nineteenth-century British verse in translation to prove it. His spectacles were round, gold rimmed and small. This outfit reached him by courtesy of a girlfriend who worked as a stewardess for Aeroflot and went shopping for him in boutiques on stopovers in New York or London, raising the capital by selling illegally exported tins of top quality caviare and small, easily hidden icons from Moldavia. She, too, must have had an uncle of some sort or another.

His poetry was influenced by a dozen or so books he had acquired from the same source: she had access to bookshops in the West about which none of us dared even fantasize. These books were, to say the least, eclectic, for the girl had no idea what she was buying as her knowledge of English was limited to *Will you have a cup of coffee?*, *Please fasten your seat-belts*, and *Thank - you - for - flying - with - Aeroflot - we - look - forward - to - welcoming - you - on - another - flight - please - take - all - your - hand - baggage - with - you - on - departing - the - aircraft*, which, Viktor claimed, she said in one very accentuated breath and which he insisted constituted a sound poem.

On Saturday evenings, we used to congregate in a murky cellar done out as an anonymous bar just off the Nevskiy Prospekt, close by the railway station at Ploshchad Vosstaniya. It was a hang-out for students from all the faculties of the university, the technical university and various other odds and sods of higher education establishments around the city. Needless to say, the KGB had a resident snoop in there. The under-barman, Sergei, was their man. Yet he was easily bribed. We also fed him spurious pieces of disinformation so he could maintain his credibility with his superiors in the city headquarters building by the Neva.

It was in this bar with no name I first heard Viktor

recite a poem. Of sorts. It was at a time when he was besotted, there is no other word for his enthusiasm, with the poetry of the American poet, Robert Lax. The poem was based upon a Coca Cola advertisement poster his tame stewardess acquired for him in a shop which, she assured us, sold only Coca Cola memorabilia. We did not believe her: surely, we argued, no one in a nation as powerful as America would be interested in collecting items related to a soft drink. We were, I know now, wrong.

The wording of the poster, which I saw, read: *Coca Cola©®TM It's The Real Thing*. Viktor's poem went thus.

Co	Co	©®TM	e	ng
ca	ca	Eee	Ree	
Co	Co	tsssss	ull	
la	la	th	Thee	

I do not lie. This was it. I saw it printed in a semi-subversive booklet of his which circulated amongst the avant-garde brigade at the university. It could be read across, down or up, according to mood or whim, so one person might interpret it as *Co ca Co la*, another as *la Co ca Co* or a third as *CoCo©®TM eng*. The ©®TM was pronounced *Krutum*. The only instructions to a reader were the *tsssss* was to sound like the bottle opening and the *ng* was enunciated with a glottal grunt, as if caused by drinking.

I have never heard a more inane work of literary art, for so it purported to be, in my life.

Yet this was many years ago, when I was young, irresponsible and seeking an identity. And Viktor was unique.

He disappeared from my life when I entered the space programme, along with so many others, fading just as friendships do when one leaves school, or university, and moves on through the tunnel of years. I wondered from time to time what became of him. Now, orbiting the Earth, I think I know. He has bought up America and impinged his poetry upon it. What we regarded as avant-garde is now accepted as the norm.

Just an hour ago, I switched on the VHF unit, chose the receive mode and set the tuner on auto-seek. The first thing it came up with was

WLKC — 98 period 4 on your C-saw-sassy Ray-dee-oh! It's 9 on the time. An' here we go wi' the new ree-lease from Mack the Jack, a.k.a. My-Kull Jack-son. Wow! Will ya listun to th' boy daynce.

My English is fluent but it took a few moments of thumping primeval drumming before I could work out a translation. *Mir* moved on, the next snatch of sound even more unintelligible.

. . .an' He sayd Go out uh th' moun-taynes and the roar-ky playces and do Mah wuk. Only in thus way can ya cum t' th' Glow-ry I prowmised ya all. An' he sayd . . .

I pressed the re-search button. The digits spun and jerked

to a stop like the images in the window of a gambling slot machine.

Downtown traffic's snarled around Jefferson and 43rd. On the freeway, it's movin' steady but there's a tail-back northbound at the junction with the throughway at . . . (static interruption) *The outside temperature's a Bee-Bee-Cueing 38 Celsius and the humidity's 79. Pollution monitors downtown give air quality a no-no today. So* (sound of asthmatic hooter being burped) *all you sufferers take care now.*

This was followed by a newsflash which went:

Police in Arragon County have made an arrest in the continuing investigation into the murder of Mr and Mrs Mishikitty in their home on Orange and 12th, Thursday night. Lieutenant Crade made the following statement to the media just this hour. (The voice changed: in the background, a siren could be heard wheeping soullessly). *We have charged Marvin James Tutsimco with the homicide of Mr and Mrs Mishikitty Thursday night. He was picked up by officers of the APD boarding a Statesline bus at the city terminal. He had in his possession a one-way ticket to Chicago, a Smith & Wesson .38 and over seventy-one thousand dollars.* (A strident female voice interjected). *Is this the weapon used in the killing of Mr and Mrs Mishikitty?* (Lieutenant Crade again). *Yes, ma'am, we believe it is.* (The original voice returned). *You heard it first on*

WMAM — morning news and views update, on the hour, by the hour.

For another eight minutes, the VHF scanned the wavelengths, delivering jingles (*Don't go for bust! Go for a must! Brand new Chevvies — the cars to trust!*), snippets of incomprehensible music lyrics, more weather reports, disc jockey identity slogans (*Stay with the Billy-Joe Eagle Show, where the sixties just won't go — away!* and *Andy Broast — the Host with the Most*) and stock market reports (*Dateline — Wall Street: at close of business yesterday, the Dow-Jones stood at 2903, up ten from Wednesday. Trading today was brisk in bonds but heavy selling overnight in Tokyo and the dip in the Nikkei Average led to an early slide. The index stands at present at 2904, down just one on the day so far. This is Herb Ascott for Dateline — Wall Street brought to you by Credit & Merchantile, the men with a finger on the dollar's pulse . . .*)

I switched off as the track of my orbit carried me over the Arctic Circle north of Great Slave Lake. For several minutes, the receiver had picked up only static and one or two signals of a non-commercial nature — military transmissions perhaps or light aircraft flying over the empty spaces of northern Canada.

So, I thought as the North Pole and the far night drew nearer, such is the world I have quit but cannot entirely leave — greedy, violent, dirty, lost and bland.

And poetic.

A man becomes a god only when he has complete control over either his own destiny or that of others. I believe in this implicitly.

It may not be a permanent state, this godly authority. He may be in such a prestigious position for only a moment, the merest flick of an eye which, if he is not aware of it, will pass him by as silently as a cat burglar, as anonymously as a fly venturing from one dung pile to the next.

I had never given deification much thought: it was Pyotr who first set the chain of ideas rolling.

We were driving out of St Petersburg in the direction of the airport, riding in the near derelict Zil he had purchased after its first life as an official limousine was long forgotten, its second reincarnation as a wedding car was well over and its third, more recent, existence as a city taxi was about to end. This gives some indication of its condition: taxis are the least loved and most abused of all vehicles, the cheap whores of the automotive world, to be used at whim when there is nothing better or more inexpensive. The engine ran unevenly, one of the tyres was through to the canvas in two places, the doors did not fit properly, the windscreen leaked, the heater ran at half setting regardless of the weather, and the rear window was decorated with a circular series of cracks emanating from a central point where the glass was opaque and a stone had struck. In midsummer, one drove with the windows open to disseminate the heat whilst in midwinter one bundled up warm and hoped the ice around the surround on the inside of the windscreen did not drip on to one's clothing or into the top of one's gloves or boots.

It was getting towards evening in the beginning of summer but not yet near the time of the white nights. We were *en route* to the village, travelling at a breakneck speed, weaving to avoid the omniscient pot-holes which test all Russian drivers and their vehicles to the extreme. Automobiles of Russian manufacture may look antiquated, be of a design unchanged in decades and offer only the barest of utilitarian essentials, but they last. I had a Russian jeep for my use at Baikonur which was eighteen years old and rattled like half a bucket of river pebbles falling down a long flight of stairs, but it never broke down, never failed to start on the coldest of mornings after a few turns on the key and was never serviced, being subjected to the oldest military maxim in the world — if it works, why fix it?

We had left the old city of St Petersburg and were now in Leningrad: despite how names have been changed, re-changed, and re-re-changed, attitudes and habits have remained constant. People who lived in the close, ancient streets Tchaikovsky had hummed in, Pushkin had strolled in, and generation after generation of nobility had sported and fornicated in, considered themselves to live in St Petersburg whilst those who lived in the rambling suburbs of Stalinist, Khrushchevian, Brezhnovian blocks of flats, factories, offices, railway yards, tram termini, artificial parks, docks, bus garages and grandiloquent socialist statues were said to occupy Leningrad.

No one and no one thing can really touch the soul of

a great city, Pyotr remarked after some minutes of silence between us.

He spun the wheel and the Zil drummed over a set of tramlines around which the metalling was eroded away. A car coming towards us swerved and rocked as it avoided a collision with us and a hole in the road at least ten centimetres deep and filled with black water rainbowed by oil.

Not even God, he added, tugging the Zil back on course.

We drove on for some minutes. A bus jammed with workers returning from the factories sped by in the opposite direction, the windows steamy with breath despite it being a balmy evening. Faces, slighted frosted with the condensation, looked blankly out at the street. A man on a bicycle pedalled furiously across the wide road a hundred metres ahead, the wheels bounding over pot-holes and cracks in the tarmac caused by years of winter frosts and spring thaws.

Look at that, Pyotr said at last, jutting his chin ahead through the windscreen.

We were approaching the massive roundabout at Ploshchad Pobedy. From the centre rose the tall obelisk of the monument to the victory over the Nazis, surrounded by groups of statues, soldiers and sailors, partisans and volunteers cast in bronze, greyed by traffic fumes, forever fervent in their determination, their valour, their triumph.

Pyotr slammed on the brakes. I instinctively grabbed the dashboard and straightened my legs. The Zil instantly filled with a stench of hot, dirty oil and singed rubber. There were a number of holes in the floor, knocked through by rust or large stones banging up from the road and catching a rotting weld, from which a thin veil of smoke wisped upwards.

Crossing the wide avenue before us was an old woman, hunched over and wearing a heavy cardigan with a headscarf despite the warmth of the sun. The car behind us squealed. I flinched, awaiting the impact. The driver swerved his car around the Zil, skidding sideways on some loose gravel towards the old woman who paid it no heed.

See! Pyotr exclaimed. The spirit of Russia!

You mean the skidding car, out of control but grinding to a halt?

No! Of course not! That's just a careless driver. He rammed the Zil into gear. I'm sure they have them everywhere. Where there is a man, there is an accident looking for a place to happen.

I mused on his philosophy. He was so right, although how much so had not, I was certain, occurred to him. Pyotr is not so much a philosopher as a letterist: he does not consider his thoughts, he just expounds them for others to make what they will of them. If he had lived in the past, he would have been an essayist or a fable-teller.

I mean the crone, he continued. Look at her.

I looked. She was nearly at the curb now, still hunched, still moving with a fragile, short step, more a shuffle than a progression of feet.

Maybe she's deaf, I ventured.

She's Russian, Pyotr retorted. A good Russian. Never mind the world, just reach the other side. She's a fatalist.

He thumped his foot on the accelerator and we jerked forwards, manoeuvring past the other car which had come to a halt, the driver stalling the engine. It wheezed and whirred as he attempted to restart it.

You know about the monument? Pyotr enquired as we circled the roundabout.

He put it as a question which I was well aware, whatever I said, he was going to answer.

Of course, I know, I replied. I have lived in St Petersburg for . . .

The front battle line between the Nazis and the city ran along here, he began. The enemy didn't come down to fight. They stayed in the low hills. Beyond the airport. Towards Pushkin. They didn't dare. They knew if they got into hand-to-hand combat they'd have their throats slit from ear to ear. The entire force of Nazism failed to destroy us, our city. They killed six hundred thousand citizens, they shelled the city for nine hundred days, they razed the palaces — but what?

He waved his hand grandiloquently over the steering-wheel.

It is still here. All of it. We are still here.

A large bus was driving towards us. It was a Mercedes Benz yet with East German licence plates: the world had no more than two hemispheres at the time. The windows were decorated with curtains draped to one side like an inverted V and the driver, we could see, wore a smart uniform.

Here's another lot! Pyotr muttered poisonously. Tourists. Come to see what? To see how we've restored the palaces, repaired the houses, filled in the bomb craters.

As if to deflate his jingoism, we hit a deep pot-hole. The Zil juddered alarming. The steering-wheel spun out of Pyotr's fingers and momentarily took on its own life, ominous clunks and thumps thundering under the floor. A piece of the panelling by my foot flexed in then out again.

You know what that obelisk is? he went on, regaining control. I will tell you. The Finger of Leningrad. The Digit of St Petersburg. The Prick of Peter the Great.

As if to reinforce his statement, he stuck his arm out the window, extended his middle finger and jabbed it upwards at the Mercedes Benz bus.

The busload of tourists had angered Pyotr and, as was his way when he was enraged, he fell silent.

As we progressed away from the monument, I looked back at it in the wing mirror held on to the door by one screw and vibrating badly, distorting the image in the glass. To me, it represented not a fuck-you finger but a consolidation of all the pain, all the screams, all the tears and, no doubt, also some laughter and sighs from lovers coupling in the dark of nine hundred nights.

Their deaths, I thought, were so impersonal, just as their graves are now. They died the worst way a man can go to find his void of eternity or seat on the right hand of God, depending on his own convictions. Without hope.

At that moment I remembered Kalat-I-Ghilzai, a fly-blown, dusty town of makeshift hovels, low mud-brick peasant houses with flat roofs, concrete government buildings in need of painting and a petrol pump on the road from Kabul south west to Kandahar.

We were flying north at 150 metres, hugging the contours of the ground and using the road as a navigation aid: the small arms fire we had flown through just south of Musa Qala had done no more damage than dent a few panels and pierce one tiny section of the fuselage. Ten minutes before, we had landed in the forward supply base at Kandahar to refuel. As the fuelling crew worked Georgiy, the pilot, stood by nonchalantly looking on, unperturbed: there were over two and half hours of daylight remaining, Kabul was only 320 kilometres away and we were carrying little weight. If the going got tough, he reckoned, we could easily rise to 2000 metres, yet he preferred to keep low and fast: the higher you were, he reasoned, the sooner you were seen and the Mujahaddin were said to be equipped with SAMs.

The massive MI-26 helicopter was making good speed, despite the terrain. Standing behind Georgiy, my hands grasping the back of his seat and that of his co-pilot, I could see the airspeed indicator reading 255kph, the normal cruising speed for the aircraft. Up above and behind me, the twin Lotarev D-136 turboshafts sliced the hot, dry air with their eight-blade rotor.

We're safe, I thought. This is the most powerful helicopter in the world with a payload of 20,000kg, the freight hold larger than an An-12 transport. Looking round the cockpit at the five-man flight crew, I felt secure.

I was a fool then, not a god: I was not in control.

The tracer fire came suddenly, one shell bouncing off the roof of the cockpit. The whole aircraft shuddered as Bujan might, like a tired dog trying to rid himself of bothersome flies on a hot day: such was the very thought which entered my head.

There was another burst and my face was hit by a flush of hot liquid. I closed my eyes and, bracing myself against the co-pilot's seat, reached for my camouflage scarf.

A voice yelled, Hydraulics! Hydraulics! Losing pressure! Losing fluid!

I licked my lips. The wetness on my face tasted of sweet iron. I found my scarf and wiped it across my eyes.

The aircraft was starting to pitch alarmingly. A warning siren was blaring somewhere near my left ear.

We're going down! Going down! the voice hollered.

Another screamed, Brace! Brace!

I hugged the seat back and let my legs go into a spring position, as a parachutist does just before hitting the ground. My scarf was screwed up between my chin and the seat back. On the co-pilot's neck, beads of sweat were standing out.

The scarf was dark maroon. I looked at Georgiy. The windscreen in front of him was smashed, the flight instruments broken with bare wires and smoke coming from the panel. His head was gone.

The co-pilot wrestled with the controls and managed to bring the MI-26 down to a heavy landing beside a gully across what appeared to be an earthen football pitch, quite devoid of even solitary tufts of grass but sporting a leaning set of goal posts draped with a goal net which had clearly once been a tank camouflage mesh. On the far side of the pitch were the first buildings of Kalat-I-Ghilzai.

No sooner were we down than we were out of the helicopter, sprinting for the cover of the gully. Bullets whipped around us. Tracers came in, sparking off the rocks. I looked at the buildings. They had no windows. People were scurrying about, doors slamming and goats fleeing.

Once in the gully, we took stock. The flight crew and I carried side arms. The twenty-man platoon of special forces operatives in the rear of the aircraft were armed with Dragunov semi-automatic sniper's rifles fitted with PSO1 'scopes, AKM assault rifles and AKR sub-machine-guns. One of them had a grenade launcher. As they deployed themselves, working with the pre-ordained synchronicity of intelligent insects, the radio operator started transmitting on the emergency waveband, repeating our position over and over again until he got radio recognition and a confirmation of signal.

When they were in position, the platoon laid down a heavy curtain of gunfire. For a short time, the Afghanis held their fire and kept their heads low. One or two grenades suggested to them they might be wise to retreat.

After about ten minutes, in a lull in the fire-play, the radio operator reported the search and rescue people would come for us in an hour and a half. I understood their thinking: drop in at last light, lift us clear by twilight, rise vertically to 3500metres and head back to Kabul by night with no running lights. The rebels might have SAMs but no missile radar guidance system, and the heat-seeking qualities of surface-to-air missiles were not infallible.

It was decided we would obtain better protection if we could make it to the buildings across the football pitch which was to be the pick-up zone for the S&R helicopters. Not only would the buildings give us cover and a chance to consolidate and re-group but the Mujahaddin would be less likely to lay down a carpet of gunfire for fear of hitting their own people. And so, as the soldiers put down a withering fire, we legged it as hard as we could go for the buildings, skidding into the late afternoon shadows and smashing open the doors on the first hovels we came to.

To an observer, it must have looked hilarious. As we burst in through the doors, the occupants tumbled out, scattering for their neighbours' doors, heading off down the street with their robes flowing behind them. Children led the way, fleeter of foot than their elders. No one screamed or shouted. They were too busy concentrating on running.

We consolidated ourselves in four or five hovels. The platoon fanned out through the surrounding low-walled goat pens and courtyards, knocking over bales of fodder, outdoor tables and charpoys to give added cover. The more shadows one can make, the more one can flit between them.

The heavier calibre tracers ceased but rifle fire continued to come in at us, yet it could not penetrate the dense mud-brick walls. Nevertheless, we kept our heads down: if just one of the rebels had an armour-piercing round filched from our forces, he could cut through the hovels like a pencil through a pumpkin.

Taras, the co-pilot, was in the same hovel as me. He sat hunched in the corner. I could hear him sobbing with rage, his teeth grinding.

The fuckers! he muttered. The fuckers! They got Georgiy. The fuckers, fuckers, fuckers!

He seemed to have no other vocabulary with which to rid himself of his anger.

About thirty minutes after we were downed, two Mig-29 Fulcrum Bs flew over accompanied by a Mig-31. The former strafed the hills beyond the helicopter, putting down half a dozen fragmentation bombs before the Mig-31 came in to fire off several racks of rockets, the explosions of which echoed in the hills. This seemed to pacify the rebels and the incoming fire gradually faded then petered out.

Now we wait, remarked one of the soldiers. Have a picnic. Have a smoke.

He took out a pack of American Lucky Strike cigarettes: how he had come to possess them I shall never know.

After some minutes of comparative quiet, interrupted only by Taras in the corner grumbling, The fuckers! The fucking fuckers! I made to leave the hovel. The soldier touched my arm.

If you want a shit, he said, smiling to me, do it by the door. Don't put yourself in view of the 'copter. If there're any of them still up there . . . Last thing you want to do is die with your pants round your ankles and your arse unwiped. Not dignified, he added.

I nodded my understanding and went into the balmy, low sunlight. There was no one about except for another of the soldiers hunched down behind a low mud wall. He wagged his finger at me, pointed to the hills and dragged it across his throat before pointing to me. I nodded again.

By the wall of the hovel was a trough for watering animals. It was full of clean but brackish water. I put my hands in it. It was as warm as a soothing bath. No sooner had I immersed my arms than red filigrees of Georgiy's blood drifted outwards from the material of my uniform flying jacket. I splashed water on my face: light red drops fell from my nose into the trough.

Taras came out of our shelter, crouched down and ran at the double towards another hovel, kicking the door open. This time, no one ran out.

I risked a look across the football pitch. The helicopter had lurched to one side. The rotors were awry, a greasy drift of smoke lifting from the fuselage door through which I could see oily flames licking and shaking in the heat haze.

One of the special forces men must have fired the aircraft to destroy the code books and radio, render it useless to the enemy.

The hills simmered, a barren backdrop of brown rocks and brown earth, the occasional sunburned bush and outcrop of shadow. Behind them, the mountains were gently going purple where the sun was abandoning the crevices and canyons.

Hey! Look at this!

It was Taras's voice, shrill with tension.

I spun round, my pistol in my hand.

From the hovel into which he had vanished, Taras reappeared dragging a youth by the arm. He was dressed in the usual baggy trousers and loose kaftan of a peasant, his head in an untidy turban, his chin decorated by the first attempts he had made at growing a man's beard. Upon his feet were a pair of Russian army issue boots, without laces.

What is it? I called softly. Keep your voice down.

The muzzle of Taras's pistol was hard into the youth's right ear.

No sooner had I spoken than I heard a replay of my own voice in my head. *It*, I had said. Not *he* but *it*.

It's a fucker, Taras said. He was almost gleeful.

He dragged the youth over to the cover of the hovel.

You! Taras commanded, jerking his chin at the hunched soldier. Take a look in that dung-heap of a hut.

The soldier weaved across the open ground and into the hovel. Taras slammed his prisoner against the wall of our building: the youth slid to the ground, his eyes fast on Taras's pistol.

Found 'em!

The soldier came out of the youth's hovel carrying three AK47s complete with several magazines bound together with tape and fitted with webbing slings.

Cover the fucker! Taras ordered me. I cocked my pistol and pointed it at the youth.

A surge of incredible power ran through me. I felt like a man who had just won a billion roubles before they were inflated, had been made Tsar of all the Russias, had been granted his every wish. My hand did not so much as waver. I was in command. This was my world, this courtyard scattered with pellets of goat droppings, strewn with wisps of straw and, I now saw, pock-marked with drops of water falling from my clothes, each one of them carrying a cell or two of Georgiy's soul.

The soldier cocked each AK, testing to see if it was in firing order.

They looked after these good, he noted.

To my astonishment, I felt my penis growing erect. I had not the merest thought of a woman in my mind and yet it was swelling, hardening, pressing against the inside of my fly buttons. I wanted to reach into my trousers and straighten it but did not. Besides, it was soon so stiff it straightened itself.

Got a hard on? asked the soldier who had been in the hovel.

I made no reply.

Taras stepped forward to the prisoner who glanced quickly at him then, deciding he was no threat looked back at me. With one swipe, Taras cut off the youth's left ear. He screamed, just the once and pressed his hands hard to the side of his head. Blood oozed through his fingers and soaked into the collar of his kaftan.

That's my souvenir, Taras said quietly. My fucking souvenir.

What are you waiting for? the soldier asked.

I heard him but it was some seconds before I realized he was addressing me.

Go on then. He did for . . . He snapped his fingers, trying to remember the name.

I did nothing.

What was the pilot's name?

The other soldier said, Georgiy.

Yeah, Georgiy. So?

I still did nothing. My cock was as hard as a broom handle and stretching the material of my underpants.

Go on, then. Shift the bastard.

Very slowly, I thought of what I was going to do and yet, in fact, I believe I thought of nothing. I gradually aimed the pistol. The youth looked at me. His eyes were dull, perhaps with the pain of his wound, perhaps with the acceptance of the inevitable.

I shall never know.

Taking up the pressure on the trigger, I squeezed ever so slightly, as if terribly afraid of the recoil, of the report, of the irreversibility of my action.

The gun fired almost, it seemed, without my assistance.

The youth's forehead exploded. He did not slump forward or slide to one side but stayed leaning against the wall. His hands fell to his lap. Blood, spurting to his left from his ear and the exit wound of the bullet, sprayed on to the mud wall which soaked it up like a sponge.

I lowered the gun.

Just for those few moments, I was a god, in complete, unequivocal control of the whole universe, of all of time, of the very essence of existence.

Every four or five orbits, I pass over Afghanistan and sometimes I think of the youth's bones lying bleached in the dry hills, his dust blowing across the football pitch.

This is a luxury only gods may have, to ride over that which they have created or caused to occur, and look down upon it and feel no regret whatsoever.

❧

I am riding Newton's cannonball.

He imagined a massive cannon, set and primed at the top of the highest mountain in the world. The charge rammed down the barrel was so great it could fire a cannon-ball so its trajectory, as it fell, followed exactly the curve of the planet. In this way, once fired, it would encircle the globe, returning to the point of its discharge. Theoretically, of course, the artillerymen would have to move the cannon by the time the shot returned otherwise the whole lot of them would have been blown to bits by their own weapon and would have looked downright foolish.

Of course, it could not work. Friction with the air would tell upon it. Even if the highest mountain projected through the atmosphere of the world, the cannon-ball would gradually slow, gravity reach out to tickle its spinning orb of iron and entice it home.

Nothing is forever, Isaac. Nothing at all.

Kelvin scotched you with his second law of thermodynamics.

It is a simple premise. Heat always flows from a hotter body to a cooler body. This is the supreme law of nature, the First Commandment God gave to the elements before he started on the morality of men with his thou shall not murder, or commit adultery or covet thine neighbour's ox or whatever.

Imagine a hot day. Pyotr has spent the morning digging up his carrots. His shirt sticks to his back with the sweat of honest toil, the sort of stuff Communism was built upon, the dignity of labour. He reaches the beaten earth yard and flops into his chair. Anna, the good wife with a scarf about her hair and Bujan at her heels, comes out and puts beside her husband a glass of lemonade. A huge chunk of ice, courtesy of Vitaly Menshikov, bobs in the liquid, waiting to bang on Pyotr's upper lip as he slakes his thirst and thanks his luck for a wife who thinks of him. Bujan sits with his tongue hanging out. He's a stupid dog, eats ice in the summer but scoffs snow in the winter.

The ice melts as the heat from the lemonade moves into it. It cannot be avoided. This is a fundamental of creation, is it not?

Have you ever seen a glass of lemonade get hot and a lump of Menshikovian ice form in it?

No chance!

If this were possible, Svetleishyi would have no need to put on his malodorous bear-skin coat in the middle of the winter and venture out to saw up the river. He would merely set a bucket up in his cavernous ice store and wait for the miracle to happen.

Just as the ice melts, so do things wear out. Pyotr's Zil for one.

The glass of lemonade with ice has no more shape than the glass of lemonade with melted ice. Leave an ice cube and it will melt as soon as there is heat to move into it. Like Pyotr's cabin. Leave it long enough and it'll be a pile of logs but, no matter how long you wait, the pile of logs will never become a cabin — not without human intervention.

What better proof of entropy exists, I cannot think. The second law of thermodynamics may therefore be summed up by saying all things wear out, from the trajectory of Newton's missile to a pair of cheap shoes.

Men think they can reverse this divine *decretum*.

Vladislav Baryshnikov, the man who runs the repair shop in the remains of a city council store-yard for street signs and lamp standards in the middle of the wasteland between Uyezdny Prospekt and the railway marshalling yards in the St Petersburg suburb of Smolenskoye, to whom Pyotr takes the Zil when something finally packs in, is one of these men.

Late one autumn, I returned to St Petersburg from Moscow after attending the celebrations for the October Revolution. Pyotr came to meet me at the airport, carried my bag to his car, dumped it on the rear seat and lowered himself into the driver's seat, reaching across to unlock the passenger door upon which I had to tug so hard to get it open the shock absorbers creaked.

It's getting sticky, Pyotr observed unnecessarily. It does when winter comes on. Like an old woman. It feels the imminent onset of the cold weather in its chassis.

We set off from the airport, turning left towards the city along the dual carriageway.

How was your flight, my friend? I see you came on the high-wing aircraft.

I shrugged. I had travelled in an Aeroflot Ilyushin IL-76.

How good is it ever, flying in a passenger jet which, when the clarion calls from the Kremlin, will instantly be transformed into a heavy-duty, long-haul military freighter? I replied.

Pyotr cast a quick glance at me.

Have you flown it yet?

Flown what? I rejoined.

You know.

I know?

Don't play games. Have you had a ride in it?

We are told not to say . . .

Hey! he exclaimed. I'm not a CIA spy or a KGB informer. I am Pyotr who grows vegetables and gives you vodka.

I flew in it last month, I admitted.

He was referring to the Tupolev TU-160 long-range strategic bomber. I had been invited to ride in one at Ramenskoye just before the celebrations began, piloted by a young man with Germanic blond hair who was to take part in a fly-past.

And? And? Pyotr insisted.

And it is astonishing, I reported. Four turbofans giving nearly 23,000kgp with re-heat. We took it up to 12,200 metres and flew at Mach 2.1.

Faster than a bullet, Pyotr mused.

Faster than a bullet, I concurred.

Then we had the accident. A lorry some way ahead of us was shedding lengths of angle iron. Dusk was drawing in and the street lights were only just coming on. Pyotr mistook a section of iron for a tramline and ran over it. There was a terrible clash of metal and the Zil seemed to slump to the front nearside.

Shit! Pyotr murmured: he is not a man given to gratuitous swearing.

We turned right at the next junction and drove straight to the repair shop, the underneath of the car clanking ominously. Baryshnikov was standing by the remains of an ex-army truck, the rear held up on a criss-cross of old railway sleepers, the axle and differential of which lay on the ground amidst filthy puddles and soil stained black with discarded oil. He greeted us by flicking his cigarette end into a puddle: I half expected it to catch alight, like the brandy poured round a pudding.

Front wishbone, he said laconically, cursorily inspecting the Zil's belly. Shot to hell and beyond.

Can you fix it? Pyotr enquired.

Baryshnikov grinned toothlessly. He lost his four front upper teeth in a fight when he was conscripted into the army.

Can I? he replied. Can I? Can a fish fuck in the water? Can birds fly?

I was about to point out whilst all fish do reproduce under water not all birds could take to the wing, but I thought better of it.

He called out into the recesses of the repair shop, his voice flat against the corrugated iron roof.

Fedya! Fedya! Have we got a left front wish' for a
'63 Zil?

There was a sound of iron being moved.

Yes. We got one.

We got one, Baryshnikov confirmed needlessly. By the
time we're done — say Wednesday? — it'll look as good as
new. There's nothing we can't fix up to last for . . . He
thought about it. The car'll outlive you, Pyotr, my friend.
It'll go on for ever.

He slapped his hand on the bonnet. I noticed a block of
rusty mud drop from inside the wheel arch and bounce off
the tyre.

So much for Baryshnikov. He thinks he can reverse
entropy, refuses to admit he is impotent against it.

For there will come a time, far into the dim dawns of
the future, when all the suns and all the stars have burned
out, when life will be impossible because there will be no
heat to move into the cold places. Everything will reach
stasis and the universe will suffer heat death.

Or will it?

There is, I admit, a slight statistical chance Baryshnikov
is correct: things may be able to reverse their decline, their
wearing out. Time is infinite and anything may happen.
The logs may become a cabin after all.

Who knows?

Be that as it may, just as the Zil is dancing with Madam
Entropy, so is *Mir IV*.

Not only do faults occur in the spacecraft but the orbit
on which I spin is decaying. Bit by bit, centimetre by
centimetre, hour by hour, the whole edifice, with me as
passenger, is edging nearer to the speck on almighty space

whence it emanated on the top of a Soyuz rocket.

This decay manifests itself by minute changes in the on-board navigation computer. Numbers alter of their own volition, never drastically but always positively, as numbers do. It appears infinitesimal: 1,454,789.176 becomes 1,454,787.893 over the duration of a ten-hour period. If I were a rich man and these were dollars in the bank, I'd give not a jot. But they aren't. They are numbers by which my life hangs in the balance.

I am able to rectify the problem. Just as I can alter the pitch of the craft, or its angle to the sun or the Earth, or rotate it so one side does not get too hot — and there we have heat moving from the hot sun to the cool little world of aluminium struts and steel bars, titanium panels and alloy sectioning, carbon fibre composite and ceramic tiles I inhabit: the eternal second law — so can I, within limited parameters, alter the orbit in so much as I have the capability to move a little further out into space.

The feat is achieved by using the TACPS, the Thruster Attitude Control and Positioning System. It consists of a cold gas nitrogen propellant in a 35,000 kg/sec blow-down system on a thruster frame outside the craft, linked to twenty-two spherical propellant storage tanks governed by quad-redundant control solenoid valves. The N_2 is stored at 2,245 N/cm^2 ±69 at 38°C in the spheres which are .13 cubic metres in volume.

Every twenty-two days, I have a trimburn, which is to say, I fire the little thruster rockets of the TACPS which repositions me and maintains my correct orbit. Without these minor adjustments, I would gradually draw nearer to the Earth and burn up.

With careful manipulation and obeying the calculations arrived at by the computer which reads the data every twenty nanoseconds, I fire the thrusters in a set pattern to reposition the spacecraft. All I hear is a brief rush of gas, like steam hissing from the pistons of an old locomotive labouring through the Urals on a landscape muffled by snow. All I sense is a movement of the sun from one window to another as the craft makes a tiny leap towards the great beyond where the stars go on and on to the place where time is made by a vindictive God with little humour and an impulsive nature.

For drastic orbit shifts, there is a liquid fuel booster system I can use but it is not intended for the purpose. The real function is to assist in manoeuvring when docking with other spacecraft or radically altering position or orbit to avoid collision with space debris.

Therefore, every so often, I have to make adjustments in order to keep my seat upon old Isaac's cannon-ball. I slip my feet into the restraints by the guidance control panel, put my hands on the red switch and, when the computer so instructs me, give it a quick flick. It snaps down then springs back. There is a pause, then I briefly hear the locomotive, from far off, as it chugs between two stands of pine trees laden with snow in the sub-light of a beautiful Russian winter. The beam of sunlight coming through the triangular window over the panel zaps across the cabin and vanishes as another of its comrades jumps through the window near the waste management facility.

That is all I do. All the calculations and positionings, angles and durations of thrust from booster III or VII, are actioned by the computer.

When the stability of the orbit has been maintained, I let my feet work loose from the restraints and, with my toes, give the merest of pushes. My body floats into the centre of my domain and I allow myself to hunch up like a foetus and spin gently in space.

The sun is constant, the Earth spins around it in a state of false joy, *Mir* reels rounds the Earth obeying laws old Isaac tried to understand whilst, inside it, I spin like a ball of flesh around the kernel of my soul and ponder, if I feel inclined to lachrymosity and self-indulgent pity, what will happen when the N_2 runs out and the liquid fuel is burned off.

I can hardly get out and push. This is no Zil with a bust wishbone and there are no inter-galactic Baryshnikovs to fix the bloody thing from scraps he's salvaged off passing missiles or filched from rocketry's parking lots.

On the other hand, I need not bother myself with such mawkish thoughts. I'm not unique. All men die sometime, because the bus driver fell asleep or the pilot misread his instruments, because the doctors were unskilful or simply because it was time for luck to run out, for Kelvin's second law of thermodynamics to be read and the sentence passed.

❧

Perhaps I have a fever of some sort, have inexplicably picked up some virus which has been travelling through the vacuum of infinity ever since time popped its evil little face out of its womb and started spreading like a cancer through eternity.

There are those who claim viruses originated in outer space, who have written learned papers and addressed august societies in echoing lecture theatres on the probabilities of it. They have cited viral epidemics coinciding with the eruption of sunspots, the explosion of super-novae, electron storms and other heavenly happenings. The appearance of comets, however, is the favourite cause of these blind theorists. If, the hypothesis goes, the tails of comets are composed of ice then there must be water, and where there is water there is the propensity for life. That cometal ice may not be water but ammonia, chloride, nitrogen or some other gas, and that viruses are not necessarily living organisms but complex chemicals obeying obscure laws, does not affect their argument. Viruses have the ability to survive in a vacuum so therefore they can travel through one: the influenza which wiped out millions just after the Great War could just as easily have already decimated the population of Zarzuela, the Cerulean culture of Oxymoron and the slimy little green governors of the planet Grumous, the third smallest body orbiting Bellatrix in the constellation of Orion.

Or some such adumbrative bullshit.

The known fact that anything entering an atmosphere at the kind of speeds required for interstellar voyaging is burned up more rapidly and more thoroughly than a feather of duck's down in a bonfire of old truck tyres seems not to have weakened the hypotheses.

Despite these fantasies, the early space programme controllers took no chances. Men returning from space were kept in quarantine for weeks in case they had picked up an alien creature which fed upon their corpuscles, sucked their plasma or infiltrated their testicles, building like replicants inside them. When Armstrong and his comrades returned from the moon, they met President Nixon through a thick glass window in their isolation module. No one knew the questions but they were ready with the answers. If Armstrong had been found to be contaminated with a virus from beyond Andromeda, make no mistake about it: he would have been killed, incinerated, his dust dissolved in acid and the acid kept more securely than ever a spent fuel rod of uranium was stored. His death would have been written off as the price of science and the newspapers would have been told of a terrible fire in the isolation unit.

The supposition my spacecraft is hermetically sealed and utterly airtight, and therefore impregnable to anything drifting through the void looking for a new host to colonize, means nothing. If I can experience such failures as I have then it is odds on there are minuscule leaks here and there, infinitesimally small cracks in seals, between riveted plates, along the seams of metal. The tiniest leaks would not be discernible to me, to the measuring instruments, to the phalanx of probes and sensors and computers but this does not preclude their existence. A virus may enter where a filament a thousandth of the width of a hair may not pass. After all, something knocked the starboard discone antenna and there is no knowing what: maybe it was a virus travelling at tens of thousands of kilometres a second, spun through umpteen magnetic fields, rich in the knowledge of a thousand galaxies, which did it. Even a virus must have some mass and if it was journeying at fantastic speeds it might just have sufficient momentum to bend a flimsy metal arm. Who can tell? It might at this very minute be infiltrating itself through the skin of an unknowing victim, preparing to set its own pandemic in motion.

Or it might be that the fever symptoms are produced not by a virus from Zeugma but one from Earth, carried up in the folds of my clothing, the intimate furrows of my body, nestled and protected, nurtured and cherished by my own flesh and blood. On Earth, it is a benign molecule the function of which is obscure — say to provide light in the tail of a glow-worm or give a butterfly the ambition to find nectar as it lies locked in its chrysalis — but up here, orbiting in zero gravity, it reacts to the titanium oxide forming on the bulkhead panels, mutating into a hungry doit greedy for my brain cells, coveting the warm rush in my arteries and acquiring aspirations beyond its station in the order of things. It is not unknown for staunch friends to turn into malicious enemies when times get tough or conditions change.

Whatever is the case, I feel feverish. My brow perspires uncontrollably for ten minutes then inexplicably stops, the evaporation of my sweat suddenly cooling me and bringing on a brief spasm of shivering: yet it is not the sort of trembling which accompanies illness but more like that which goes with fear, a deep and rumbling tremor seeming to start in the bones. If I were a planet and my soul a molten core, this would be the start of an horrendous earthquake sufficient to eradicate species, alter climates and bring down mountains. No sooner has it started, however, than it ends and there is no harm done.

When the last shivering attack hit me, about an hour

ago, I positioned myself in my usual day-dream position in the centre of the cabin and hung perfectly still. I have found when these attacks occur, my skin is for a short time incredibly sensitive, as if I had spent an hour in a good Russian *banya*.

How I would relish an hour in a traditional bathhouse right now! The steamy air hot from the fires, the brass basins burnished like gold, folded sheets and towels laid out next to the wooden tubs white with decades of scrubbing. And the birch twigs. Little bundles of them, clean and dark and supple. Even the memory of the sound of them swishing against my skin promotes a nostalgic frisson of pleasure. After the heat and the thrashing would come the scrubbing and rinsing, the massaging of tired muscles and bones that wish they were dead. And then, the agony and the ecstasy over, an hour's dozing on the hard wooden benches, listening distantly to others chat about the state of the nation, the state of the world, the state of their mother-in-law's bunions or their brother's deal which fell through.

Lying in weightlessness, I closed my eyes. The shivering continued. Not for long. I would guess the bouts did not last three minutes: but what three minutes they were!

At first, just as my eyes closed, I heard a voice.

Good-evening, Alyona Ivanovna, I . . .

The words had a slight resonance to them as if they were being spoken in an empty room by someone lacking in self-confidence. It was a young man's voice and I knew it came from within me although it was not me speaking. At least, not initially.

127

I have brought you something. Had we not better pass into the room where there is more light?

There were two sets of footsteps: one was heavy and firm, the other light and scampering in a rodent fashion.

Do you not remember me, Alyona Ivanovna? I have brought you the pledge I promised just the other day.

There was a pause before the voice living within me continued, Why are looking at me as if you didn't know me? Do you want it? Take it or leave it. I can go elsewhere. I haven't the time to waste.

The voice was peeved, impatient, somehow afraid.

It's a silver cigarette case, the voice went on. Don't you remember I told you about it the last time?

None of Alyona Ivanovna's words came to me. It occurred to me a conversation was taking place but I could hear it only as a soliloquy, privileged only to hear my own side of it. Yet, despite this, I knew what the other was saying: she was asking why I was pale, why my hand shook, whether or not I had just come out into the cold air from a hot *banya*.

Fever, the voice replied and now it was me speaking. I felt my lips move as I hung in the weightless air. One can't help looking pale if one hasn't eaten. Another pause followed before I went on, It's a cigarette case, a silver one.

She complained it was not heavy enough to be silver and wanted to know why I had tied it up so tightly in a ribbon.

My hand slid along the side of my cosmonaut's overalls. My fingers gripped the handle of a hatchet. My eyes blinked. The shivering increased within me.

I knew who I was now. My name was Raskolnikov and

I was a poor student who was about to control the world. Just for a moment or two.

My arms were weak. I raised them over my head, the action bringing them strength. With a swinging motion, I brought the blunt back of the hatchet blade down upon Alyona Ivanovna's head. The handle jarred. I struck again, again and again with the measured, methodical beat of a drummer at a military funeral. I heard the smack of dull metal on bone, a slight whimper, a thump.

I stopped and through my closed eyes saw her head gushing blood, her eyes popping out from her face like those of a scared hare. The force of the hatchet striking had dislodged them from their sockets.

There was a sort of musical sound, a small unmelodious chiming. I recognized keys jangling. This was followed by rustling and shuffling feet, drawers opening and closing, a heavy object being tugged across floorboards.

In my hands, blotched with blood, were gold chains, gold watches, gold bracelets, gold rings, gold bangles, gold hairpins, gold cufflinks . . . They flowed over my fingers like the sun on the sap of the fir trees.

Another face appeared, a younger woman's face which twitched spasmodically. The eyes stared at me unseeing and the mouth opened but no sound came out. The lips were as white as the teeth behind them. I raised the hatchet once more. This time, the edge of the blade did the job. It split her forehead open. Blood and greyish-pink foam oozed through the crack.

The feverish shivering was gone but there was a sharp pain my head, just behind my right ear. My eyes opened. I had indeed swung my arms about my head, the momentum sending me across the cabin and into the bulkhead next to the second crewman's sleeping restraint. A small angle on the side of one of the storage lockers had impacted itself against the back of my head.

My heart was pounding hard, my breath coming in short gasps as if I had just been involved in some extreme exertion.

Twisting round, I pushed myself towards the food table, strapping myself into the seat with the lap restraint. I felt I had to sit down even though, in space, it is not essential to be seated to relax. The need to do something normal, something terrestrial and human in the face of such grotesque inhumanity, was overwhelming: old habits die hard.

Very carefully, I calmed myself down, taking breathing exercises to lower my respiration and heart rate. In a few minutes I was back to normal, yet the quandary remained as to why I had been suffering shivering fits, why I had hallucinated such an act and why I should have chosen — or had it been chosen for me — for three minutes in outer space, to become a fictional murderer.

❧

My grandmother's name was Zinaida, but everyone knew her as Zina. She was a petite, delicate woman whom one might have assumed to have come from the aristocracy for she had about her, even in old age, a certain air of refinement. It was not that she was an aristocrat but she had rubbed shoulders with them: my great-grandfather had been a footman to the Tsar posted to the palace at Petrodvorets and his daughter had frequently experienced the life of the nobility at second hand. From time to time, the servants were allowed to take home to their families platters of food left over from a banquet or a ball and it was, in this vicarious way, that my grandmother came to develop a taste for the finest caviare, the most delicate vol-au-vents and the tenderest cuts of meat.

It was so beautiful, she would recall, sitting on the edge of her bed with her flannelette night-dress loose about her old bosom and tumbling in folds in her lap, her stick-like legs bare from the knee down to the cracked leather slippers my grandfather had worn. She spoke each syllable slowly, drawing it out as if by lengthening it she could imitate what she saw as the long, golden, lazy days of monarchy.

Tell me about it, I would request, humouring her but secretly satisfying my own yearning as well. Fantasies of riches and power, princesses and emperors fill every young man's mind, even that of a Communist.

The palace, she would begin, was built above the shore of Finskiy Zaliv by Peter the Great. It was the greatest palace in the world, Misha.

My name is not Mikhail, yet she always called me Misha: at least, towards the end when her mind was slowly losing all its faculties, as a flower drops its petals when the water in the vase gets low, and all she kept inviolate beneath her thinning wisps of hair was the story of Peterhof.

After declaring the palace's magnitude, she would pause and look upwards, her eyes moving across the ceiling as if Peter himself was looking down at her from a heavenly chariot as it rode by on the clouds. If she were alive now, she might gaze up into the sky to see if she could spy me speeding past well above the clouds.

He declared, she would continue, he wanted a palace and a kitchen garden — those were his very orders — to better those of the King of France at Versailles. He had visited the French king and had seen the wondrous palace he lived in. So they moved millions of cubic metres of clay and transported in by barge piles of earth and horse dung to replace it and give the gardens substance. Tens of thousands of trees were imported from all over Europe — fruit trees from France, chestnuts from Prussia, maples and lindens, apples and pears. Storms battered the trees. Frosts killed them. Winter snows buried them. They were replanted. A canal was dug for the fountains. You know how Peter loved fountains.

She spoke as if we both had known him, her words a reminder as if he were a long lost friend of whom details of friendship might be fading with the passage of time.

At this juncture in her story, I was always tempted to inform her how four thousand soldiers and indentured serfs dug the canal, living in tents and makeshift shacks on the shore, were fed the barest essentials and given only a modicum of fuel in the winter. They dug and sweated and cursed and starved and died of cold, of malnutrition and of disease. Yet to tell her this was to ruin her story: besides, she would not believe it. The history books, she claimed, were wrong, written by politicians with grudges to bear and professors with old scores to settle.

Instead of being belligerent I would ask, for I knew she wanted to show off her knowledge and tell me, Who built the fountains, *babushka*?

Who? she would splutter. Who? The greatest engineer in the history of Russia. That's who! Vassili Tuvolkov. He went to France, studied how the French made fountains and, in 1720, he began to construct his hydraulic system. Pipes ran for twenty-three kilometres from Ropsha. Then the greatest European sculptors and builders came. Stakenschneider, Benois, Shubin, Kozlovsky, Martos, Voronikhin. Even the Italian Rastrelli. They built statues for the fountains, buildings in the grounds. Oh! Such wonderful men!

With this outburst she would fall silent as if in temporary mourning and would not go on until after at least a minute's meditation, her eyes glazed and her lips curled in a wistful half-smile as if she was travelling back to walk in the grounds again and feel the mists of water drifting on the breeze to cool her face.

There were hundreds of fountains, she would start again, her eyes seeing me once more. One had a dog chasing ducks, another men blowing trumpets. There were men fighting sea serpents and young girls — such pretty young girls, pouring water forever from amphorae. And they were all gold, Misha, solid gold.

I did not disabuse her of the knowledge: at best they were gold leaf upon lead.

And there was the trick fountain.

She leaned back on her bed. Her hands gripped the metal frame beneath her shallow mattress and she laughed.

There was a tree surrounded by pebbles and hidden

spouts in the stones. If you trod on a certain pebble, it released a jet. Right up your skirt! Ha!

Her breath came in bouts, her happiness translated into little bestial snorts.

Which was the biggest fountain? I would ask. It was an accepted prompt for which she waited, the culmination of her discourse on the subject.

The greatest was never seen by Peter. He died in 1725 and it was not made until 1735. It was Samson, Misha.

Peter the Great wanted a statue of Hercules wrestling with the nine-headed Hydra but instead they fashioned Samson prising open a lion's jaws. It was an allegory, Misha. Samson was Russia, you see, and the lion was the beast from the Swedish coat-of-arms. For Peter beat the Swedish in the Northern War. The greatest plume of them all shot up from the lion's mouth. Like a roar.

Her arms rose up in a kind of supplication. The flesh of her biceps sagged where the short sleeves of her night-dress ended.

And the water roared, Misha. Oh! How it roared.

She would wave her fingers in the air, her arms beginning to shiver with tiredness.

They were gold, those statues. Every one of them. It's true, my boy. I've seen them, Misha. I've *touched* them.

Quite suddenly, her arms would flop down like a puppet's when the strings are cut.

I would ask her about the palace buildings but her memory was not so sharp. She could remember the pantries stocked with hanging sides of beef, carcasses of pigs and barrels of apples, the kitchens and the maids in their trim uniforms with the footmen in livery. She reported wandering the rooms and corridors with her father when the Tsar was not in residence. I think the sheer grandeur of it all must have overcome her: it was too sumptuous, too miraculous, too rich in imagery for her memory to retain specific details. The only room she could recall with clarity was the Hall of Muses, the floor inlaid with delicate marquetry, the walls and ceiling decorated with the portraits of the muses surrounded by gold filigree.

Whenever I visited her, and we talked of her childhood, I always asked her if she would like to go back to Petrodvorets.

She never called the place Petrodvorets, as it was known in later years. To my grandmother is was always Peterhof. Peter's garden, Peter's yard.

Yes, she would reply pensively. Yes. To see where I was a little girl. Just one more time.

A casual listener would have thought she was royalty and perhaps pondered on how she had survived the revolution.

Grandma Zina died so long ago now my best visual memory of her is a photograph in my mother's album with the faded satin cover.

Thinking of her now, I consider how she longed once more, upon her death bed, to visit Peterhof and wander the long corridors, dance and twirl alone in the Hall of Muses and pretend she was young again, and a princess.

As for me, I have visited the palace to stand in awe at the grandeur of its architecture, admire the opulent extravagant beauty of its rooms, the exquisite perfection of its gardens but I have no desire to see them one last time, as she did.

Instead, I would like to be able to watch the low

autumnal sun striking at an angle along the furrows in the fields around Pyotr's cabin, not long after the ploughing, turning the sods the colour of burnt umber and promising another harvest after the blight of snow and the cruel whistlings of winter. And see the firs run golden.

❧

A new problem has arisen.

At first, it manifested itself as a very slight tang in the air, something almost indiscernible. It was like walking down a crowded street and momentarily being aware of the merest whiff of a woman's perfume; akin to being in a crowded room and smelling the raw, secret scent of recent lovers without actually being able to pinpoint the source.

It came upon me as I was shaving, a time of deep concentration for me as I have always been loathe to cut myself during my toilet. To enter the cosmonauts' mess with a small sticking plaster on the chin or neck led invariably to great badinage: shaving has always been a tricky task for spacemen and the attitude was, if you nick yourself in the shower at Baikonur, you are just as likely to slit your throat in space.

In the early days of the Soyuz project, experiments were conducted to decide the most effective way of keeping a smooth chin in a weightless place. It was not just a matter of shaving as on Earth for the stubble had to be contained. It was dangerous to have the fine rough splinters of hair drifting in the spacecraft. Being capable of conducting electricity, the shorn stubble was a short circuit risk: worse, if one of the cosmonauts inhaled it, it could not only be uncomfortable but also dangerous. Tests conducted on monkeys showed inhaled stubble not only irritated the lining of the throat or nose but, if it got as far as the lungs, it behaved like tiny splinters, working its way into the mucous lining of the bronchioles to cause irritation, inflation and ultimately haemorrhaging of the lung.

Sevastyanov and Nikolayev tested dry blades coated with a stubble adhesive, but they scraped and hurt. Electric razors with aspirators to suck up any stubble and pass it through the air filters were tried but they did not give a close shave and the circular blade wheels, being made of inferior steel, quickly blunted. Finally, it was agreed the best method was an ordinary safety razor used in conjunction with a specially prepared shaving cream which looked like hair gel and was dispensed from a tube like toothpaste. It was soap free, obviating the need for wet wiping, and deliberately unperfumed although it did have a certain slight oleaginous smell to it.

I like to take my time over my personal hygiene. Some men rush it, step smartly into the shower and vigorously rub themselves then efficiently switch off the taps to get out and energetically towel themselves down. I prefer to stand in the shower, letting the warm water sluice over me, course across my chest in runnels, form drops on the hairs of my nipples and rivulet down my thighs. When I lather myself, I enjoy watching the bubbles move down my length in waves of white froth, stealing away the dirt and detritus of a day's work in the space laboratories, an afternoon's labour in Pyotr's vegetable patch or an evening's love-making with Shura in the wheat-fields.

Of course, such a luxury is lost to me forever now. On *Mir*, I have alternative options: first to 'wash' myself with wet wipes then dry myself with dry wipes, which is unsatisfactory and leaves me still feeling slightly soiled. Second is to make use of the partial body cleansing facility which is a hand-washer: a measured quantity of water is squirted on to a cloth then wrung in a squeezer unit to remove excess water which is safely sucked away to the waste management collecting tank. There is even a soap dish upon which sits a block of wax-ish soap which appears in both colour and consistency not unlike Lenin's face in his tomb. It looks most out of place not because of its similarity to Communism's Messiah but because, unlike everything else not nailed or screwed or clipped down, it does not float off its dish. The designers at Baikonur, wanting perhaps to give cosmonauts a reminder of their home gravity, have made the soap dish from steel and embedded in the block of Lenin's flesh a carbon magnet.

Third is to take a shower. Of sorts.

The personal shower facility is a mockery of the real thing. It consists of a cubicle around which may be drawn a cylindrical door in lieu of a curtain. The shower, which would suit the efficacious washer, is of the soak-soap-suck variety, though little soaking is done.

Once encased in the cylinder, with my feet arched into the hoops on the floor to stop me drifting about, I switch on the hand nozzle which delivers exactly one thousand millilitres of lukewarm water under pressure, shooting it in a slightly expanding spray. This I have to rub over my body before it drifts off to be sucked into the waste management system through a series of small holes above my head or below my feet. Once dampened — one can hardly say wetted — I lightly rub myself down with soap which is then rinsed off with another one thousand millilitres, the water from each operation being collected from my body by a flexible hose attached to a vacuum nozzle.

The whole operation takes less than five minutes. It is hurried in the way all military affairs are chivvied along.

So, when I shave, not being bound to routine or doctrinaire procedures, I take my time. I can make a personal hygiene session last from Cape Town, over the North Pole and almost down to Hawaii.

It was whilst shaving over Alaska I sensed the tang in the air. I was concentrating on the blade, watching in the mirror as it slid over my skin just as I was sliding over the world, smoothly, silently. My mind was blank of any thought. Shaving is a little like love-making: if done properly, it can be so auto-erotic in a non-sexual way it has the capacity to empty the mind.

It was hard to define, not an unpleasant smell, more an obscure animal odour. For a moment, it vaguely reminded me of musky wine and I tried to assess what might have such a smell in the spacecraft.

Then it dawned on me. Malfunction.

When he breathes, a human exhales over four hundred separate chemical compounds — carbon dioxide and monoxide, water, acetone, methane, hydrogen, acetic and carbonic acid, hydrogen, volatile and sometimes toxic oils — not to mention bacteria and viruses. As long as he lives, and even after his death, tiny flakes of himself break free as dust.

Ally these to the various sealants, seals, plastics, adhesives, lubricants, solders, insulations, coatings and polishes used in the construction of *Mir* and one is left with a dangerous aerosol of potentially life-threatening dusts and particles.

To cope with this lethal cornucopia, the Atmospheric Control and Management System continually re-cycles, rejuvenates, filters, heats, cools, dehumidifies or dampens the air I suck into my lungs and pollute.

Should this go wrong, I am doomed.

As soon as I realized the malfunction, I knew what I had sniffed. Good old vinegar. It was not the tart variety but the sweet kind Anna provided for Pyotr to pickle his cauliflower heads in.

Quickly completing my shave, I stroked my chin to satisfy myself the job was well done — as if I was likely to be kissing any pretty girls! — and set about unscrewing the wing nuts which hold the ACMS inspection plate. With it removed, the taint of vinegar grew a little stronger. With the spanner clipped to the inside of the plate in my hand, I unwound the filtration unit retaining bolts, placing them in my pocket to stop them wandering off to play by themselves.

The filter, when I got to it, was clogged with a fine mess of grey slum rather like one finds down the plughole of a particularly noxious domestic drain.

Bloody hell! I exclaimed.

This sludge was not some divorced gunk which had vicariously collected here. It was me. Every bit of it had once been a part of my body.

I recoiled from it. If it had suddenly come together to form a space creature which reached out to me with slimy tentacles and tore a living creature like itself from a cavity in my sternum I could not have been more repulsed.

Not being sure of the procedure for cleaning the filter, and not finding this mentioned in the computer files, I turned to the manual. It offered no specific cleaning routine but I noticed one paragraph which has made me distinctly uneasy. It read:

> *The atmospheric filtration unit filters are fine mesh grids situated in compartment II-B of the ACMS housing in front of the ACMS extractor fan assembly.* **!WARNING!** If removing the filter, be aware of the EFA directly behind the filter which does **NOT** have a protective grille covering. The filter should not require attention during MSF (the abbreviation for 'manned space flight'). *If it becomes over-saturated with dust, remove this with a vacuum nozzle capable of dry-stuff evacuation.* **DO NOT DISCARD THE FILTER.**

At no point did it mention the filter trapping liquid. Clearly, if the dust was liquefied, there was something wrong: what, I could not tell.

Very carefully, not so much to avoid the high-speed fan blades as to stop the slum escaping from the filter, I removed the assembly and floated with it to the faecal collection unit where I scraped off as much of it as I could with the spanner and dumped it in the faecal collecting bowl, the suction vent whipping it out of sight into the waste management collection sack. Ideally, I should have rinsed the filter but there was no means by which I could do so safely except by taking it into the shower with me, and this alternative sent thrills of disgust up my spine. Besides, I was not sure I should risk wetting what was clearly designed for dry dust only.

When it was as slime-free as I could manage, I rubbed it down with a disinfectant wipe which I also allowed, against operating instructions, to vanish down the faecal collecting bowl. It seemed only right somehow that the detritus of my outer body should go the same route as my inner bodily wastes.

With the filter fitted back in place, the smell dissipated. Yet the fact remains: there is something wrong. The dust should have been dry and it was not. Dry dust would not clog up the filter, would still allow air to pass through it. Wet dust will not.

I shall have to keep an eye on the filter. If I do not, I will surely poison myself.

One moment, I shall be fit and free, the next I shall be endowed with a wandering mind and, five minutes later, I'll be as dead as a bolt in a bulkhead.

How ironic it would be, with all the unique opportunities I have in space for choosing a dramatic and honourable death, to shuffle off my mortal coil like a common suicide who connects the hose-pipe to the exhaust of his car, puts it through the passenger window, slams the garage door, sits behind the wheel and starts the motor.

❧

In three places within the shell of the egg carrying me on

my never-ending spin round the Earth, there are what is officially referred to as PEAPs — Primary Experimental Activities Packages. Each package, the smallest no bigger than a substantial briefcase but the greatest the size of a dowager's cabin trunk, is not all it seems.

Take the smallest: PEAP I appears quite innocuous, an aluminium box with a lid on it held in place by three spring-loaded steel clips. There are no warning labels on it, no little radio-active propellers or skulls. Open the lid and, within, there is a number keypad no larger than that of a desk calculator and a liquid crystal display capable of showing ten lines of read-out. A paper spool can be ordered to print out what is tapped into the keypad, by way of a check. And that is it. No fancy electronics peek tantalizingly through the frosted perspex cover in which the keys are set, no circuit board offers its gold-plated maze for inspection, no microchips sit squatly on their brown or green base.

The box is anonymous. No mention is made of it in the vade-mecum of the flight manual, no instructions exist on how to operate it, save within my head. It is not attached to a computer screen, has no speaker to issue requests or instructions in a metallic voice. If *Mir* were to be obtained intact by the Americans — or the Martians, come to that — there is no way they could infiltrate the contents for the box is booby-trapped. The removal of so much as one screw from the bodywork causes first the invisible microchips within to erase themselves then sends a hefty charge from a capacitor through the whole circuitry, overloading it and burning out certain sections of it. This much we were warned about in pre-flight briefings.

It is a state-of-the-art device the function of which is to

flim-flam about with radar profiles and signals. I have not the merest clue as to how it achieves this miracle but, in effect, it nullifies the strategic advantage of such aircraft as the American Northrop B-2.

The B-2 looks less like a multi-role bomber and more like a folded paper plane made by an ingenious and precocious child with a few lessons of origami under his belt. It has no tail, consisting of a thick supercritical wing resembling a boomerang with a serrated rear flight edge. Constructed not of aluminium like most aircraft but of carbon fibre and Kevlar, only the high-stress sections are formed of metal: titanium is used. The entire airframe is covered by a radar-absorbing composite skin. Even the engine efflux nozzles are so placed that the hot exhaust gases emit over the inboard trailing edges to reduce heat emission. The head-on radar profile is less than ten per cent of the nearest radar-fooling aircraft and every external feature has been designed to present the lowest radar, infrared and electro-optical signature possible. In effect, it is near radar-invisible.

PEAPI makes such aircraft radar visible.

The second PEAP consists of several boxes and compartments attached to each other by wiring conduits. The equipment therein measures a very wide waveband in the electromagnetic spectrum, covering every wavelength from the ultra-violet >0.29mm, through visible light and infrared to microwaves >2.0m. This gadgetry, which includes a multi-spectral photographic system in addition to several other cameras, relays through a television and radio link network to ground control. With such capability, science staff in Baikonur and other tracking stations can access non-imaging multi-spectral radiometry data, multi-spectral aerial photography, multi-spectral vidicon television transmissions, multi-spectral line-scanning output and synthetic aperture radar or active imaging microwave information.

All this allows for extensive earth resource study, mapping, planning and analysis. Land use classification, crop identification, plant disease recognition, crop damage detection and even yield estimation is possible. On top of that, soil quality and type can be assessed, forests studied, maps updated or, in some instances, written, urbanization traced, pollution and pollutant drift studied, geology and mining information realized, ocean currents observed and the sea floor mapped, fishing shoals guarded or exploited, weather patterns recorded and volcanoes or floods scrutinized.

From my elevated seat against the star curtains of eternity, I can watch quite dispassionately as car fumes gas hundreds in Los Angeles, bush fires burn thousands in Africa, ash clouds smother ten thousand in the Philippines and the Ganges drowns a hundred thousand in Bangladesh.

What is more, like any omniscient being, I can prove the lies: those fields I romped in with Shura cannot, believe me, produce the yield level those party newscasts used to trumpet and the coal of the Ukraine is going to run out in the not-too-distant future. As for a good war in the making, I can be the holy adviser. This is my divine declaration — presidents and kings, power-brokers and priests, do not waste your time over the Persian Gulf, starving out marsh-dwellers and bombing Bedouins. Instead, concentrate on the South Atlantic. The seabed bears more oil than you need to drive your cars and spin your turbines, foul your countries and poison your futures.

Perhaps this is to be my role as I move, as we all do, inexorably towards death — to guide my own kind towards their Armageddon, play with them as the cat does with the mouse, or the mongoose with the snake, or the wanton boy with the fly. Or as a god does with his creation.

The third and biggest PEAP is the one I like the most. It is a fantastic technical achievement consisting of a powerful image-rendering and re-analysing computer, a colour television screen (with the inevitable Earth-bound link which is scrambled for security purposes) and three television camera assemblies mounted on the outer fuselage. It goes without saying it was invented and installed for the sole purpose of espionage.

Of all mankind's most useless occupations, spying is the most futile. Billions upon billions of dollars, roubles, pounds, deutschmarks and, no doubt in ancient times, cowry shells and dolphins' teeth have been expended gathering information about one's enemies, opponents, antagonists and even friends. As soon as the information is acquired, it is invalid: men change, worlds change, circumstances change. The only benefit I can see arising from espionage is that it has kept novelists and film producers, actors and cameramen, printers and publishers gainfully employed: and journalists, who occupy the next rung down the social ladder from beggars and whores, for whom a good sex-and-spy scandal sells more papers than a ritzy royal wedding in London or a public presidential indiscretion in Washington.

Of course, as soon as *Mir IV* was mooted and the design team sat down at their tables, the military boys met with the boffins and the payload was determined: so many tons of electronics, food, water, human flesh, experiments and what was always referred to in coded armyspeak as MPAMs — Military/Political Advantage Modules.

PEAP3 is more officially known as an Image-Rectifying and Intensifying Remote Sensing Video Recognition System. In short, it can take vidicon photographs of locations on the ground, the computer assessing and correcting the image until it becomes as sharp as a snapshot taken by a cheap camera in the hands of a tipsy uncle at a family picnic. And this is not all. It can, in the right conditions, zoom in so close as to recognize objects less than half a metre in size. In other words, if the sunlight is not too diffuse and the shadows not too deep but sufficient to give a three-dimensional quality, and the air is not too polluted or the image not too fast-moving, it can just about recognize and record the tipsy uncle's beer bottle standing on a folding table by Auntie Olga's handbag.

The military potential for such a tool is enormous. During the Cuban missile crisis — as they called it — the Americans were able to photograph what they thought were missile trucks in what purported to be jungle clearings next to what might have been construed as missile workshops. Now we (and, be sure of it, they as well) can read the lettering stencilled on the rear fin of the smallest missile and watch as the missile truck driver nips across to the roadside ditch to take a piss.

During the first phase of the mission, when the others were aboard, we had a number of tasks to conduct with the PEAPs. Whole swathes of Siberia were scanned with PEAP2, the seabed of the coastal regions around

Novaya Zemlya and Novosibirskiya Ostrova were mapped and Kazakhstan was surveyed for soil water levels. On three occasions, and at short notice, whilst passing over the western United States, we were scrambled to operate PEAPI.

I was in charge of these tasks.

The form was simple. In a bleak bunker on Mount Klyuchevsk, a man sitting at a dented steel console with a set of earphones clamped to his crown and watching a radar picture beamed to him from an early warning reconnaissance aircraft somewhere over the Pacific noticed an anomaly, smelt a rat or had the strings of his instinctive violin plucked. He depressed a button and a light went on in Baikonur. Another man, seeing the light, twirled a dial and a series of co-ordinates raced through the skies to strike *Mir IV*. A buzzer in the PEAPI sounded and I flipped open the catches, pressed the red knob and, according to the numbers read out to me by Gavriil, punched the data into the keyboard.

From there on, the process was automatic. The numbers in the liquid crystal display flickered and changed like those of a national lottery reader. Gradually, over the space of sixty seconds, they grew less and less and were replaced by an elastic grid which altered shape. A blip would appear momentarily somewhere on the grid which would then centre on it and start to reform. At last, the blip would be constant, a line of figures printing out below the now frozen grid. From the buzzer emanated a broken *brss-brss* sound, like a lazy summer wasp trying to get through a pane of glass.

Gavriil took the numbers from me and relayed them

to Baikonur who passed them on to the man with the earphones. In ten minutes, a voice would congratulate me, as if I had been the king-pin in the proceedings rather than merely the typist.

Every time we achieved a firm blip I could not help thinking, if this was war, I would have just, by merely typing numbers into a box, made visible a hidden aircraft and eradicated a man. The thought never failed to briefly chill me.

Why, I cannot say now: it is the role of gods to give life and to take life away. It is our velleity, our bounty, our responsibility. It is also our primary entertainment. I know for I have been so entertained.

It was, however, PEAP3 which provided us with the most staggering results, for none of us had any notion of its capability before blast off.

We had, of course, been trained to use the IR2-SVRS as it was abbreviated from its initials, subsequently shortened further to IR2. Settings and parameters, control codes and operational codes were easily learned as were the techniques of aiming, focusing and guidance. Yet at no time had we seen the equipment operating for real. All of our training was conducted in a flight simulator either ground-based at Baikonur or installed into a specially adapted Tupolev TU-204 going into free fall from 40,000 feet to simulate weightlessness. In short, we were accustomed to going through the operating routines but not with seeing any genuine hard-copy results.

It was not until some time in the second half of +4 the signal came through for us to switch on the equipment and use it. Vladislav was on duty at the time whilst Gavriil,

Stepan and I were taking a rest period, snug in our sleeping restraints.

The other two were, in fact, dozing but I could not. I was not tired and found the enforced rest periods, built into our activities schedules, tiresome. I have always been a man to keep my own hours and even months of training had not blotted out the most ingrained urges of my biological clock.

I hung — or lay: have it as you will for, in space, certain verbs are obsolete or ambiguous — in my restraint, my eyes straying around the cabin, my mind drained of all thought. It was not until I cast a glance at Vladislav I stopped and paid attention.

He was suspended before the television monitor attached to the PEAP3 assembly and, although one's muscles tend to be relaxed in weightless space unless actually being used, I could sense he was tense, excited and even a little apprehensive. No sooner was the realization in my mind than he turned and saw me looking at him. For a long moment, our eyes met: his were slightly staring, like those of a man exiting a cinema after a horror film during which he has been excited to the point of fear yet always known the blood was fake and the werewolf created by clever make-up.

Come, he mouthed at me: it was a part of the mission programme no one be disturbed whilst sleeping, yet it was patently clear I was awake.

Waving his hand around his wrist like a traffic policemen on junction duty, Vladislav beckoned to me. There was an urgency in his action. I unzipped the sleeping restraint, tidied it quickly into its retaining cover and pushed myself across to his side.

Look at this, he whispered, his mouth close to my ear.

There was on the screen a moving colour image but I was not quite able to work out what it was: to gain a clear view of a picture, one has to be directly in front of the monitor.

Incredible! Vladislav remarked, his whisper slightly louder with his excitement. It's just incredible!

I gently nudged him aside and moved into position. On the monitor screen was an aerial view of what was clearly a military establishment. On one side of a low, oblong building were parked six or seven cars and a flat-bed truck: the cars were black, red and silver but the lorry and one large saloon beside it were painted khaki. Two bushes stood to the side of the parking area which was metalled and, behind them, a tree cast a short shadow over what I took to be sun-scorched grass. Between the tree and the building was a flagpole from which an American stars-'n'-stripes flag was pensile in folds against the wood, the colours obvious despite the flag not moving. I would have guessed the camera taking the picture was fixed at an altitude of about thirty metres.

What is this . . . ? I began.

Vladislav looked at me then reached across to press the shift control. The view started to shift as if the camera was panning. The car-park and building disappeared off screen right as the view altered. A pathway of white concrete cut in a straight line through more bushes and beneath a scantily-leafed tree. Some steps were arrived at which went down into a trench and stopped in deep shadow. The pan continued. Into sight came a semi-circular plate then, beyond it, a hole in the ground about five metres in diameter. Poking up through it was the nose of a missile.

I don't quite understand . . . I said.

Vladislav replied, his soft voice quivering, It's a silo. In Nebraska. In America. About forty kays north of a town called Grand Island. There's a complex. About ten silos.

Yes, I interrupted quietly, I can see that much, but where is the image coming from?

He nodded at the monitor.

I turned to face the screen again. A man was walking across the ground towards the semi-circular silo door: he moved with a determined step, was obviously a military man. After a few steps, he looked up as if some sixth sense made him aware he was being observed. I could not quite make out his features but his hair was fair.

What is this? I asked again, my voice slightly louder now.

It's what we can do, Vladislav rejoined. The IR2 is taking a video film of what you see and relaying it back to Baikonur.

A video film! They never showed us this in training. It was always . . .

Stills, Vladislav interrupted. I know. They kept it from us.

But it looks as if . . . I said, my eyes held by the monitor.

I know. But we're not forty metres up. We're at — he checked the read-out on the orbital positioning unit — six kays off apogee. That's 404 kilometres up.

I returned my gaze to the screen. The figure had reached the door, stepped on to it, gone to the edge and was now, it seemed, calling down to someone within the silo shaft. For a moment, I wondered if I might not, by turning a knob, increase the volume. It was too amazing to believe I was not watching a piece of ordinary film.

How long does it sustain the image? I asked.

Vladislav said. For about three minutes. The tracking locks on . . .

I know, I replied, all the cameras have forward movement compensation and frame/lens rotation. But this . . . This is astounding.

Of course, Vladislav continued, it can't film over the horizon.

Sure enough, as he spoke, the signal commenced breaking up and, over the course of fifteen seconds, the screen image was lost to a snow-storm of interference.

With over an hour left of my rest period, I returned to my sleeping restraint and buckled myself in yet I did not sleep. I could not remove the image of the silo from my mind. Now, in the calm, I could recall details which had not been apparent at the time but which had impressed themselves upon me. The walking man had been an officer: I had registered the fact he wore silver on his shoulders. The missile in the silo had the letters U and S painted on the fuselage. Of the cars, the red one was a convertible two-seater sports car with the roof open. I could clearly remember the matching red leather seats and the steering wheel, a driving mirror mounted on each door. Finally, I recalled, although I had not been conscious of it at the time, a shape under the tree which I now realized was a dog lying on its side in the shade.

And it occurred to me how very similar the scene was to one of ours. Around our silos — I have visited a number of them, built into the flat steppes or cornfields of the

Moscow Basin just as the American one was dug into the wheat-belt prairies — officers and men park their cars, although admittedly not fancy racers such as, perhaps, the officer on the door owned, and certainly I have seen dogs belonging to military personnel about the place. Our stores were in low, oblong buildings and, not infrequently, a nearby flagpole bore a flag. I could, I thought, have been looking down on Mother Russia were the cars more drab, the trees less full and the dog less well fed.

Now, alone in space, I use the IR2 for a completely different purpose. Instead of spying upon officers and armaments, soldiers and secret installations, I arbitrarily take a three-minute long peek at wherever I might be traversing.

On my penultimate orbit, I trained my space eagle eye upon Los Angeles.

I do not seek out especial co-ordinates as Vladislav was instructed. He was ordered to look at a certain pinprick on Earth to confirm intelligence reports: sometimes he found the intelligence proven whilst, at other times, he was left staring at a vacant expanse of desert, field or waste ground. What I do is take a general co-ordinate of the land below me then, adding random figures to bring the field of search down as small as possible, set the apparatus in motion and take pot luck.

On occasion, I hit nothing of interest but this time I struck fortune.

After a minute of searching and waiting for the co-ordinates to come into range, the screen flickered and I found myself observing a riot. It being summer in California, the air is hot, the sun is high and tempers are strained.

How the riot came into being is, of course, something I shall never know: but, for three minutes, I saw the full action.

There was a wide street along the kerbside of which were parked cars, end on to the sidewalk. Running about between these cars were several hundred people, many of them either black or very dark skinned. As they ran, they paused and threw objects back the way they came. Several of these erupted into flame on the road surface and I took them to be Molotov cocktails, another purportedly Russian invention. Panning the camera, I shifted my view on to the target of these bombs. Advancing down the road was a cordon of police, patrol cars following behind them with numbers blazoned on their roofs. Iridescent red, violent white and electric blue flashes issued from the lights bar over each windscreen, bouncing off the paintwork of the parked cars. Every policeman was helmeted, the front phalanx carrying shields. As I watched, one of these men fell. He must have been shot. Instantly, a thin veil of smoke was thrown up by the police as they returned fire. I panned back. There were a number of bodies on the roadway, some lying still, others writhing, trying to crawl to the cover of the parked vehicles. A dull flash appeared in the centre of the road down which an intermittent yellow line was painted. White smoke belched from the site of the flash. With this, which I took to be tear gas, the rioters dispersed and the image on the screen began to disintegrate.

I was not shocked by this exposé of raw humanity, nor was I saddened or even made sympathetic by it. I was quite detached for this is the way with gods. We look down from heaven and we see what is happening to creation and we are dispassionate for, at heart, we are cold and calculating. And cruel.

Do not believe what you read in the various scriptures of the religions men have forged for their own peace of mind.

The reality of deity is otherwise.

❧

+198:19:46:00.

Today, I am Konstantin Eduardovich Tsiolkovsky. Allow me to introduce myself.

I was born on 17 September 1857 in the village of Izhevskoye in the province of Ryazanskaya. My father was a forest ranger and no lover of the Tsar which cost him his job. My mother, Mariya Ivanovna Yumasheva, was a beautiful woman who bore the rigours of marriage to an anti-tsarist with stoical dignity. Later, I moved with my family to Vyatka where I learned to swim and dive in the river and jump from floe to floe as the thaw came.

They called me Ptitsa — Little Bird — because I was restless.

How much a name can prophesy.

When I was ten — I think it must have been about then — I caught a cold, then scarlet fever, and was made deaf. The world was muffled, my friends left me and I was lost.

I suppose my real self is not unlike Ptitsa flying high, lost in the void, abandoned to my fate, unable to hear a human voice unfettered by a beam of radio waves.

Three years on, my mother died and I was forced to leave school. But then, at sixteen, I went to Moscow, rented a third of a room from a laundry-woman for fifteen kopecks and started to read in the public library. I was poor, half starved, dressed in rags and as near as dammit as deaf as a post but I taught myself integral and differential calculus, advanced mathematics, statistics, spherical trigonometry, algebra. I married Varvara Yevgrafovna Sokolova and took a teaching job in a primary school near Kaluga. And I experimented. And I slept short hours. And I was short with my wife. And I dreamed of the skies. And I wrote.

My dreams and words were about flying in space beyond the ensnaring octopus of gravity.

In March 1883, I wrote

There is neither up nor down in free space because down is the direction in which bodies travel at accelerating speeds. There are no vertical or horizontal places. There are no mountains or chasms. No stone ever falls into a chasm, nor does any unwary animal. Just as the moon hovers above the earth without falling down to it, so a man there can hover over a chasm which would be frightening to earthlings.

Already, I was voyaging to the moon. I designed an aeroplane with a petrol engine and a spaceship with a rocket motor: and, in our house on Georgivevskaya ultisa, was my *vozdukhoduvka*, my wind tunnel for experiments on wind resistance and aerodynamics. My articles — *Exploring Space with Reactive Devices, The Duration of Solar Radiation, Air Resistance and Aeronautics* — became known when Mikhail Mikhailovich Filippov published them. Mendeleyev praised me. My formula on the motion of rockets was accepted and named after me.

Yet all this is in the past. For, today, I am not the hungry crank in the village school but an old man, a member of the Socialist Academy, honorary member of the Society of Friends of Natural Science, honorary professor at the Zhukovsky Air Force Academy. I am a hero of the Soviet Union, the Father of Cosmonautics.

The street outside is steep and cobbled. Few cars drive this way, down to the river Oka. In winter, it's as treacherous as a glacier until someone salts it and strews it with gravel: in the summer, camomile and buttercups push through between the stones. In the gardens, behind the fences, gnarled apple trees grow and cows graze the river bank.

Someone is stepping up to my door. I can just sense their footsteps resounding on the planks of the veranda. The strident doorbell rings tentatively, almost cautiously. Whoever is out there is afraid of me, or in awe of me, or afraid of themselves. With equal, though differently motivated, caution I move slowly to the window and push the curtain aside. My hands are old: my fingers, thin and as yellow as parchment, have nearly run their course of writing words and typing reports, scribbling numbers and tapping pencils as they await the next instruction from my brain.

Of course, I cannot see them. Foolish me! If the bell has rung they are, *per se*, out of sight. Such a collapse of logic! No car is parked on the cobbles, crushing the weeds.

I look around my room. The walls are lined with books, folders, manuscripts and the desk where I sit for quiet hours at a time now, a creature not so much of thought as contemplation and habit, is cluttered with a slide rule, an ammeter and drawings of machines which may never work except in the fantastic chambers of my soul.

There is a knock upon my study door. I glance in the glass of a photograph hanging on the wall and see an old, grey-bearded man with a hollow chest, steel-rimmed spectacles perching on his nose. I settle in my armchair and balance the book I was looking at rather than reading upon the arm.

Come in, I say at last, louder than normal, as a deaf person does when he forgets the rest of the world can discern a sparrow's fart at twenty paces.

A young man comes in. He wears a flyer's uniform with medals from a war I do not understand.

And he is me.

We talk about mathematics and the concept of space, about drifting in time, about progress and Einstein. I cough frequently as he listens and he is polite enough not to interrupt me when I mumble or lose my train of thought for a moment. My slow speech races ahead of my mind and I get lost from time to time. My shoulders hunch a bit.

Our conversation moves inexorably towards rocketry. It always does with visitors: they do not want to hear about my aching back or tired eyes, my life with Varvara Yevgrafovna, my disappointments and failures.

I put my listening trumpet to my ear to hear his words which are my words. He tells me of rockets and I laugh, with my eyes. It hurts my throat too much to laugh aloud. When he is done, I tell him of my route to Mars, the place to land on Saturn, what to find or look out for on the surface of Venus. Or Mercury. I continue to assure him mankind will not live only upon Earth, that there will come a time when humans inhabit other planets, will conquer inter-solar space. Satellites will not merely carry telephone calls from businessmen and lovers, parents parted from their children and generals requesting strategies, but also helioelectric power cells beaming clean power to sub-stations down below. In vast glasshouses circling the sun, rare plants will grow, rare seeds germinate and food be grown for all men equally. The scent of tropical orchids will mingle, I assure him, with the fragrances of the stars.

Or, I think, not. Who cares? Not I. Not any longer.

We drink a little tea. He gives me some token of esteem. It is a model of a rocket three-quarters of a metre long, fashioned in aluminium and correct in every detail, down to the rivets and vanings on the fins. I thank him for it, assert I shall always treasure it.

Little Sasha next door shall have it. He is a destructive boy and can hurl it through space to crash land into the dung-heap created by his father's cows.

At last, my visitor goes. We shake hands. His is firm, mine has gripped enough congratulatory paws.

He is shown out and I hear his shoes upon the stairs, in the hallway, on the veranda and then the cobbles. I do not get up to see him go up the street although I am sure, for I have seen it in the past, he will stop at the end and look back contemplating his meeting with the man who dreamed of travelling to the moon and sent him there.

+198:21:18:14.

That is over with. I have come out of my selfish trance

suspended in space and am myself again, a single figure, not married to a whim.

It is time to eat. I drift to the storage lockers and remove a main meal, variant 2. This is one of eleven different menus. I know them off by heart: variant 2 is liver pâté, *borshch*, chicken with prunes (puréed into a sort of coarse stew) and cream cheese *zapekanka*. The pâté has to be spooned out of an hermetically sealed tub, the soup has to be reconstituted with hot water, the chicken has to be rehydrated and heated whilst the *zapekanka* has to be eaten from a tinfoil cup. It goes without saying these bear little similarity to the real thing.

I strap myself into the restraint at the table and begin to prepare my repast. Out of the window above my head, the horn of Africa is sliding by with a string of clouds, like the tail of a comet, peeling off from the peninsula and curving out towards the Yemen. The land in view is the colour of liquid raw sugar whilst the sea is a dark, royal blue verging on black.

As I insert the nozzle to inject hot water into the plastic bag of *borshch* powder, just for a moment, my hands look like those of an ancient. I blink. Now they are mine again. I squeeze the trigger and a measured quantity of water squirts into the bag. My hands are shaking as if, despite being in early middle age, they belong to a senile old fool too prone to pedantry and monopolizing the conversation at dinner parties.

Suddenly, I am afraid to glance towards the mirror. Like Dorian Gray, I am terrified of what I might see. Instead of a cosmonaut in the prime of life, in need of a shave and perhaps a little pallid from not being able to tan himself by the rays of a benevolent sun, I might catch a glimpse of an old cosmonaut. Or Academician Konstantin Eduardovich Tsiolkovsky, long since in his grave.

Not that it will ultimately make a jot of difference. I am whoever I am, man or god, sucker or scientist, dreamer or dumb-arse and there's not a thing I can do about it.

❦

The train journey from St Petersburg to Archangel took two days in the depths of winter. It is a twelve-hundred-kilometre route and not direct. The railway goes first due east for about six hundred kilometres to Vologda where it joins the line from Moscow.

I have only travelled that way once, during the early days of my cosmonaut training when it was demanded of me that I undergo a four-week Arctic survival course. It was intended not only to save me should my re-entry module go off course and hit the ice cap but also to toughen me up, test me and my comrades, sort out the sheep from the goats.

As would-be spacemen, we were all afforded privileges usually reserved for senior party officials, apparatchiks and members of the nomenklatura, the wives and mistresses — and boyfriends — of Politburo bigwigs, deputies and men with large pockets and capacious wallets.

There were five of us taking the course under the instruction of a specialist Arctic warfare unit based in a camp on the shore of the White Sea north of Archangel. We had not met prior to our coming together in the railway station in St Petersburg and, as we were introduced, we eyed each other cautiously for we were in competition. Only three of us could pass through to the next stage of space training.

Well, now you know each other, Colonel Dogonkin said after we had exchanged pleasantries in a waiting room reserved for officialdom, I'll leave you to it to go and get your balls frozen off.

He pulled his *papakha* down over the top of his ears. It was made of lamb's fleece, pinpricks of light catching the melted snowflakes in the fur.

One thing, he remarked as his aide-de-camp opened the door for him, it'll be a bloody sight harder up there with Major Livanov and his frost-bitten crew of killers than it ever will be on the dark side of the moon. Survive the next month and you'll face hoards of Venusian cannibals with equanimity.

With that, he was gone and we exchanged nervous glances.

Army crap, said a voice quietly.

I turned. It was the first time I set eyes on Vladislav Cherkasov for he had been relieving himself in the officials' toilet as the rest of us were introduced.

You think so? I queried.

Sure! He shrugged. Those Venusians can suck your brains dry with one telepathic nod. I bet there's not a single weapon in the secret arsenal of the entire Red Army capable of *that*.

On the train, we were assigned a four-berth sleeping compartment each. This was luxury indeed. One of the top bunks was folded down and laid with crisp sheets and several deep quilts whilst every light socket had a bulb in it, dimmed by a switch near the door. In the corner, by the window, was a triangular porcelain basin set in a mahogany case, a small bar of lavender-scented soap placed in the dish above it. The blind was pulled down on the window so I raised it and, for a while, stood looking out at the platform along which passengers were hurrying, loaded down with cheap suitcases, bundles and packages tied with cord.

To watch them passing was to observe a cavalcade of all the Russian peoples. There were businessmen in suits under camel-hair overcoats, peasant farmers or foresters in thick padded jackets and scarves, old hags in long dresses and heavy coats, young women in furs reaching below the tops of their lined boots, red-faced soldiers encumbered by satchels and rifles, sailors with their belongings neatly stowed in kit bags. Most were of European stock but there were others on the platform, hurrying as the seconds to departure ticked away — Siberians and Georgians, Azerbaijanis and Turkestanis, Armenians and Kazakhstanis and those clearly of Mongolian ancestry. There was even an African, most probably a foreign student for, at the time, the USSR was encouraging them to visit the best universities and learn chemical engineering or mining and the true worth of the teachings of Marx and Lenin.

At just before midnight, the train horn sounded and the couplings clanked as the locomotive took up the strain. Very slowly, the platform began to move backwards, the light from my window catching the faces of those waving goodbye or just standing watching bleakly as the carriages gained speed.

It was snowing hard outside the station and, before we

crossed the Neva, white cancers of ice began forming on the window-pane. Behind them, the occasional weak glow of a street lamp shone through the developing blizzard.

Pulling down the blind, I turned on the light over the bunk and unpacked a book from my case. I forget what it was but I do know it was a western novel in English for when there was a discreet knock on my door, I guiltily hid it under my coat.

Come! I called out over the slow staccato rattle of the wheels across a junction of points.

The door opened and an attendant entered carrying a tray of tumblers filled with steaming tea and cardboard boxes the size of those in which shoes were sold.

Good-evening, *tovarishch*, he greeted me.

We were all comrades in those days.

So you have a samovar on the go somewhere? I replied.

In the next carriage, comrade. If you should need anything, do please ring.

He nodded to a white button set in a polished brass surround above the seat on which I was sitting.

Thank you, I said, going on, how old is this compartment?

How do you mean, comrade?

How old is it? I mean, it has a bell and the fittings, I nodded at the basin, seem rather antique and not a little . . .

Luxurious, comrade? he suggested. This carriage, I believe, dates back to before the war. He smiled, almost patronizingly. They don't make them like this now.

No, I agreed. I feel rather like the Tsar travelling in such style.

He smiled again and added, So long as you don't end up like the Tsar, comrade. Or behave like him.

Quite! I answered sharply.

Whilst we were talking, he unfolded a table from the wall beneath the window and, resting the corner of the tray upon it, off-loaded two tumblers and two of the cardboard boxes.

I am travelling alone, I said, noticing what he had done.

Yes, comrade, he replied. It's a long night.

And with that he left the compartment, sliding the door closed behind him.

I took a sip of the tea. It was piping hot and, as I swallowed it, I realized just how cold I was. Despite the efficiency of the heating in the compartment I was still suffering from the waiting room and the cold walk through the station. The outside temperature was at least −20°C.

There was another knock at the door, just as soft as the attendant's but somehow more insistent.

Come in, I called out, not as loudly as before because the train was now riding rhythmically over a straight length of track.

My expectation was to see one of the other potential cosmonauts standing there, perhaps with a bottle of vodka in his hand, grinning over his shoulder. Instead, the door slid open to reveal a young woman in a thick, dark brown fur coat and matching hat with a small overnight bag in her left hand.

Yes? I said.

Is this compartment six? she enquired.

The number was plainly marked on the door.

It is, I began, but I feel you may have made a mistake. This is reserved . . .

She stepped over the lintel and slid the door closed behind her, shrugging off her coat and lying it next to where I was sitting.

My name is Zhenia, she introduced herself, without invitation.

As she spoke, she checked a scrap of paper which might or might not have been a ticket, holding it at an angle to the light before raising her eyes to meet my own.

Compartment six, she said, tilting the ticket in my direction but giving me no chance to verify it.

She sat down opposite me across the table and warmed her hands momentarily on the second tumbler.

It is a very cold night, she commented.

Yes, I agreed.

She removed her fur hat and placed it on my coat. Her hair fell to her shoulders.

And a very long one, she added.

Having said this much, she daintily sipped her tea, put the tumbler down and opened one of the boxes.

Are you hungry? she enquired. We each have a box but . . .

Reaching across, she undid mine and peered inside.

. . . as I thought. No two boxes are alike. Shall we pool our resources?

Before I could reply, she had rung the bell and the attendant, who must have been hovering outside, knocked and entered without waiting to be invited in.

Could you bring us a large plate, please? she requested. And my case.

He nodded obsequiously, murmured an affirmative in a most deferential voice and disappeared, to return in a few moments with an oval silver-plated dish and a small aluminium suitcase. Placing the case by her legs and the dish on the table, he nodded once more, to each of us, and closed the door.

With long, delicate fingers, Zhenia removed a variety of *pirozhkis* and *vatrushkis* from the box, putting the former to one end of the dish and the latter to the other.

There are three salmon and wild mushroom *pirozhkis*, she said. We shall have to decide who eats the odd one.

I was so taken aback by this confident young woman I could make no reply. I just sat and studied her. She was, I guessed, about twenty-one, but it was hard to tell for sure for although she looked so young she had the manner and self-assurance of someone ten years older. As tall as I — my medical card put me at 1.81 metres — she was slim with small breasts under a light blue cashmere sweater. Her hair was half-way between blonde and auburn, cut to just below her shoulders. It shone with a healthy lustre in the dim compartment lights. Her skirt was short and tight, made of a black material with a sheen to it. It could have been silk. The stockings on her long and shapely legs most certainly were. Her waist was narrow, her arms not too fleshy nor too thin, her eyes hazel. Although the lights were low, her high cheekbones cast narrow shadows on her face which bore a discreet modicum of cosmetics.

Do you know why the lights are dim on Russian trains? she asked, breaking into my inspection of her.

To economize, I suggested. There is much demand upon power resources in the winter.

No, she said, that's not it. It's because bright lights are cold and dim lights are warm. A dim light encourages the body into thinking it is warm and, if that's the case, it will be warm. The dimmer the lights, the less heating is required.

That's a preposterous suggestion! I blurted out. You can't think yourself warm if the air's below zero.

She laughed. Her teeth were even and white, her lips, like her arms, not too full but not too slight.

But, she went on, her laughter vanishing, you can think yourself happy if you are sad and calm if you are angered.

That's different, I retorted. Those are states of mind, not physical realities. You might just as well think you are dry when standing in a shower.

She laughed again. There was a teasing glint in her eye and I, too, laughed.

I am still right, I said.

Really?

Still right, I reiterated. If your surmission is correct, and the lights are low to encourage psychological warmth, then this still saves power by necessitating less heating.

Are you a professor of logic? she enquired.

No. I am an air force officer.

There are few aeroplanes in Archangel at this time of year.

How do you know I am going to Archangel?

This is the Archangel train . . .

It was half a question, as if she was suddenly worried she had embarked upon the wrong service. There had been another train standing across the platform as we pulled out.

This is the Archangel train, but how do you know I am not going to Moscow, for example? I asked.

Via Vologda? she replied, with a hint of strained incredulity. In midwinter?

She picked up one of the little pastries.

I'm hungry.

Very daintily, she popped the *pirozhki* in her mouth.

They're very good, she remarked, wiping her mouth with a cotton handkerchief. As good as my *babushka's*.

Nothing is ever as good as one's own mother's — or grandmother's — cookery, I declared.

Perhaps, she allowed; then, reaching under the seat, she pushed the heater control handle to the hottest setting.

We ate the rest of the pastries and drank our tea without speaking. I wondered who she was, what she was, where she came from and where she was going. In those days, one did not ask such pertinent questions even of close friends, never mind passing acquaintances on life's wicked whirligig.

When we had finished the food and drunk the tea, I rose to my feet.

If you will excuse me? I said.

She nodded.

I left the compartment and, sliding the door closed, stood for a moment in the corridor. The windows were totally frosted over with patterns of ice. Snow was building up in the corners of the frames. The train was not travelling at any great speed, indeed not above fifty kilometres per hour, but even this was sufficient to compact it into every angle of the carriage exterior.

After a moment, I turned right to make my way towards

the lavatory at the rear of the carriage. The thought occurred to me to knock on Vladislav's door. I felt I needed to tell someone my compartment had been invaded by a pretty young woman verging on the beautiful: no wrong conclusions could then be drawn when the fact leaked out, as surely it would. In those days, everybody in the military minded everyone else's business when they could. One never knew when such information might come in useful.

Having seen him enter compartment three, I paused by the door and was about to knock upon it when I heard voices within. One was feminine.

Leaning against the window, I smiled inwardly to myself. Most probably, we each had a nocturnal companion. Either we had been cleverly targeted by up-market whores working the station or these were girls provided by Colonel Dogonkin.

When I returned to my compartment, I discovered from which source the girl had arrived. The pastry boxes, dish and empty tumblers were cleared away and in their place stood a silver-plated ice bucket with the neck of a champagne bottle protruding above the rim. Two glasses stood beside it with a little tray of *khvorost* sprinkled with sifted sugar powder.

Zhenia was sitting on the seat beneath the open bunk. She had hung up her coat and mine on a hook and was reading my western novel.

You are a naughty boy! she rebuked me, holding the book up.

Do you read English?

And French and Finnish. And a little German.

I stopped myself from remarking how seldom one came

upon an educated hooker. Yet this, I thought, was no street tart with the ability to offer poly-syllabic pillow-talk: this was a Party party girl, one of the best, able to hold her own with ambassadors and arms dealers. I smiled at the pun: it would not be her own she was used to holding.

Why are you smiling?

Nothing, I said. Just a thought.

And the book? she asked. There was no edge to her voice.

When I was a schoolboy, I replied, sitting next to her, we used to have sexy books circulate amongst us. Swedish books. Very explicit. Now . . .

Now you have western books.

Now I have western books, I concurred, and they do no more harm to me than those dirty books did in secondary school. A story by a western author is hardly likely to turn me into a raging capitalist. I have also read *Animal Farm* and *1984* and I am still a good Communist. One has to know one's opponents to act against them.

She put the book down and looked at the ice bucket.

Open the champagne.

I took the bottle out of the ice, the cubes clinking metallically on the bucket. It was a French champagne, Piper-Heidsieck, not one of the superior brands but then I was not a senior officer. The cork popped and I poured out two glasses.

Zhenia took hers, helped herself to one of the little biscuits, bit it in half then sipped the champagne.

I like to drink sparkling wine with *khvorost*, she said.

Later, as the train rumbled steadily through the frozen night towards Cherepovets, we stood naked in the gently swaying compartment, running our hands over each other's bodies. She was an expert, knowing just where to press with the ball of her thumb, where to lightly scratch the skin with her nails, where to momentarily slide her forefinger in. Despite the weather outside, we were sweating. At length, she insisted I took her on the folding table, lifting herself on to the polished wood and placing her feet on each of the seats, opening herself out to me. I stood between her thighs and pushed myself into her. She was wet and warm, as smooth as satin.

Go in all the way, she demanded in a husky voice so quiet I could only just discern her words over the sound of the wheels.

I did as I was told. She murmured a few times at her first orgasm then, satisfied, turned her attention to me, her fingers playing with me, teasing and enticing, squeezing and rubbing.

Afterwards, we lay side by side between the crisp sheets. She slept but I remained awake, thinking of Russia covered with snow, the eyes of wolves bright as stars against a jet backdrop of endless forests.

Gradually, the wan light of a winter's day eked through the frosty windows. From the next compartment, I could hear voices raised in laughter but was not able to comprehend the gist of their humour. The sun rose, filling the compartment with a weak flush. Opening the window a few centimetres, I gazed out at the monochromatic landscape. Telegraph poles went by with monotonous regularity. A small railway halt slid past with a man standing by a neat pile of logs thatched with snow. His lips were taut against the cold. The steam of his breath was suspended in the air before his mouth like a swarm of white bees about the slit entrance to their hive. Apart from the occasional field or cleared ground by the track, the world appeared to be covered in nothing but birch trees and ice. Nothing moved except, every now and then, a black bird of some sort which flew away from the train towards the safety of the forests.

The attendant served us tea and *kalachi* an hour before we arrived in Vologda.

Do you get off here, Zhenia? I enquired as the locomotive slowed on entering the outskirts of the town.

We were on first name terms now.

No. I am going through to Archangel with you.

We alighted from the train to stretch our legs on the platform. It was bitterly cold. Ice started to form on my upper lip and I had to blink to keep my eyes irrigated.

Come, Zhenia said and we went into the restaurant, crossing through the jostling, steaming, heaving mass of travellers at the cafeteria counter towards a door to the rear.

Zhenia knew her way about. There was an attendant at the door but, as soon as he saw us approaching, he opened it for us, giving me a glance of pure hatred as I passed through. I might, I considered, have been a tsar after all.

The room we had entered was rather like a sparse private drawing-room. A green and cream tiled traditional stove stood in one corner, emanating heat and a smell of pine pitch. We slipped off our coats and draped them over a chair. A second door opened and a waitress entered, a white apron tied round her waist. She said nothing as she placed a tray of *zakuski* on a table with a small bottle of vodka.

No sooner had we sat down than Vladislav entered with a petite blonde girl holding his hand. She wore a coat of grey rabbits' fur.

Good-morning, he greeted me and nodded politely to Zhenia who half-smiled at him.

Good-morning, I answered. We are half-way there.

The two women fell to talking quietly to themselves so I stood up and went to Vladislav's side where he stood warming his hands against the stove.

Dogonkin has flair, he said quietly to me. Never mind riding *in* a train. I've been riding *on* one. She goes like the trans-Siberian express.

That fast? I said.

Come along, friend! he retorted. Have you ever been on the trans-Siberian express? Fast? Never! Slow and rhythmical, takes its time, sways and rolls. You know what's the best thing could happen now?

Tell me, I suggested.

A blizzard, somewhere around Nyandoma. That's what we want. North of the junction at Konosha, anyway. A real country-closing, wolf-running, bear-hugging bugger of a blizzard with a strong wind, drifts five metres high and the snow-ploughs stuck in their sidings. Then we'll have to sit in the train for twenty-four hours and I can take the trans-Siberian railway all the way to Vladivostok. And back.

He looked up at the ceiling of the room where an old-fashioned light fitting hung down, coloured panes of glass surrounding two light bulbs, one of which was flickering.

Grant me this, God, and I'll kiss every icon and light every candle in St Isaac's Cathedral. That is, he justified himself, if we return with our balls unfrozen.

What if they get worn out instead? I asked. It's a long journey.

A chance I'll take . . . he said.

Vladislav was saved his kisses and candles. No blizzard intervened. For the rest of that day, and into the night, the train laboured northwards. Zhenia and I sat in our compartment. She read my western novel whilst I dozed or read a poorly written biography of Tchaikovsky someone had been selling on the platform outside the cafeteria: it evaded most of the controversial issues about his death and his penchant for picking up peasant boys and lovelorn sailors in dark alleys.

At dusk, which came not long after we left Vologda, the attendant served us a meal after which we drank vodka and talked, fondled and eventually fornicated.

We were used to each other now, had a rudimentary understanding of the other's preferences and pleasures. The first time, she wanted it standing up; the second, she lay on one of the seats, moving me in and out of her in time with the motion of the train; the third, we lay on the bunk, oblivious to the harmonies of the track, testing its mounting hinges and causing the wires supporting the outside edge from rings in the ceiling to loosen then twang tight.

As the train pulled into our destination, I asked the same question a thousand men ask of lovers and whores every day of the year wherever there are bordellos and loneliness.

Lifting Zhenia's case off the seat for her, I said, Shall I see you again?

Perhaps, she smiled. One day, when you are a famous cosmonaut and you need to take a train from St Petersburg to Archangel.

I had not mentioned, nor had she enquired after, my job. Yet she knew. Like every well-qualified courtesan, she knew.

And if I do not become a famous cosmonaut? I asked.

She kissed me lightly on my cheek, as if she really was in love with me, and said, Who knows?

Of course, I never saw nor heard of her again. After our month's training, we returned to Moscow by train but, this time, there were only three of us and we were obliged to share a compartment, piling our cases on the spare seat. The attendant did not serve little boxes of pastries and, when the train stopped in Vologda, the private rest-room was locked. I know, because Vladislav tried the handle. He was always a chancer.

Such is the way of all life. We meet, we touch, we part and that is an end to it. Nothing is more transitory than human relationships. It is all just a process of being cast together, later to drift away. The only variable is the length of time.

Right now, outside the triangular window next to the command console, it is colder than ever it was on the outer surface of the train. The frost would be inches thick were there water out there to form it.

And I am alone and yet I am not actually lonely. Not so very long ago, Zhenia was here for a few minutes, in her fur coat, with her legs spread wide. I saw her in my mind and fleetingly tasted her in my mouth. She had the flavour of champagne and *khvorost*.

So far as I know, there is one experiment which has never been attempted. Fucking in a state of weighlessness. It would surely be exceedingly difficult. One would have to grasp one's partner very tightly or there would be nothing upon which to gain purchase. Friction is essential to sex as more than just an erotic aid to carnal pleasure.

Possibly the Americans have given it a go. They are past masters at innovation. Who knows? Maybe their space shuttle has FRHs fittings — Fornicatory Restraint Harnesses.

Sitting at the food table, idly tossing the velcro darts at the dartboard without caring whether or not they stick or hit the bull, I recall what Shura said as she put on her shoe. The wheat-fields were like an ocean of mercy.

I never understood exactly what she meant until now as I realize, spinning through space with my future laid out like a Persian carpet before me, that train journey to Archangel was my first voyage upon its waters.

❧

It is one thing for the spacecraft to start to malfunction but quite another when I follow suit.

On three occasions over the last twelve days, I find I have been hallucinating. This is not a matter of having my floating dreams or patterns or colours: those, for want of a better term, are controlled fantasies. These others are distinctly uncontrolled, involuntary events over which I have no say.

My latest session of delusion occurred just over an hour or so ago, as I was using the Lower Abdominal Negative Pressure Unit.

The LANPU is one of the bio-medical experiments installed in *Mir IV*. It consists of a metal cylinder into which the subject inserts the lower half of his body to the waist, sealing himself in with a flexible rubber diaphragm just above the solar plexus. The pressure in the cylinder is then reduced by a pump mechanism until the negative level is equal to the effect of the ordinary, earthbound hydrostatic pressure experienced by a man standing upright in a IG gravity field. The data so gathered through capacitance gauges attached to the legs, and a strap around the upper arm containing a small microphone, records the subject's blood pressure and pulse, LANPU pressure, changes in leg volume, body weight, heart rate and body temperature — the microphone picks up Korotkoff's sounds. When data is being collected, the results are beamed down to Baikonur as well as being recorded in the on-board computers.

There is no need for me to use this equipment for experimental purposes but, by placing myself in it every ten days or so I can judge how my basic life functions are faring.

I had wiped the back rest, waist diaphragm seal, inner walls of the cylinder, seat and foot restraints down with an antiseptic swab and was just settling myself into the cylinder when my head began to spin. I was not dizzy. The effect had nothing to do with balance. It was my mind that was spinning, not my brain or the liquid in my inner ear.

Optimistically pressing my hands to my brow, as if this might have some result, I tried to stem what was going on within me but was powerless.

My eyes grew heavy and my muscles relaxed, so far as I could tell, and I wondered, in a lucid moment, if this was a reaction to the pressure being lowered on my nether regions but this could not have been so for I had not even sealed the diaphragm about my waist, never mind started the vacuum pump.

I have never been hypnotized but I imagine what I underwent was a similar experience but without the expertise of a psychiatrist or the chicanery of a fairground magician — or is it the other way around?

A series of images drifted through my subconsciousness: this is the only way I may describe what happened. At first, my mind was quite blank then, as suddenly as if someone had switched on a movie projector, I saw a face which was both familiar and yet utterly strange. For one moment, I knew it and was ready to welcome it but the next it was alien to me and I sensed an anger at it for having infiltrated my presence. It did not say anything, nor did it move save to blink. There was no expression upon it at all. I stared at it and it stared at me.

Gradually, it transmuted into another equally ambiguous face which was quite genderless: the first had, I now considered, probably been masculine.

Over a space of eight minutes, for I noticed the time on the counter just before I started to have these illusions, a number of faces drifted in front of my mind's eye. Some faded before the next appeared, others cut off immediately, some subtly changed from one into another.

Most were human faces, or so I thought. In retrospect, some may not have been. It is not that they were animal exactly, or even non-primate visages: it is more that some implied to me they were other than human. I suppose the nearest I can explain this is by using as a metaphor the sighting of auras.

There are those gifted people who claim to see a coloured aura about a person, the shape, hue and puissance of the glow denoting their temperament, honesty and strength of personality. I cannot vouch for the veracity of this gift having never possessed it and, being of a scientifically and unemotionally curious bent, I am sceptical of it but, this notwithstanding, I believe if such an ability exists, and if auras are real, then what I saw in those eight minutes was akin to it.

One or two of the faces remain with me, an hour later.

A child emerged at one point, leering brat-like and thrusting his face towards mine — it was a boy — in a pout of defiance. This was, I thought detachedly, the face of a lout in the making, a child ready to flaunt authority. He had been caught masturbating behind a hedge or touching up the girls in his class behind the school wall and, rather than accept his crime he was prepared to justify it, defend it on a point of logic. I could hear him, although his mouth did not move, belligerently arguing his case on the basis boys were males and possessed of an inordinate sexuality, and girls were the object of the sexuality. Therefore, he claimed, sticking his finger in their knickers and tossing himself off afterwards was merely a biological function, a part of the learning curve of masculine behaviour for which he should not be punished but praised for having had the audacity to test out his theories.

He would have made a fine lawyer.

No sooner had this pugnacious little oaf gone his way than Pyotr's face appeared, the only one of the invisible parade whom I recognized for certain, a quizzical smirk playing on his lips, his eyes glinting in the way they did when he was about to recount a joke or make a contentious statement.

My friend, I heard him say, quite distinctly, what is the difference between a dead rabid dog lying in the road and a dead lawyer lying in the road?

I do not know, I responded, listening to myself as if I was speaking from far across an echoing hall.

Then I will tell you. It is the tyre skid marks in front of the rabid dog's corpse.

Before I could laugh, or remonstrate, or come back at him with a riposte he was gone and, in his place, was another face which might or might not have been my mother's. She gazed at me with the despair of parenthood then altered into what I thought was her brother's face, my Uncle Stanislav.

With a fierce determination befitting a man who had worked his way up through the ranks of the KGB to head the office in Volgograd, he interrogated me. His questions were unintelligible and my answers just as obtuse yet they appeared to satisfy him for he grinned and melted into thin air like a soap bubble bursting, a few little specks drifting down from the minute implosion. When he was gone, I realized the gist of his cross-examination had been my alleged misbehaviour with some girls in a playground.

He was the last one. After his departure, my mind emptied and I came to as if from a trance. My body had drifted out of the LANPU cylinder and was lying alongside the bulkhead beside it. The cleaning swab I had been using floated near my right shoulder. Grabbing it, I thrust it into a waste disposal bag then spun the bag into the waste management airlock, closing the door on it.

Punching the control panel for the airlock beside the door, I listened for the hiss of the outer hydraulic hinge and the hollow suck of space as the outside vacuum tore the bag away, the contents decompressing as the air in the swab was voided. The noise was like the prayer of an exorcist, ridding me of the faces I imagined to be soaked into the material.

Attaching sensors to my skin and connecting these to the bio-instrumentation panel, I set the equipment to monitor. It took only a few minutes to produce a complete bio-medical profile.

My body temperature was low at 35.6°C, my heart rate was down to 62 and my blood pressure was below normal for a cosmonaut in zero gravity.

There was one factor in all this I could not determine which was bothering me. If the hallucinations came first and resulted in my cooling and slowing down then I was not so concerned: I had, presumably, woken up so to speak because the alarm bells were sounding in my system to say I was getting too cold. On the other hand, if my temperature had been dropping and I was not aware of it, the fantasies indicating a biological ignorance of the cooling, then I was at risk. Studying myself in the mirror in which I shaved did not suggest I was hypothermic: my skin was not red and I did not feel lethargic.

To be on the safe side, I provided myself with a hot drink, sucking it down as soon as I could without scorching my mouth. It warmed me — the digital thermometer took me up to 37.8°C — but somehow I did not sense it would prevent further phantasms from needling their way into me.

With my body now back to a comfortable state, I am

reasonably secure but I must not be complacent and must be always conscious of the fact I am possibly beginning to go the way of my spacecraft, starting to wind down, break up and cease to exist.

On the other hand, perhaps I have a greater cause for concern. It might not be my body which is emulating *Mir* but my mind, slowing developing hair-line cracks, stretching at the seams, pulling apart under unforeseen tensions and stresses. The collapse of my body is something I can accept, as every man must: the time will come when it simply will no longer work efficiently and I am ready for my heart to stop beating, my lungs to cease sucking air, my kidneys to give up filtering my blood. What I am most reluctant to conceive is the deterioration of my sanity.

A man, after all is said and done, is nothing but a bag of functional bones, not all that different from a pig in a pen or a hen in a hutch. Save in one respect. He possesses an intellect which divides him from bestiality, and I would not become a beast by losing it.

❧

Pyotr turned his derelict Zil away from the cart track, let it freewheel to a stop and switched off the engine.

Here we are, he remarked, adding somewhat tongue-in-cheek, A place as yet undiscovered by women.

We were halted on a flat promontory which, after a few more spring floods, would become an island as the meandering river changed its course, slicing through where the Zil had come to rest and turning the fast flow before us into an ox-bow lake.

You sure women haven't been here? I replied. That's a very considerable statement to make without foundation.

Stands to reason, Pyotr defended himself. If they had, they'd have settled here, or at least ruined it for the likes of us before moving on. No, look about you, my friend. Do you see the hand of any woman at work here save Mother Nature?

I had to agree. It was an unspoilt scene. The promontory was covered in short grass, the shore of the river lined here and there with clumps of reed and sedge. Across on the far bank, the deciduous forest reached almost to the water's edge whereas, on our side, the trees were kept at bay by the track made by the vehicles and feet of lumberjacks.

No time to waste, Pyotr declared. There are only eighteen hours of sunlight today and we've used up three getting here.

I looked at my expensive Japanese digital watch, obtained from a friend with a diplomatic posting overseas: it read 07:14.

As Pyotr opened the car door, a flight of ducks took to the wing from behind the largest rank of reeds. He raised his hand in mock imitation of a revolver and imagined them falling dead at his feet.

Now there's something to keep you busy, Bujan, he said as he opened the rear door.

The dog jumped languidly out to sniff the grass then, there being no bushes close by, cocked his leg against a rear wheel and let fly a squirt of pungent yellow urine.

Damned dog! Pyotr cursed, swinging his booted foot

half-heartedly in Bujan's direction. We're in the middle of a forest and he chooses to piss on the car.

He's only marking his territory, I commented, giving poor Bujan an excuse.

No! Pyotr exclaimed. He's marking *my* territory. The car's not his. If he wants a territory, let him go off in the forest and find it.

Together, we removed our weapons from the Zil: Pyotr had brought his old shotgun and I had an equally ancient Mosin-Nagant carbine on loan from Anikushin, a remnant of his service in the war against the Nazis. It still bore a rusty bayonet folded along the right side of the barrel.

If you can't hit anything, Pyotr observed, looking at the blade, you can stab it to death. It's sure to die of blood poisoning if you don't hit a main artery.

He slung a small wooden box with a carrying rope fixed to it over his shoulder, working the rope above his head and across his chest like a bandoleer: then he filled his loose-fitting jacket with cartridges from a hessian sack in the car.

You've got rounds for that . . . That thing? he enquired.

Thirty or forty, I replied. All Anikushin still had. The brass on some of the cases is black with tarnish.

Well, he's got no use for them, Pyotr retorted, what with his love affair with caterpillars and sparrows.

From beneath the front passenger seat, I took out the can of oil Pyotr kept in the car: the Zil consumed a litre of oil every two hundred kilometres or so, most of it being belched out in a smokescreen of filth every time the accelerator was depressed. Trickling a few centilitres on to the carbine, I rubbed it in with my finger, working the bolt to and fro to loosen it. Like the bayonet, it was rusty and badly in need of lubrication.

You should prepare your gear, Pyotr remonstrated, before you get in the field. Nothing worse than lining your sights up on a fat deer only to find your gear's not up to it. Don't they teach you that? If you get to be a cosmonaut, you'll have to take special care of everything. Let that go and . . . He thrust his hand up and exploded his fingers open. *Pooph!* End of flight!

A decrepit rifle borrowed biannually for one day is hardly the same as a spacesuit, I contested.

Pyotr grimaced. This line of argument was beneath him.

He slammed the car door and locked it.

So! Today we wander the forests and catch our weight in game!

I shrugged and said, Today we walk a lot of kilometres and drink some vodka. Any creature we bag will constitute a bonus.

Standing on the bank, I studied the river. It was about fifty metres wide, the steep sides a good metre or two high in places, lower at others where the spring torrents had eroded them or where a tree had been washed out, roots and all, to start its long journey to the sea or, more likely, some old lady's stove in the village twenty kilometres away. The water level was low and although there were a number of deep pools and stretches of slow currents downstream from where we had stopped, the water also flowed quickly over some rocky stretches.

Let's go! Pyotr ordered, calling over his shoulder, Bujan! Bujan!

He walked a little way upstream and stepped into the river, the water rising against the side of his boots.

Taking my time, I waded after him, feeling with my feet for a solid footing. He, on the other hand, just marched across the river as if it was nothing more than a wet road.

It was agreed we should walk about fifty metres apart, one keeping to a pathway, the other ranging through the cover: after an hour, we would change over. Starting off, Pyotr took the pathway and I had a hard time in the forest keeping abreast with him whilst at the same time making as little sound as possible. When we swapped positions, he noiselessly forged ahead through the undergrowth and I found myself walking at a fairly swift pace along the track.

By ten o'clock, neither of us had seen anything to which it was worth raising our guns. Pyotr was frustrated as he rejoined me where the path, a wide woodsman's track, entered a clearing of dappled light and short grass.

This is a farce! he muttered. I've seen a couple of pigs and one deer. Heard the buck sniff. No barks or foot stampings so he wasn't that alarmed but I still can't get close enough for a clean shot.

I've only seen a few moving shadows, I replied.

He gave me a mildly recriminatory glance and said, You need to move more silently. I can hear you on the path. You sound like a man riding a second-hand bicycle. Perhaps that damn rusty carbine squeaks. Or your boots do.

Wriggling my toes and rocking up and down on my heels, I said, I don't think my boots squeak. They're well broken in.

Then it must be your bones, he retorted. Too much of a soft life, that's your trouble.

He sniffed himself as if, by some sympathetic magic, this might encourage the game to show itself.

Perhaps they get wind of Bujan, I suggested.

Pyotr looked at the dog by his side. Throughout our hours' abortive hunting, Bujan had stayed with his master, moving always just a few paces behind him.

No, Pyotr declared. Bujan knows his bushcraft.

There was a distinct edge of accusation to his voice as if the dog was up to the task but I was not.

If I didn't know better, Pyotr continued, I'd swear women have been here. The animals are so — he searched for an adjective but could not find one — elusive!

For a few minutes we reconsidered our campaign then sat in the sunlight on the short grass with our feet out in front of us and opened the wooden box.

At least the mosquitoes aren't abundant here, Pyotr commented. The women have driven them off, too.

It's strange, I said, how the grass is so short. You'd think it would be longer by this time of year.

That's it! Pyotr exclaimed, slapping his hand on the lid of the box and startling a large bird in the nearby trees. That's it! Goats. It's been grazed by goats. Or sheep. And you know what that means. Where there's goats, there's women.

He spat into the grass, reached into the box and removed a square tin. Inside were half a dozen slices of black bread and a lump of veal and liver pâté wrapped in a piece of cloth.

Anna, he said quietly, makes the best pâté I have ever known. Once, she was under contract to one of the best restaurants in St Petersburg. Everyone likes what she makes. Top Party officials requested it at banquets.

And now? I asked.

Now they don't. The restaurant has gone foreign, he said with a certain chagrin.

Gone foreign?

French food, American food. Or they eat in the Grand Hotel Europe in Ulitsa Mikhailovskaya. And what do they eat? *Blinis*? *Pelmeni*? Ukrainian *varenyky zvyshneyu*? Like hell they do! They eat *coq au vin* and T-bone steaks with a side salad.

We started to eat the pâté, smearing it thickly on to the bread with our fingers. There were knives in the box but Pyotr likes to think he is living primitively when he goes hunting. In his book, only wimps use knives.

Good? he asked, with his mouth full.

Good, I ratified.

The pâté was delicious, smooth as thick cream and with just the right hint of nutmeg in it.

Of course, we had vodka with us but no ice. To cool the bottles, Pyotr had tied them in a sack on the end of a rope and submerged them in a forest pool a little way off. When he retrieved one, he pulled the cork out with his teeth and shot it with an explosive blurt out of his lips and into the pool where it bobbed for a short while before gradually making its way to the bank.

The sun rose towards its meridian, our guns lay abandoned on the grass, the mosquitoes began to increase in number. Pyotr rummaged in his cartridge-filled pockets and produced a small bottle.

This keeps the little bastards at bay, he assured me and,

rubbing some of the oily contents on his hands, stroked his head, neck and forearms.

I took the bottle. It contained oil of cloves.

Now we smell like the docks of Zanzibar, Pyotr announced as I gave the little bottle back to him.

How do you know? I said. You've never been to Zanzibar.

I've never been to the moon either but I know what it's like. Dry as a witch's tit and grey as old wall plaster. When you get there, you'll find out I was right.

The moon's the moon, I answered. You can see it and judge it. But Zanzibar . . .

What's the difference? I know what the docks of Zanzibar are like. Hot and busy with black folk. It's in Africa so it stands to reason. And there's a smell of the sea. It's an island. And the place smells of cloves because that's all they grow there. There's no airport so they must ship them out. Therefore, there are docks. And, as much of the world's supply of cloves passes through those docks, it's a foregone conclusion the place stinks of them. *Quod erat demonstrandum*, as they say in the best universities. And you should know.

For a while, we did not speak. When the food was consumed, we propped our guns side by side on the box, lay back on our elbows and drank. Bujan scuffled about in the shade or ambled off down the track only to return with his tongue lolling out, flecking the grass with canine slaver.

Tell me, Pyotr asked at last, what do you regret in life?

Regret? I said. Everything and nothing.

Elaborate. That's too vague.

I thought about it for a few minutes before replying.

I regret not having worked harder in my final year at the air force academy. I missed being top student in my year by one mark. One percentage point. Instead of me, Artem Strizhov took top honours and I was obliged, as second place, to buy everyone a round in the mess afterwards. Needless to say, they ordered the best. One failure cost me a fortnight's salary.

Were you disappointed?

I was more angry. With myself. There was no time for disappointment. Within days, I was being posted to the operations HQ in Kabul. But it niggled. Just one per cent!

Has it affected your career?

Not one bit.

Then why fret about it? All you missed was a silver-plated cup or the first medal on your chest which will be lost amongst all the others during a military career.

I'm not fretting about it.

You are. It still rankles.

It does not.

Then why are you so bitter about it?

I'm not.

My friend, you are. Believe me.

I had had enough of this and turned the conversation.

What about you, Pyotr? What do you regret?

He looked across the clearing to the point where the track, after crossing the sunlight, turned into the forest once more. I expected him to tell me of some massive creature he had aimed at and lost on some hunting trip long ago.

I regret, he began, then he stopped.

You regret . . . ? I prompted him.

I regret not taking Tatiana Pervozvanskaya to bed.

I must have looked amazed for Pyotr had never spoken about his sexual conquests. He must have sensed my surprise for he glanced at me and grinned.

She was a fellow student of mine. Tall. Aristocratic. Unattainable. If we still had a monarchy, she would have been a countess or a very highly-prized courtesan. Yet, for one night, I could have had her. Yet I did not.

Why not? I enquired.

Don't you want to know the story? Pyotr said sharply.

Of course, if you want to tell it.

Well, it's quite simple. We were on a field course in the Urals, west of Serov. On the lower slopes of Mount Solikamsk. You recall I studied geology. Anyway, the weather came down quite suddenly and we were separated from the others. She and I took shelter in a small hut on the edge of a ravine. It was a crude little shack really, probably some herder's temporary quarters or a forest workers' rest house, but it contained the bare essentials and we were carrying knapsacks and blankets. I lit a fire — there was a supply of kindling and logs in the place — and we spent the night huddled in front of the flames whilst the storm outside lashed down with rain and blew grit under the door. We dozed off in each other's arms. We weren't tired, just contented in each other's company. Half-way through the night, she kissed me on the neck and slipped her hand inside my shirt. Her fingers were like icicles but they warmed up. I kissed her hair, just the once. Had I built the fire up, for there was abundant fuel, had I not dozed off, had I established a closer relationship based upon that single kiss, I could have had her naked in twenty minutes in front of a blazing hearth and spent the night warming more than her fingers.

Why didn't you? I repeated.

That, Pyotr replied, has puzzled me ever since.

Perhaps you loved . . . I began.

At that moment, out of the corner of my eye, I saw something. Pyotr slowly turned his head, making no sharp movement. Bujan had crouched down in the short grass.

Roe buck! Pyotr whispered. They're coming out to feed.

For ten minutes, we lay quite still, our guns close by our sides and Bujan watching every shadow with an alertness of which I would never have believed him capable.

Five deer appeared after the buck. They were not fifty metres off, browsing on some stunted bushes and sweet saplings growing around another small pool. Utterly silent, they might have been deer ghosts.

Signalling with his fingers, Pyotr made antlers on his forehead then pointed to himself. I understood. Very slowly, he then advanced towards the deer through the grass, crawling on his elbows with Bujan moving stealthily along on his belly behind him. Armed with a shotgun, Pyotr had to be closer to ensure a clean kill.

I watched. After he had gone about fifteen metres and shifted his position a little to my right, he stopped and slowly raised his gun to his shoulder, balancing it on his left arm. I brought the carbine up and slipped the safety catch off, my nerves taut. We had to fire simultaneously.

I lined my sights up on the largest doe which was standing broadside on to me chewing a twig, held my breath and took up the slack in the trigger. The moment Pyotr's gun emitted a wisp of smoke, before I heard the explosion of his cartridge, I pulled the trigger its last fraction of a millimetre.

Got him! Pyotr shouted, rising to his feet in a cloud of shotgun smoke, Bujan already bounding clumsily across the grass, his old canine self again.

The doe was dead, too. I had hit her squarely in the head just below her ear. The lead slug had made a neat entry wound no greater in diameter than a pencil but where it had exited at the rear of the cranium there was a jagged bloody hole.

Designed for men, Pyotr observed. Do as much damage as it can.

Her eyes were large, dark and emotionless in death, her pointed narrow ears still pricked up for the danger she had never sensed. I touched the black, wet muffle around her nose. It was still warm. The pelt, close up, was tinged with ginger like a fox's fur in the early spring.

Using his hands as an expert masseur might, Pyotr emptied the bladders of both animals then slung his across his shoulders.

Let's go, he suggested. Nothing'll come back here for hours now and besides, I'm too old to carry two of these. Mind you, there was a time . . .

For the rest of the afternoon and into the evening, we made our way slowly back to the car, pausing every now and then to shift the weight of the carcasses across our shoulders and, in another clearing, pausing for an hour for Pyotr to bag half a dozen wood-pigeons for another of Anna's pâté recipes.

Reaching the Zil as the sun touched the horizon, we

sat on the banks of the river to paunch the deer and clean the pigeons.

Now I call that a good day's hunting, he exclaimed.

We've hardly hunted, I said.

That's just it! A good walk in the forest, some excellent pâté, cold vodka and enough meat to fill the belly of a butcher for a week. And Anna's going to be busy. We'll sell the surplus. Or barter it. That Netuzhilov, who has the plot next to Minarsky's, has grown far better cucumbers than I have this year.

There was as distinct hint of resentment in his words. Pyotr usually took a pride in his cucumbers and to be out-grown by a neighbour galled him.

For a while, as we slit the deer open and removed the offal, we did not speak. Several crows arrived to strut about at a discreet distance, eyeing the bloody guts as we dumped them on the ground. Bujan growled half-heartedly at them then went back to sleep. He made no attempt to snuffle about in the carnage, knowing his share would reach him eventually.

Do you know about the Ukrainian whose car broke down on a country lane? Pyotr asked as he dug his fingers into the deer and started to unravel its intestines. Pyotr slid his knife into the cavity of the buck's chest to slit the diaphragm and get at the heart and lungs.

In the Ukraine?

Where else?

The man was driving along when suddenly the engine spluttered, wheezed and died. The car drifted to a halt. The fuel gauge read half full and he knew it was right because he'd filled up not a hundred kilometres ago. So, he got out and opened the bonnet. He didn't know a thing about engines. He was a Ukrainian. However, he thought if he saw an obvious fault like a broken wire, he could fix it and get himself to the next town. But there was nothing amiss he could see. Just then, a voice said, 'It's the carburettor.' He looked round. Up and down the road. Nobody. He looked into the field by the car. There was a white horse chewing grass but no horseman or groom. He put his head under the bonnet again. 'I told you,' says the voice, 'it's the carburettor.' The Ukrainian looked up again. 'Carburettor,' the voice said. 'Check it over.' The Ukrainian was flabbergasted. It was the white horse talking. Anyway, he got a screwdriver, undid the top of the carburettor and saw the little petrol reservoir was filled with dirt. He wiped it out with his finger and a grass stem and put back the cover. 'I told you,' said the white horse. 'Lose power like that and you've got dirt in the carburettor.' The Ukrainian got back in and tried the engine. It started first time, he thanked the horse and drove off. Shaken by his encounter, he stopped at the first inn he came to and went inside. 'You look like you've had a bit of a shock,' said the innkeeper. 'I have,' said the driver. 'My car broke down and a white horse told me how to fix it.' 'Carburettor, was it?' the innkeeper said. 'Yes!' blurted the driver. 'How the hell did you know?' 'Had to be,' came the innkeeper's reply, 'the only other horse we've got round here's a black stallion and he knows fuck all about carburettors.'

Pyotr tossed the buck's entrails into the river. Half a dozen of the crows cawed peevishly and made an attempt to rush for the blood clots and bits of fat on the grass:

Pyotr waved his hand cursorily at them and they flapped off. Where the intestines splashed, the water threshed as small fish fought over them.

I laughed at his story though it might have been the vodka in me which found it as humorous as I did.

Right now, I could do with his Ukrainian talking horse. Preferably the black one. *Mir IV* has no carburettors.

An hour ago, at +202:03:41:00 or thereabouts, one of the molecular sieves in the Atmospheric Control System failed. Indeed, it disintegrated.

The system works like this: humidity, excess heat generated by the electronics and my body, carbon dioxide, odours and generally dirty air are removed every hour by one of two molecular sieves in the ACS working in tandem on alternate hours. First, a compressor and pump force cabin air through a filter which captures large particle contaminants. This done, the air is passed through a heat exchanger which cools it and removes some of the water. Next, the air passes through a molecular sieve which takes out water, CO_2 and an activated charcoal canister to catch odours and microscopic contaminants. At the end of the hour cycle, the molecular sieve bed and the charcoal canister are exposed to the outside vacuum which removes any CO_2 and microscopic contaminants by voiding them into space. The water is recycled.

All has been well until the last cycle changeover when the voiding valve opened and the vacuum of outer space removed not only the contaminant contents of the molecular sieve bed but the whole lining to it as well as half the activated charcoal in the canister.

I still have the second molecular sieve and canister to use

but they will operate only every other hour. This will raise the CO_2 level in the cabin and make it pretty unpleasant towards the end of every second hour. I shall, therefore, have to watch the clock and CO_2 sensors, cutting down on my physical activity when the level gets too high.

It is no small surprise to me I bother. I am going to die. It's an inevitability. Yet just as my stoicism is a part of my masculine behaviourism, so is my determination to live. No matter what, I shall go on striving to keep myself alive until I know the odds are too greatly loaded against me.

Such is the difference between the man and the god I would — I could — be. The man accepts the odds like a gambler, in desperation, placing his last chip on the zero.

Any god worth his salt would fix the wheel, but they never do.

❧

I remember the speech as if it was only yesterday.

There were thirty or so of us gathered in the lecture theatre, sitting in rows on the hard wooden benches, pads and pencils arranged neatly before us on the work shelves much as prayer texts and bibles are laid out by the doors of country chapels. Indeed, we might have been sitting in pews and, in a sense, we were yet the deity of this house of worship was not a bearded Jew or a be-turbaned Arab but an idea invented and elaborated upon by a German *emigré* sitting in a library in London, dreaming of Socialism and the international community of men.

Uncle Karl, your dreams of Marxism have a lot to answer for.

We were a select group, drawn for the best part from the army and air force: only two of our number had naval backgrounds. At least half of us were flyers of some sort — ungainly combat helicopters, sleek jet fighters or cumbersome transports. Of the three hundred who had sat the initial tests, undergone the initial medical examinations and justified ourselves, we were all who were left.

The door opened and General Nezlobin entered. He was a big man, befitting his rank and reputation. The left breast of his smartly tailored uniform jacket bore at least fifty square centimetres of medal ribbons. If each one had been earned in combat, rather than in orgies of Party self-congratulation, there would be not a single enemy of Russia left outside the most impenetrable jungles of the equator. By his side strode his ADC, a thin, ferret-faced yes-man with a leather-bound dossier under his arm, his uniform crisp from the barracks laundry, with plenty of room for the honours he hoped to eventually win.

We stood stiffly to attention. Nezlobin mounted the dais. The ADC placed the dossier on the speaker's lectern, switched on the reading light and faced us.

Be seated, he said in a quick voice, high-pitched with arrant authority: men with power speak slowly, in deep voices, whilst those with authority but little power go up one and a half octaves and rattle off their orders.

We sat.

Nezlobin took his time opening the dossier. I wondered if he was expecting something to fly out of it. There was a tentative precision about his every movement. He then removed a pair of bifocals from the breast pocket behind the multicoloured ranks of glory and started to speak to us.

Comrades, he commenced, then grunted.

The ADC scuttled to his side with a glass of water poured from a jug on a side-table. I was certain Nezlobin needed no drink: the cough was an exercise of power, not a clearing of the throat.

Comrades, he began again, you are gathered here as the cream of our armed forces, men chosen by your peers and superiors, and by your own efforts and dedication, to accept the ultimate challenge. You are to be the draft from which shall be taken our next generation of cosmonauts.

You will be following in the footsteps of great men. Yuri Gagarin, Andriyan Nikolayev, Alexei Leonov. And women. Valentina Nikolayevna Tereshkova.

He paused. The part of women in the cosmonaut programme was something, I sensed, he was either keen to overlook or forget.

Of you, great demands will be made, great sacrifices expected. Let us not forget the ultimate price paid by your predecessor, Vladimir Nikolayevich Komarov.

He paused once more, letting the first public death in space remind us we were not embarking on a game of soldiers. Or airmen.

Five minutes to eleven o'clock in the morning, Moscow time, on 12 April 1961, he continued. I was there. The capsule came down through the sky, through the clouds, to a soft landing about a kilometre from some trees, on flat, grassy land. The parachutes blossomed behind it. The hatch was opened by the receiving team and, after a minute or so, Comrade Gagarin emerged. He waved, briefly. I do not mind admitting to you, comrades, I cried. I was not the only one. There were even tears in Khrushchev's eyes when they came to shake hands. These were tears of pride, comrades. Tears shed for joy, for the USSR.

He sipped at his glass of water, another timely break to give us the chance to digest the import of his words.

You are now the bearers of our nation's pride. Upon your heads rest the laurels of history and upon your brows shall furrow frowns created by the puzzles of the future. And yet there shall also rest the crowns of greatness as yet unrealized. Never before, throughout the annals of humanity, has such a responsibility been placed upon so small and so young a band of men.

I looked around: sure enough, there was not a woman in the lecture theatre. So much for socialist equality and sexual emancipation.

You carry not only your nation's pride but also the hopes and ambitions of every living man, he went on. Over the centuries, men have pushed back the boundaries of their horizons. Columbus sailed to the edge of the world convinced he would strike land, his crew growing mutinous for they feared they should fall off the rim into oblivion and the maws of dragons. Vasco da Gama sailed into the unknown, circumnavigated Africa to find a way to the Indies. Men whose names remain unrecorded sailed the wide oceans in search of the unknown, to realize their dreams. You shall be amongst them in the pages of history.

Sitting listening to this rousing address, I considered my place in history. Little did I know then how prophetic the pen in the hand of the general's speech-writer would be:

sure enough, with my mission a failure and the top brass of Baikonur pretending I no longer exist and wishing me dead in the worst of manners — with detached disinterest — I will indeed go down in history along with the nameless ones.

You, the general continued, will push back those horizons, eradicate them and set new boundaries in the far depths of outer space. You are the explorers of the last unknown, the frontiersmen of infinity, the pathfinders whose ways will be followed by generation upon generation of mankind. You are, comrades, the cartographers of the future.

For you, there will be only the best. Your training will be more thorough than any other single man's, your access to the latest technology will be unreservedly unrestricted, your knowledge gained will exceed anything you could have ever thought of.

In exchange, comrades, we want the best of you. We expect, in fact we demand, your every effort, your unstinted dedication to the tasks set you. You will be expected as a matter of course to give of your best and more.

Your reward will be the honour of serving your country at her most glorious hour, the satisfaction of realizing your own personal glory, and immortality. I salute you.

In truth, he did nothing of the sort. Instead, he closed the dossier at which he had not glanced once. It must have been as much of a prop as the glass of water.

Without so much as a final glance in our direction, Nezlobin turned and walked sturdily, firmly towards the door. We all got rapidly to our feet and stood to attention. The ADC quickly picked up the dossier, tucked it back under his arm, switched off the reading light and, clicking his fingers at one of the future heroes of the Soviet Union, bearer of laurels and candidate for immortality, pointed from him to the glass of water and marched off after his boss, opening the door for him and disappearing in his wake.

None of us spoke. We were numbed, I suppose, by the realization of what really lay ahead of us. Yet we were all fired by pride, were prepared to face whatever space threw at us. We were ready to conquer or die.

How gullible I was, how ideologically blinkered. I did not see through all the claptrap. I believed every single word of it with the intensity and devotion of the most bigoted zealot.

Mind you, as I recall, no one put the glass of water back on the side-table.

I do not regret my cosmonautical career, not one moment of it. The training was always fascinating, the challenges always testing, the rigours always demanding. The cosmonaut programme made a man of me, saved me from myself, from a banal life in a grey Stalinist block of flats in a Moscow suburb, riding to work each day on a bicycle or a crowded train, teaching classes of students for whom dreams would soon be shattered as my own had been or shuffling papers in a military office, my trigger-finger itching to escape the typewriter. I am certain I would have ended up trapped in a marriage of convenience or social necessity, my spouse a clerk or a fellow teacher, a career officer in some woman's corps or a dowdy little creature with no interest save in washing powders and wiping the noses and arses of the spawn of my loins.

Worse, I might have ended up as Ilya Golubev did,

womanizing without knowing why, drinking without being thirsty or lonely or afraid, having no friends save those for whom he had 'done favours' in the past.

No doubt, Ilya is now a high-flying entrepreneur, pulling on his strings of contacts, pulling his women who are still aged twenty, though he is pushing forty-five and has the flabby gut to prove it, held in place by a slick western suit. I would not be like him for all the world.

Yet I do rue having been suckered by Nezlobin, falling for his salesman's patter of comradeship and patriotism.

I am up here, sailing round until eternity claims me as her son whilst they get on with it down there, busily enmeshed in the hugger-mugger of the New Russia where prices go up by four per cent a month, teachers earn less than newspaper vendors, redundant soldiers sell their military uniforms, dancing bears entertain tourists, the pot-holes remain unfilled, the drainpipes are not repaired and bananas cost a week's salary.

At this very moment, I wager somewhere under the solar panel I can see through the window, moving like a gold-plated admonishing finger across the face of Russia, Nezlobin is sitting in a Moscow bar with a glass of chilled American beer and pretzels before him, discussing foreign currency transactions and pyramid savings scams with Ilya who is drinking Coca-Cola, with ice and a twist of lemon, imported by The Viktor Asheshov International Trading, Import & Export Corporation of Riga: and Ilya is busy scheming how he might get the better of him.

Now that, indeed, would be poetic justice.

❧

Normally, I assiduously avoid tuning in to Russian radio wavelengths. It is not so much a loathing of sentimentality which prompts this, for I am occasionally prone to a luxurious wallow in nostalgia's muddy pond, but a desire to cut myself off.

I no longer consider myself to be a Russian.

This is not an act of treason. I have not and I will not defect. Defectors do not become Americans or Britishers, they merely come to be a travesty of themselves, Russians trying hard to fool themselves into believing they are what they are not. A change of passport cannot eradicate inherited traits — an in-built love of music, a taste for salted herring and *kartoshka*, and a distrust of men in full-length, leather overcoats — which will last for centuries, passed on through their children like an aberrant gene.

I once met Kim Philby, Hero of the Soviet Union and master spy. We were at a party in Moscow to celebrate some glorious achievement or other — it might have been my first space walk, I don't recall — and he came across the room to me, his right hand extended, his left grasping a glass of Scotch whisky without ice. He congratulated me on my success, speaking with all the pride of a true Russian, extolling the virtues of our space programme and superiority over the Americans in this or that technological field. Yet there was something about him: he was just a little too sincere, a little too praising, a little too proud.

Urbane, polite, and well-spoken, he conversed with me in both English and Russian, in which he was completely fluent yet without any real trace of an accent. An English gentleman to the day of his death, he was no more able to rid himself of the shackles of his nationality than a cat can get shot of the tin tied to its tail by sadistic village boys.

What is more, my disclaimer is not an act of desertion or hatred. It is not in my nature to leave friends in the lurch and I am not one to harbour a grudge. Far from it. I have remained a loyal friend of Pyotr's despite his Ukrainian jokes; and where someone falls foul of me I tell them straight out what I think of them, exchange a few blows if necessary and that's an end to it. Thereafter, we merely keep our distances.

Nor has my abnegation of nationality anything to do with my impending deification, for want of a better word.

In short, a man with a nationality cannot become a god.

Gods do not carry passports, ID cards, Party cards, union cards, business cards or, come to that, credit cards. They are above all this. They are omnipotent, omniscient, unbothered by such petty details as border guards and watch-towers, customs officials, immigration clerks and airport security checks: not for them the x-raying of baggage, the humiliation of the body search, the metal detector and the scrutiny from behind one-way windows and television camera lenses.

They breeze through international boundaries with the equanimity of ghosts.

As do I.

In the course of 71 revolutions, every 118 hours or so, I

pass over — which is to say through, for nations lay claim not just to the land upon which their houses are built and the sea off their shores, but to the sky over their heads as well — every nation on Earth.

Therefore, I am a god or, at least, I have the international gift of gods.

I listen to Russian radio as indifferently as I do to any other nation's wavebands, to find out, in the manner of a god, what is going on.

At present, the radio is off for I am over Japan and cannot understand a word of what I would hear were it switched on.

Fifteen minutes ago, however, I was over the CIS and tuned in.

How life has changed in the land of the Red Flag. For a start, the golden hammer and sickle of man's noble labour has been hauled down off the flagpoles, thrown away, burned or hoarded by faithful Leninists against the time when it might flutter once more.

Of course, life had already changed when I was thrust into space on the top of a nuclear bomb-load of propellant fuel, but I had paid it little attention. None of us had. We were sequestered in Baikonur, up to our eyebrows in the final eighteen months of mission training. When our lives were to depend on how efficiently we tightened a latch bolt or secured the seal around the helmet of our space suits, you can be damn sure we had little time to read *Pravda*, watch television or sit around in bars setting the world to rights. Politics and the state of the rouble did not affect us, or so we thought.

Such was my first mistake, to assume the politicians and the money-lenders had no influence. All four of us have been hit by our naïvety. I am stuck up here, turning into a god whilst they are down there, poor bastards.

I try not to think of them, but the occasional radio programme puts them temporarily back in mental sight. It is not hard to imagine Vladislav Cherkasov, the eroto-opportunist on the train to Archangel, struggling to make ends meet in his quarters, his pay staying level but the money in his pocket losing value as fast as mercury slides off a steel plate. Gavriil Asanov, if he is lucky, will be flying Aeroflot Airbuses: he was a certificated commercial pilot. His passengers will be lucky, too: he is unmarried and will not, therefore, have a fifteen-year-old son to whom he can hand over the flight controls whilst he nips out of the flight deck to stretch his legs, get a drink or talk to the passengers. According to one snippet of radio newscast I picked up a while back, a flight from Moscow to the Far East went down, all killed, under just such alleged circumstances. As for Stepan Kukolnik, he will be back on his father's farm, tending the pigs and collecting the eggs for delivery to the co-operative which all the farmers in his area have maintained in order to get better, higher prices in the market. At least Communism taught them that united they get rich, divided they get screwed.

And I bet none of them, not even Gavriil in his cockpit, ever looks up to the sky and wonders.

My latest eavesdropping on the ether concerned a report on the collapse of MMM. It seems — there was serious static at some stages of the newscast — an above-average entrepreneur cottoned on to a scam to lighten the wallets and purses of Russia with a dream.

So what's new!

Dreams are more expensive than a top-of-the-range Mercedes-Benz studded with diamonds. They always have been and they always will be.

I know. I ride a dream up here and it's costing me my life.

The basis of the confidence trick was simplicity itself: it was a pyramid of deceit. Dividends were promised at 3000 per cent and those who got in early, and got out early, made a killing, as they say in the West. Yet they were the clever ones, or those on the take, in the know. The dividends paid to the early shareholders emanated from the income of the next line of investors in new share purchases. All the wide boys and young, hip entrepreneurs, aware 3000 per cent was a gimmick to trap the not-so-smart-arsed, bought in at the bottom of the market and sold at the top. For the rest, it was money down the Neva on a rip tide.

The news reporter on the radio programme I picked up was interviewing a few of the fleeced masses.

Look at me!

It was an old man's voice coming up from the world below, rising to me like a prayer.

Look at me. I'm seventy-seven. I'm a good Russian. I saw the adverts on the television. I saw Lyonya. He flew to America in a big plane to see our boys win at football. I saw him buy his wife a fur coat and he's going to buy a house in Paris.

In some respects, it was a prayer. He was desperate and desperate men turn to their god as a last resort. Every one of his words was forged on the anvil of an anguished life: his belly had rumbled in the great famine of the Stalinist years, his ears had heard the gunshots purging good men, his nose had smelt the cordite blowing over Leningrad and his eyes had cried for Russia.

The interviewer interrupted, beginning, For those of you who have spent the last six months on Mars . . .

He's talking to me, I thought. I'm not on Mars but I might just as well be.

. . . Lyonya Golubkov is the big man in a vest who stars in the MMM commercials. He has a wife called Rita who loves chocolates and a brother who drinks too much vodka. The part is played by the actor, Vladimir Permyakov.

The old man's voice returned.

So I thought, I have some savings so I invested in MMM. I don't want a house in Paris, but I would like to buy my wife a fur coat. My Luba feels the cold badly with her rheumatism. So I bought some shares.

How many did you buy?

Eight hundred thousand roubles, the old man replied, his voice dull with disappointment.

And now?

And now? Now it's all gone. Every rouble. Nothing to get back. I thought it was a savings club. It was a hole in the water. Now I can't pay my rent. My landlord wants us out. I must move in with my daughter and her husband. And my wife. What's to become of us, eh?

A twenty second burst of static cut the transmission: when I picked it up again, the old man was gone, a news reporter in his place.

. . . Moscow this morning. Sergei Mavrodi, said to be Russian's fifth richest man, was arrested at his apartment by hooded special service police and militia. As he was led to a car, he waved briefly to a crowd of newsmen and angry investors in MMM. Shares in Mavrodi's company have fallen in value over a hundred times since Monday last and now stand at 1000 roubles. The company had suspended all dealings in its shares. The collapse of the company, which had over five million investors and shareholders, will not only affect the pockets of ordinary men and women. At least four major companies are expected to go down with MMM and confidence in the free market liberalization and economy is undermined. Calls are being made now to ask why the government did not intervene to close down the television advertising campaign which had lured so many into parting with their meagre savings. Meanwhile, throughout Moscow and other major cities, police are having to control large crowds of irate shareholders milling around MMM offices demanding their money back.

I flicked the switch and the radio signal snapped off.

There is nothing so foolish as a dreamer and nothing so ripe for plucking, other than a full-bodied plum being busied about by wasps, as a greedy dreamer.

One lesson has yet to be learned by my erstwhile countrymen, my one-time comrades, my fellow citizens of the now-defunct USSR. They have yet to discover what the Americans have known for decades. There is, as I am told they say in the movies, no such thing as a free lunch. For every bunch of flowers given as a gift to a pretty girl, you may rest assured she'll have to return a lot more kisses than there are petals and open her petals for a number of quick-time wasps.

I allow myself to spin slowly around the long axis of my body. My eyes scan over the experimental packages, the computers, the control units and the bulkheads. I breathe in my allotment of oxygen. I listen to the silence which goes on forever outside my little life-guarding capsule.

Such technology surrounds me, such artistry. Every rivet and screw, bolt and soldered connection was planned by a human brain, executed by human ingenuity, fashioned by human tools and assembled by human fingers. It has taken me into space.

One would think, with such powers, humans would have learnt more about themselves than they have.

Then, just as I put my hand out to halt my gentle spin, a hexagonal 3 millimetre nut floats by. It is time to start the hunt again for a naked 3 millimetre bolt.

So much for the procession of history, the progress of humanity. Even would-be gods are held to ransom by the inadequacies of men.

❧

A hurricane is raging along the line of the Lesser Antilles. The tell-tale catherine wheel of clouds stretches from the delta of the Orinoco to Puerto Rico.

For seven days, I have watched it develop from a low pressure area about six hundred kilometres north east of Cape de São Roque into first a deep depression due north-north-east of Belém then a severe tropical storm north of Paramaribo, gathering strength and anger as it headed along the coast of South America, making for Trinidad.

Now it is venting its rage, doing its worst to those little

shards of land strung out like a necklace of dark green jade, a cutlass-shaped chain stretching from Venezuela to Florida, the greater islands of Hispaniola and Cuba like fat gems in their design. I can imagine the sea risen to great heights, dashing upon the yellow sands of ten-kilometre-long beaches, tossing the palms as if they were tufts of dune grass and tearing the banana trees out by the roots. Everything is cowering down there, submitting to a force it cannot control, cannot accept, cannot understand. Men will be cursing their gods but simultaneously praying for their houses to remain standing, their crops to survive through to harvest.

They blame nature and yet they possess just such awesome destructive powers themselves. The difference lies in the destruction which lingers for decades after a man has done his worst and the renewal which springs back after the eye of the storm closes, the clouds dissipate and the sun shines once more from a blue, never-ending sky.

Before the farmer has re-established his rows of plantains and rebuilt the roof on his shack, the cashew nut trees will be in flower and the pods on the vanilla orchids will be swelling once again. The insects will have fed upon the storm-dropped mangoes and new fruit will be starting to form whilst from every snapped twig a shoot will be pulsing out bearing a tiny spear of green.

We never learn, we hominids. We ruin without a thought for the future, decimate for the sake of destruction, not for the sake of renewal. Nature is quite the opposite: she razes in order to reconstruct.

Some dozen or so orbits ago, I switched on the module in the PEAP2 which includes the multi-spectral photographic system. The MPS consists of a unit of a number of six-channel 80 millimetre cameras colloquially termed the ASE (for All-Seeing Eye) and the Earth Terrain and Topography Camera, the ETTC. The latter has a single lens with a focal length of 460 millimetre, has programmed rotation to cope with the spacecraft's movement and shutter speeds of 5, 7, 10 and 15 milliseconds. It is especially designed to assist cartographers and, to a lesser degree, espionage operatives.

Such has always been the case with every human discovery from a sharpened stick to a split atom. For each beneficial use there is an equally destructive one: a pointed stick pokes out eyes as readily as it pokes tasty termites out of their mud hill. Men, of course, have always chosen to exploit the former before the latter, or retain it: long after a new device gathers more termites the eye-poker is still in useful employ. You can count on it.

Where the ETTC takes only one picture at a time, the ASE takes six simultaneous photographs of the same target area, each in a different wavelength. There is no film in the equipment: Vladislav and the others were ordered to take the stock back with them. Yet this does not make the equipment redundant for, as a check, each photograph, as it is taken, is relayed on to a monitor so the photographer can ensure he has the right target in frame. Now, although I can take no hard copy, I can still use the cameras as single image grabbers.

Swinging down one of the folding seats which are bolted to the bulkhead by the PEAPs, I held myself in with the lap restraint and powered up the ASE. It takes a minute or so to prepare itself. With the aid of the navigation computer, I calculated a series of sets of co-ordinates over different areas of the planet below and fed the data into the search and lock facility.

The first picture to appear on screen was of an area of about a hundred kilometres square to the north-east of Corsica, including Elba and the rest of the Toscano Archipelago.

Through the visible light unit, the view appeared quite normal, the contours of the islands sharply defined and the change in sea depth between Bastia and Elba easily noted. It was when the different spectral filter channels were switched in the truth appeared.

Off the Italian coast and the north shore of Elba, there appeared a magenta hue to the sea which, in places, tended towards the purple. Instruction I had received in the air force in the interpretation of false-colour photography told me what I was seeing: the sea was rich in vegetation but not seaweed. This was algae, a thick soup of it feeding voraciously on fertilizer run off from the land and sewage pumped into the sea. A worse picture appeared a few minutes later: almost the whole area of the Gulf of Venice was a similar colour only richer, more intense.

Using different channels, I travelled the world, looking at the filth being generated below me. Cities were hazed with carbon monoxide and sulphur dioxide, industrial zones appeared as artificial rainbows of corruption. Nitrogen dioxide blew in clouds invisible to the naked eye but all too plain to my filtered system. The soot of chimneys and exhaust pipes drifted across thousands of kilometres, settled over desert valleys which had never seen a car or a factory. Fields of crops which should have shown bright red as the vegetation emitted infra-red radiation registered as a faint pink whilst urban areas, especially in the northern hemisphere, shone with a blue as intense as the finest sapphire signalling the vast expenditure of heat energy.

The oceans off the mouths of rivers were not the dark blue expected of clear water but light blue or even white with the suspension of sediments caused by erosion or industrial waste. A fan of filth spread out from the delta of the Danube into the Black Sea which was no longer black but greyed and sickly, like the skin of an old man left alone too long in the isolation ward. The stain on the sea spread from the border between Romania and Bulgaria to Sevastopol.

It was not just the industrial world which appeared debased. Whole swathes of South America and Africa, which I expected to see a healthy red, appeared as faint blue or yellow, devoid of wholesome vegetation and gradually turning into arid grassland. Fingers of dying soil inveigled their way into the rain forests and the veldt lands, tentacles of sand wormed southwards from the Sahara, tendrils of dying corals insinuated themselves into reefs along the coasts of Australia, Kenya and Tanzania.

Above all of this, the shifting dance of ozone hung, moving north, swinging south, leaving swathes of the world beneath open to the cruel burning glass of the sun.

At length, I closed down the ASE and leaned back in my seat. I was never again to suck in the mucky air of my home planet, would never again unwittingly swallow dirty water or bathe in a sea suspended with heavy metals, organic poisons and the shit of my own kind.

I rubbed my eyes which were sore from peering too long at the monitor and, when I opened them, found I was looking through the window facing away from Earth. By now, I was passing over the side of the planet in night and could see, through the centimetres-thick pressure glass, the black vastness of deep space interrupted only by the pricking lights of far-flung galaxies and thriving suns.

It all seemed so clean, so untouched, so pristine. There were no deliberate acts of destruction out there, no atomic bombs filled with hatred, no factories shovelling out ordure. Only hurricanes the size of worlds destroying and recreating, continuing the cycle of repair and regeneration.

A formidable guilt struck me then: what a terrible legacy resides in me. My reason for being where I am, orbiting my planet, is not so I can improve the lot of my fellows but extend their empire, conquer and colonize those little silver lights, arrive and settle, destroy and move on.

We met in the officers' mess, the harsh glare of the compound lights casting bars across the room from the venetian blinds. There had been a power cut earlier in the evening and the air conditioning had yet to cool the room. As was customary, the lights in the mess were not switched on.

There were twenty-seven of us seated around the dining table at the far end of which was placed a wooden kit box with steel brackets at the corners. The mess steward had thoughtfully put a folded blanket under the box so the brackets did not scratch the veneer. A vase of nondescript flowers, wilting from the heat, stood half-way down the table, a small photograph in a steel frame propped against it.

At 21:00 hours exactly, I entered the room and was shown to the box. Tarasov took my cap and Gordeev, his forehead still swathed in a bandage, produced a key and undid the lock on the box.

Staring ahead of me down the table, I looked at the photograph and said, in a clear, emotionless voice, Comrades, we are gathered here in honour of our fallen friend and companion, Vassily Kapranov, to acknowledge his passing from us and to share in the bounty of his life.

It was tradition not to mention the rank of the deceased, nor to outwardly grieve. We all accepted we were in the military to die and had known the odds were against us the morning our transfer orders arrived.

As is the way of our unit, I went on, it is now my responsibility, as his room-mate and friend, to offer amongst you the effects of our comrade and to remind you you are honour-bound to dig deep for the sake of his memory.

Without looking down, I dipped my hand into the box, my fingers closing on the case of a camera which I raised level with my chest and displayed to the assembly.

A camera, I said. Fairly new, with a 50 millimetre lens, leather case and carrying strap.

Tarasov, standing to my left and a little behind me, watched the room.

Thirty roubles, Bratsev offered.

Forty, Aksionov raised him.

Fifty-five, Velichko chipped in.

The bidding rose to seventy-five roubles. Tarasov collected the money, dropping it into a manila envelope and handing the camera to its new owner.

So the auction progressed, Vasya's belongings passing out amongst his erstwhile companions. Everything went. We were obliged by an unwritten code of practice to purchase everything he had owned which was not retained for return to his family. Even his socks and spare pairs of underpants went to the highest bidder along with his belt, spare flying boots, uniform buttons, compass, knife and fork set, penknife and the few books he had been reading.

When the sale was over, the steward came round with glasses of vodka handing one to each of us and placing one before the photograph. We toasted Vasya's memory, tossed back the drink and set our glasses upside-down around his image. The last act was for me to take his vodka and pour it on the floor.

As the others filed out of the mess, carrying their purchases, I turned to Tarasov.

How much is in the envelope? I enquired.

He looked at the flap where he had been keeping tally.

Six hundred and twenty-five roubles, he informed me.

A good sum, I said.

Volsky spent the most, Tarasov continued. He's had a winning streak lately playing against the boys in the vehicle pool. Vasya's death has given him the opportunity to restock his own kit box.

He picked up the envelope, licked the flap and sealed it.

I'll be going now, he murmured. I'm sorry. We all are . . .

With the door closed behind him, I sat down and gazed at Vasya's photograph. A shaft of light cut across his face giving him a sort of square halo. I thought how much his image looked like a little black and white icon. He was half smiling as if he had been told a good joke and was now at the end of the laughter it had raised in him.

Slowly, my tears welled up and the room became hazy, the bars of light running into each other. I did not sob nor did I cry. My shoulders did not heave and I did not catch my breath any more than anyone might who has a raw throat. When I did suck air in, it was mingled with the taste of the vodka and the scent of the flowers.

Reaching forward, I was about to take up the photograph when one of the withering blossoms fell from its stalk to the table, resting on the top of one of the upturned glasses. I placed it on the table before me, smoothed out the petals, removed the backing of the photograph frame and, inserting the flower behind the picture, closed it once more.

Just then, from somewhere far off outside the compound, there was a burst of automatic fire and a muffled explosion. A siren started to wail. Gathering up the photograph, I quickly left the mess and headed for the nearest shelter.

Back in my quarter, sitting at the writing table by the window which I had shared with Vasya, I collected the few personal possessions I had deemed should be sent to his family. They were trinkets really, of little worth — his wrist-watch, the glass freshly scratched when he parachuted into the ravine, his medal ribbons, the Parker fountain pen of which he was so inordinately proud, his dress uniform cap, a bundle of letters and a little sketch-book in which he had drawn some portraits of his fellow pilots,

Afghani women and views of villages and mountains like those amongst which he had died. The last items were the framed photograph and an anonymous stone.

As the helicopter landed and the medics ran after me towards the depression in the boulders, crouching low in case we came under fire, I bent down and grabbed a smooth pebble the size of an egg.

I do not know why I did it. Perhaps I am superstitious.

With everything put into a tough plastic wallet, I added the envelope of money and started, for what must have been the tenth time, to read my accompanying letter.

Dear Mr and Mrs Kapranov, I began,
I write as your son's best friend, and at the behest of his commanding officer, to respectfully inform you . . .

There was no need to read it again. I put the letter in with the rest and closed the flap.

I wonder, remembering that hot evening in the mess, if my former cosmonaut associates have had an auction of my possessions. I am not sure which of them would take the auctioneer's place, hold up my cigarette lighter or the sextant I had retained after my first term in the academy. Not one of them was a real friend.

Vladislav Cherkasov would buy my camera, that's for sure. He always envied me it. He could use it to take pictures of naked girls on trains to remind him of his youth. Gavriil Asanov would bid low and probably come away with the cheapest item no one else wanted which he would subsequently discard. As for Stepan Kukolnik: I never knew him well enough to judge his taste.

At what stage, I ponder, will they hold the auction? After my death is discreetly announced in an obscure military publication perhaps, or after they see a bright meteor slicing a midsummer night sky which suddenly reminds them of me and the fact they have yet to hold the sale.

There again, they might have already divided the spoils amongst themselves, having given me up for dead, and poor Pyotr and Anna will have received a second little plastic wallet of ephemera and an envelope of roubles nowadays worth next to nothing.

❧

Maurits Escher: that was the painter whose name I could not remember.

It came back to me as I was in one of my suspended day-dream sessions, drifting without touching anything.

At first, I went through the usual few minutes of pattern dreams and colour journeys, nothing extraordinary happening or appearing before my inner eye then, as one misty scene dissolved, it was replaced not by another mixing of hues and tints but by a silver disc which transmuted into an opaque orb with a pointed upper surface. Gradually, the opacity cleared, the orb took on a three-dimensional quality and I realized I was looking at a vast droplet of water.

In my thoughts, or perhaps in reality for I do not know what I do when I am day-dreaming, I reached out to touch it. Had it been water, the droplet would have broken and run down my fingers, yet it did not and

I was able to cradle it in my palm as one might a rare and exotic fruit.

No sooner did I come in contact with it than a vision appeared on the surface of the drop, distorted where the edges rounded away from me.

A voice I sensed rather than heard said, quite conspicuously, With the compliments of Mr Escher.

The vision was a reflection of the front of Pyotr's village house in which I could see him sitting on a chair, Bujan lying at his side and elongated by the curve of the droplet. The wall of the house stood in the background, the division between each log easily discernible. I was in the centre of the droplet, to the forefront, holding it up.

Pyotr moved, Bujan got up and the view instantly changed to the inside of *Mir* illuminated by sunlight coursing through one of the windows. Every detail was clearly defined – the monitor screens, computer read-outs, banks of switches, lights and buttons, locker doors, EPCs and, in the distance, sleeping restraints. Yet I was excluded.

A panic came over me, sufficiently strong to bring me out of my reverie. I came to in a cold sweat, a memory not only of this droplet but also of Peter the Great's throne, the room where my image was missing from the mirrors.

Foolish though it was, I actually touched myself to reassure myself I really did exist.

Now, twenty minutes and a quarter of the world further on, I realize the experience has made me conscious of my predicament. To those below, whom I once knew, I do indeed no longer exist.

For Pyotr and Anna, standing as the sun goes down on the firs and missing me, Anikushin and his patch of carefully nurtured weeds, Dogonkin riding the Archangel train with a floozy in his compartment, Major Kozyrev and his conscience — for all of them, I am trapped in history.

In fact, I am trapped, in a manner of speaking, not in history but in a bubble of water vapour, of air gradually getting a little more stale by the orbit and high tensile metal, tangled by fate but more free than any other man who ever lived.

❧

It is +214:05:09:35 precisely.

I have woken from my last rest period with an astonishing feeling of power. Invincibility seems to ooze from me like honey from the hive.

If it is true the possession of extreme power makes a despot of every man, enlivens the Nero which lurks in every soul, then I am reborn this hour.

I am Adolf Hitler with my SS dogs barking at my side, straining at their leashes and baying for the blood of the Israelites. The smell of the gas chamber is in my nostrils, the stink of the boilers of Auschwitz as they dissolve the flesh of the abhorred and the despised, the feared and the envied.

Or I am Pol Pot with my rice paddies fertilized by the brains of my enemies, the pig-sty walls made of glued skulls and the fences round the cattle pen a grille of femurs. The temples ring with the silent chants of dead monks and the birds in the trees no longer sing for I have torn their tongues out for bookmarks in the volumes of violence.

Now, as the snow falls, I am Joseph Stalin with my
fawning advisers and my distrustful narrow eyes, searching
here and hunting there for traitors, for those who might
be stronger than I, for the children of fathers who might
harbour grudges and the wives of husbands who vanished in
the long winters of hatred. Every shadow holds an assassin's
knife, every corner gives cover to the murderer's gun and
the only way to survive is to shine a bright light into every
cranny and round off all the corners.

The minutes spin and I am Benito Mussolini with
my fat jowls shaking, Francisco Franco with my stark
generalissimo's smile, Idi Amin cramming the unborn babies
of Africa into my gullet and Saddam Hussein gassing and
draining the marshes of the first rivers God ever cut on the
face of creation.

I am Christ resurrected, have pushed aside the stone
and risen to sit on the right hand of my father's throne
and gloat.

No longer am I afraid of being someone else. The first
time, when I thought Napoleon was spending his vacation
from hell lounging on the beaches of my soul, I was terrified.
If I were a superstitious Ukrainian, a ready butt for Pyotr's
jibes, I would think the devil was after my soul but,
being a level-headed Russian, and from St Petersburg, I
know better.

Perhaps I am going mad, entering the early stages of what
they call being star-happy: the Americanism is, I believe,
spaced out.

A human body seriously out of kilter, lost to its
equilibrium and no longer in tune with its surroundings,
is doomed. It can no more survive than an ant can on an

iceberg. But the human mind: that is a different matter. It can suffer infinitely more than the body, can see out a million days of anguish. It is limitless, its boundaries those not of the bone dome of the skull but of the Pandora's box of the imagination.

No. I am not losing my mind. I am gaining knowledge.

What was it Voltaire wrote?

What is insanity? It is to be in possession of specious perceptions yet to have the power to reason correctly from them.

❧

I could kill myself. It would be a solution to the interminable problem of waiting for something to happen, counting down the aluminium trays of reconstituted sliced bacon in aspic and baby-mushed apple and rhubarb purée. It is true men may return to infancy in senility and must be prepared to accept the eventuality but I am not yet senile and I resent being fed infantile pap.

Up here in space, my suicidal options are somewhat restricted. Like most men of my cultural background, I am denied the common bullet, the hose-and-exhaust pipe and the walk into the sea with a pile of cheap clothes enigmatically folded into a pile on a beach at dawn. Jumping off the platform as the Moscow express trundles through is out: so is leaping off the tourist-infested walkway around the top of St Isaac's Cathedral. Sadly, I am unable to drink myself to death with a case of vodka.

However, I do have a few alternatives which might almost be classed as traditional.

First, I could poison myself. There are pain-killing drugs in the Medications Storage Locker and the dental kit. As these are stocked for the welfare of four men, and as I have as yet to use any of the contents, there are copious supplies of paracetamol and, better for my purpose, ampoules of morphine. Four of those injected in quick succession should do the trick, if I can stay sentient long enough to get them all in. Death would arrived fairly quickly and carry me on a magic carpet of blissful oblivion.

Second, I could go the honourable way. Falling upon my sword would be rather difficult without the convenience of gravity but I could open my veins.

The Roman emperors, or those who fell foul of them, took this course. They ran a hot bath, got into it, slashed their wrists under the surface and watched as their life flowed out of them in crimson submarine flowers. Eventually they were found, blanched as an etiolated weed, honoured for their manhood and carried to a neat sarcophagus along the Appian Way.

Not having the facility of a bath, I would have to suspend myself in the shower. The result would be rather messy but of no consequence as no one is likely to discover me.

To die in such a fashion would be fitting for a god. The emperors of Rome thought they were gods and I am on the road to deification so it might be appropriate.

Yet both possibilities are somehow mundane. I, the cosmonaut in control of the world, the master of technologies beyond common comprehension and the arbiter of infinity, should really go in a much more scientific, state-of-the-art manner. Being in orbit ought to give me a certain unique edge over all the other sorry would-be suicides down below.

So, thinking along these lines, I have decided, if I so choose to top myself, as gangsters say, to allow myself to accept death's kisses through outer-space hypothermia.

It is an ingenious way to die, almost glorious, not unlike a death by overdose but avoiding all the mucky vomit and loosening of the orifices which occurs when the body knows it's going and tries by reflex to get rid of its danger. Hypothermia is much neater.

Humans must maintain an inner-body temperature to keep functioning normally. Even in extremes of heat and cold, the internal temperature of the body, governed by blood flow, skin hairs and layers of fat, seldom varies more than two degrees either side of 36.8°C. Even the outer surface shell of the body is rarely 4°C off the norm. If the inner temperature at the core of the body reaches above 42.7°C or below 28.8°C, death is assured. In order to maintain the correct levels, the body burns fat and fuel to keep warm: shivering is the alarm bell, telling the body through reflex muscle spasms heat is being lost quicker than it is being restored.

The biological process is controlled by a thermostat at the base of the brain. At the onset of hypothermia, this bio-system instructs the body to withdraw heat from the outer layers and transfer it to the inner. Hands and feet grow cold, the muscles hardening. Blood circulation slows and the brain is starved of oxygen and nutrients. Gradually, the brain loses activity, the shivering stops and irrationality begins. Death is not far off but its victim has no worries for the mind is accepting the fact. In the next stage, the pulse grows irregular and drowsiness leads to semi-consciousness then eternal unconsciousness.

It is a painless way to go to the river and hail the boatman.

When the SAM missile hit, it took the starboard vertical tail surface clean off Vasya's Sukhoi SU-27. I saw a terrific flash through the corner of my eye which momentarily lit up my cockpit, even though it was mid-afternoon on a cloudless day, and I thought he had been hit in one of the engines. I pressed the radio transmit button and was about to signal the downing when there was a rush of furnace-hot air around me and the world turned over. The next thing I knew I was hanging limply from the strings of my parachute. Vasya's fighter exploded some fifteen kilometres off, a little puff of black smoke and a spurt of ignited aviation fuel in the barren Afghan mountains. My own aircraft was nowhere to be seen. I presumed it was already down over the mountain ridge to the north and hoped it landed on some Afghan village, wiping out a large number of the be-turbaned sods we were fighting.

Squinting against the sun, for my visor had disappeared from my flying helmet, and squirming round in my harness, I searched for another parachute. Finally, I spotted one a thousand metres or so below me and about four kilometres off, the dull-coloured canopy almost invisible against the browns of the sunburnt landscape. It was rushing towards me on what must have been a strong wind current into which I was also descending.

Sure enough, several minutes later, the wind caught me and by the time I landed on a hillside to the east I was less than a kilometre from where I thought Vasya had come down.

I removed my harness, gathered up the parachute and stuffed it into a crevice in a gully: then, from the cover of a boulder, I took stock of my surroundings.

The mountainside was quite bare of vegetation and I could make out no signs of habitation nearer than the hazy distance of the valley floor below me. Down there, a rough track meandered across a dusty plain devoid of fields, stock or even temporary nomads' camps.

Checking my survival pack and touching my water bottle to reassure myself it was not leaking, I set off walking in the direction of Vasya's landing. In half an hour, I found him. Not being able to steer his parachute, he had descended into a ravine and smashed his right ankle and elbow. His flying jacket was torn and his left shoulder was bleeding, although not profusely.

How bad's my neck? he asked.

Once I had helped him towards a depression behind some boulders, which would not only afford us some cover from prying binoculars but would also shelter us from the sun, I took a look at his wound.

Your neck's fine, I reported. It's your shoulder and it's superficial. A flesh wound, nothing more. A few stitches at the most. And a lot of bandages. You'll be off to Moscow by the weekend.

Has your beacon triggered? was his next question.

I felt in my flying jacket and took out a small metal box, shielding it from the sun with my hand. A red diode was flickering on it.

Yes, I said, almost cheerfully.

Good, he said. Mine's fucked.

He eased his right arm with his left hand.

How's it feel? I enquired.

Fucked, he said again. And my foot.

Hurt?

He hummed affirmatively and asked, How long before they get a 'copter out, do you think?

I thought about it. We were approximately three hundred kilometres from Kabul. The rescue beacon was on but the mountains would block the signal. To find us, they would have to send up a spotter, engage the signal, pinpoint it, relay the information and then scramble a rescue flight. I glanced at my watch. It was 15:41. There was no possibility they would get to us before nightfall and no way they would fly after dark. We were here for a good eighteen hours.

We'll be back in Kabul for a shower before either of us turns into a pumpkin, I lied. I'm afraid we'll miss the evening meal, though.

Pumpkin?

You know, the story of Cinderella. She turned into a pumpkin at midnight.

You're wrong, Vasya said. Her coach turned into a pumpkin and the horses became mice. She just lost her ball gown and her shoes.

He grinned painfully and tucked his right arm into his flying jacket.

You never were very good at story-telling, he chided me.

No, I thought, I never was, but I could lie faultlessly.

I applied a field dressing to his shoulder wound and

offered him a shot of morphine: we had two small doses each. He declined it saying he was able to bear pain and would rather live with it than fall into a drugged sleep only to wake to it later.

As the afternoon wore on, we did not talk much. Every hour, we had a gulp of water and sucked a boiled sweet from our survival packs. Eventually, Vasya lay in the shade, half-dozing and I went off to recce our surroundings and search for a level spot where they might bring the helicopter in.

The hillside was steep, ranging between forty and sixty degrees from the horizontal with some small, eroded cliffs which were near vertical. Brown lizards several centimetres long scuttled about: I could not imagine what they ate for there were few insects and the only vegetation I discovered was the odd clump of desiccated grass or bush of leafless twigs.

A few hundred metres from our hideout, I found a patch of hillside with a slope of about ten degrees but it was strewn with boulders up to the size of a large suitcase. I also came across the dented tail fin of a mortar round and some fragments of shrapnel. These heartened me. A skirmish had obviously taken place here so the spot was not unknown to our side. I decided to come back after dark and roll as many of the boulders as I could down the mountainside, clearing a landing pad.

What have you found? Vasya wanted to know as I rejoined him.

A place for them to get a 'copter in.

He smiled then winced.

Elbow? I queried.

Ankle, he answered. I think it's in a bad way.

No worry. The medics'll fix it.

We sipped a little water and waited. A few aircraft flew over at an altitude of about 8000 metres. The sun went down behind the mountains.

I suppose we're here for the night, Vasya remarked as the first stars appeared.

I suppose so, I replied. But that's not bad news. Under cover of darkness, at least we're safe from the testicle-eaters of Takhar and all their merry brethren.

At 20:00, by the light of a thin, new moon suspended like a white eyelash against the black sky, I left Vasya and made my way back to the semi-plateau. For nearly two hours, I worked up a sweat as I laboured rolling rocks down the hillside and shifting the larger ones to the side. By 22:00, I had cleared an area more than adequate to accommodate a Mil MI-26.

Returning to our boulder hide-out, I found Vasya crouched upon the ground in a foetal position. I thought at first he was asleep and took care not to wake him but he was only dozing lightly.

It's cold, he said as I settled down next to him. Can we light a fire? It'll not be seen in this depression except from above.

I considered this: he was right. It would not give away our position for I was certain there would be no one on the moutain above us. On the other hand, there was hardly anything to burn.

Scavenging about, I uprooted half a dozen of the twig bushes, broke them by stamping on them and made a small fire. It did not last more than thirty minutes. The wood was so dry it flared up and was fine grey ash within minutes, no embers remaining.

As the night went on, the air temperature dropped dramatically. I huddled up against Vasya but this only caused his injuries to hurt more. I flapped my arms against my side but to no avail. At least, I thought, I was keeping alive. Vasya, on the other hand, was in a bad way. He could not move and make his muscles create heat. He shivered loudly, muttering to himself.

I'm fucking freezing to death, he moaned. Can't we light another fire?

I got to my feet, went out and ranged about for more bushes, finding two of them. I lit another fire as close to Vasya as I dared and, using the metal box of his broken emergency beacon as a mug, warmed some water and helped him drink it. It revived him somewhat but he was soon cold again, his extremities numbing.

Going to the ravine, I cut the cords off the parachute and, bundling it up, took the nylon back to the depression where I lay down on the ground beside Vasya, fitting my body into the curves of his, as close as a lover. This done, I tugged the material over us, tucking it in, folding it double, trapping as much air as I could in it which I could heat with my own body.

Keep your hands to yourself, won't you? Vasya murmured.

Those were his last coherent words.

For an hour, he mumbled every so often, his body twitching once or twice, but by the time the sun came over the valley, heating the rocks again and warming the air, he was dead.

For me to die as Vasya did is so uncomplicated.

All I have to do is cut off the heater system and fractionally open one of the vents to lower the pressure inside the spacecraft. This will have the effect of rapidly cooling what air remains. I will go through the symptoms of hypothermia pretty rapidly and should be unconscious in a matter of minutes. Thinking about this, however, I question why I have even considered it. There is no need to accept this surrender, follow this weak man's way. It is just simply too melodramatic.

Like every other living creature, I am waiting upon the inevitable. If anything, I am more fortunate than most. I can assess my lifespan in aluminium trays, drops of water and molecules of air.

It is better to go to death knowing what is happening. Only the foolish or those unappreciative of their good fortune surrender control over their destiny.

❧

I discover I have a fellow passenger.

Every so often, as part of the bacterial control programme, I check the quality of my drinking water. This is simply done by extracting a small quantity from the main tank through a withdrawal valve, adding it to a reagent in a small plastic vial, shaking it and checking the iodine concentration is not below three parts per million. If it is, I have to add a solution of iodine to the drinking water supply pipe, leave it for an hour to act as a sterilizer then vent the contents before topping up the level of the solution in the tank to the required strength. To accomplish this, I insert a soluble iodine pill into the injector mechanism, having first unscrewed an inspection panel close to the head of crewman #3's sleeping restraint.

Behind the panel is a space just big enough to allow me to put my hand in to operate the injector. There is no light in the panel: all actions must be done by touch.

When I last carried out this drill, and finding the system needed attention, I withdrew the screws with the power-driven screwdriver, for they are a tight fit, unlike many in the spacecraft, allowing them to drift with the plate whilst I fumbled to get a pill into the slot on the injector. Not for the first time, I had difficulty introducing the pill into the injector and it slipped from my fingers.

During training sessions, such an action was easily rectified. One looked about underneath the injector for where the pill might have dropped. Gravity does one a lot of favours. Up here, in mid-mission, the problem is compounded for nothing drops. It merely floats off. To find it one has to look everywhere, in three dimensions. Certain the pill had not escaped the mechanism housing, I set about fanning the air with my fingers, starting at the rim of the panel mounting and hoping to net the pill wherever it was drifting.

Instead of the pill, my fingers snared on a fine mesh. I could hardly feel it at first but, as my hand shifted, I sensed it tugging infinitesimally at the hairs on the back of my wrist. Very carefully and, I have to admit to myself, with a degree of apprehension born of watching too many science-fiction films as a teenager, I withdraw my arm. Snagging the back of my hand was a fine spider's web.

Under normal circumstances, I doubt I would have seen it but, with the atmosphere of the spacecraft being enclosed and dust laden until it reaches the filters, it was decorated by fine particles of what was once my skin.

I stared at it in wonder for a while before starting my hunt for its maker.

The iodine pill was, for the moment, forgotten. I grabbed hold of one of the high-powered spotlight torches provided for emergencies and in case of primary electrical circuit failure and set about shining it into every nook and cranny of the potable water circulation system. I did not find the spider until I was into the night segment of the orbit when, at the rear of a pipe duct, the torch caught a momentary silver glimmer. Looking in, I found another, almost pristine web yet, despite its cleanliness, it was a sorry affair. There was little symmetry to it. Threads of gossamer linked pipe mountings to bolt-heads, retaining clips to wire junctions but there was no delicate spiral ladder of fine cord, no sense of proportion or design. The whole thing was a failure.

The spider squatted to the rear of its disorderly mesh, its legs bunched up as if it was contemplating a leap for freedom. If, I thought, it was a jumping spider then it was in for a shock. One clear bound and it would hurtle across the cabin and squash itself on the opposite bulkhead.

Very slowly, I pushed my index finger through the apology for a web and rested it next to the spider's head. Much to my surprise, the spider did not back up but, after tentatively testing my skin with its legs, stepped on to my fingernail.

Clear of the pipe ducting, I held it close to my face and studied it. With its legs outstretched it would perhaps have covered the surface of a St Petersburg Metro token. Its thorax was a dull yellow colour, rather like old mustard congealed on the side of the pot, whilst its legs were blackish-grey and its abdomen, although predominantly the same colour as the thorax, was shot through with fine, dark maroon lines. Its multiple compound eyes glistened like chips of burnished jet.

Anna had a thing about creepy-crawlies.

Wasps she swiftly despatched with a home-made swat constructed of a square of thin leather fixed to a length of dowelling; flies she killed in a similar manner. Her aim was steady and her flick of the swat so delicately accurate she killed them with one swipe but never squashed them, so there was no mark of insectial body juices on her scrubbed deal table. Bees she ignored unless they threatened either to sting or sink their proboscii into her new-made preserves. Moths she hated and drove out of the room with a duster. Butterflies she admired from a distance and crickets she captured in a tumbler to release outside in the grass. Mosquitoes and gnats she wiped out with a quick clap of the hands.

But spiders: she worshipped spiders.

The ceiling of their cabin was a maze of cobwebs crossing and re-crossing, decorating the heavy beams and funnelling like tiny tornadoes into cracks between the planks. Every work surface and stick of furniture was polished, every book dusted, the floor swept thrice daily. Unless you gazed up, the house looked as pristine as an operating theatre: but cast your eyes up and there was spider city suspended over your head.

Once, not long after I had cemented my friendship with them, I arrived early at their house in the village before Pyotr returned from the forest. It was a day of grey drizzle and sombre skies. Anna showed me in and sat me down at the table.

How are you? she asked. Keeping well? How was your drive from the city? How is your training going?

I am fit and well, I replied. My drive was tedious and overlong. It took me four hours.

Four hours! Pyotr does it in three and a half. In that wreck of his. And your training?

It's coming along, I admitted.

What are you doing now?

It was theoretically forbidden for us to speak of our work outside our immediate circle of fellow trainees and lecturers but no one obeyed the rule.

Theories of spatial navigation. It means not just measuring and navigating by distance and altitude but also by time. We don't say, 'The moon is 368,000 kilometres away.' Instead, we say, 'The moon is 73 hours away at an average velocity of 5287 kilometres per hour.'

It sounds difficult.

It is, Anna. Very difficult because you have to take into account orbits and gravitational forces, not just those of the Earth but also of the moon, trajectories and angles of approach. It is rather like throwing a stone at a galloping horse. Hurl it directly and it falls behind him. Throw too far ahead and you miss.

She tut-tutted, pushed the kettle on to the hob and tapped the ventilator on the chimney. Through the open door of the stove, I could see the flames gutter then start to burn more fiercely.

You'll have some coffee? We have coffee.

I nodded. Bujan appeared at the door. He was a young dog in those days but he was rehearsing for his old age. He sauntered in, nuzzled his spittle-soaked muzzle in my hand then collapsed in front of the stove, dropping his body as a tired knacker might dump a load of bones in front of the glue pot.

Pyotr won't be long, Anna predicted. Ten minutes.

She busied herself with the coffee and a plate of *vatrushkis* she had made.

I am glad you come to see us, she said after a minute's silence. Pyotr likes your company and I . . . She seemed embarrassed and did not look at me as she continued, Our Vasya was . . .

Yes, I answered. I know. I was there.

Anyway, with him gone — well, now we have you.

Turning, she smiled her mother's smile. It was then, I think, I came to realize I loved the pair of them.

She put the plate on the table. A spider appeared, lowering himself from the spider metropolis of arachnids overhead, paying out his life-thread from his spinnerets with his rear legs. I bent down, removed my shoe and was preparing to get rid of it when Anna, turning from the stove, issued a little squeak of indignation and horror.

Put your shoe on! Now! This instance! Don't you know it's terrible bad luck to kill a spider?

You sound like my grandmother, I retorted, doing as I was told.

A sensible woman, then, Anna rejoined.

But why . . . ? I began, intending to remonstrate with her.

Why? Because. That's why. And I will tell you. A spider brings good fortune. If he was to settle on your coat, you would know you would soon receive money. On my table — well, then I will get money. If you had killed him, you would bring on rain.

I looked out the door. The drizzle was consolidating itself into a light downpour.

It is raining, I said, trying to suppress the belligerence I would not have disguised had I been talking to my grandmother.

Then maybe you've killed one already today, Anna rebuked me.

She put two tumblers of sweet, black coffee on the table. Just at that moment, Pyotr walked in, his coat sopping, his trousers clinging to his thighs and water dripping off the barrel of his shotgun.

Have you killed a spider? she accused him.

How the hell should I know? Pyotr said bluntly, sitting down by his glass of coffee. I've been walking in the forest since dawn. I've probably trodden on hundreds of the little bastards.

There! exclaimed Anna, looking pointedly at me. You see?

She on about spiders again? Pyotr asked, glancing up at the mist of overhead webs.

I said nothing.

If every one of those damn spiders did his job, we'd be millionaires living in the lap of luxury, not living amongst peasants in the lap of horse dung.

He pushed his boots off, displayed his socks to the stove for a moment then tucked his feet under Bujan to warm them further.

If you see a spider making his web, you'll soon get new clothes, he said, half-mimicking his wife's voice. Well, I've sat here of an evening and seen most of that — he jabbed his finger upwards — being spun and I'm still wearing a jacket my father wore.

He slurped his coffee and ate a *vatrushki* without seeming to even bite it. His Adam's apple gulped as he swallowed.

In the old days, Pyotr went on, peasant women — and I'm not talking about when the tsar was just a twinkle in his daddy's eye! I'm talking about the Khruschev years. As recently as that! — peasant women who suffered from rheumatism or asthma used to go about with a little cloth bag full of living spiders hung around their necks. So much for the efficacy of medical science and the copious number of icons in the Russian Orthodox Church worn thin by kissing and polished by the spit of old hags.

Anna gave her husband a filthy look and muttered, If you wish to smile and thrive, leave the spider running live.

Once I had inspected it, I pondered what to do with my cosmonaut arachnid.

To kill it would have made best sense. It could short circuit something with its inquisitive legs and yet I could not help hearing Anna's voice warning against it.

In the end, I emptied one of the surgical equipment boxes, which have perspex covers sealed by a zip strip, dumped the contents into a waste disposal bag and introduced the spider to it, closing the cover. I could now observe the spider and keep it alive without risking it getting up to mischief.

Now we are two, the spider and me.

We share this little haven in space: and that is not all. We shall share the same fate, too. As assuredly as I shall eventually die, so shall the spider. There is not a fly to be had in *Mir*.

However, I have done my duty by it, saved it from a frazzling between two connectors and ensured it will survive at least as long as its god will let it.

Every now and then, I give the box a quick look. Partly, I want to make sure the spider is still securely inside it. Partly, I gain a sense of companionship from knowing another creature shares my predicament.

❧

Are you ready? Pyotr enquired.

Do I look it?

He walked around me, studying me from toe to crown. The exhaust on the Zil clicked and snapped as the metal quickly cooled in the freezing air. Brilliant low sunlight glanced off the remaining patch of chrome on the rear bumper.

Are you warm? It'll be as cold as hell out there.

I am sweating in here, I replied. And hell is not cold. It is hot.

That depends, Pyotr retorted. For Italians or Britishers, Americans or Africans, hell may be hot but for Russians? Believe me, Russian hell is cold.

He completed his inspection and punched my arm.

You'll do but, he turned serious, which was unusual for

him, if you feel yourself getting cold, you must tell me. Then we'll come back to the car and switch on the engine, have a swig of tea. Something like that. You know the drill. You were trained . . .

He stopped talking, reached into the trunk of the Zil and removed an old canvas knapsack.

Yes, I confirmed quietly, I know the drill.

Pyotr carried the knapsack of gear and a canvas bag of kindling wood. I carried our stools, a two-metre broomstick, a heavy *kolovorot* to carve through the ice, an auger and a large brown paper bag done round with twine. Side by side, we set off down the slope from the road, trudging through the snow which reached up to our knees.

We should have brought snow-shoes, I said after we had gone a little way.

Nonsense. Only another hundred metres to the bank then another hundred on top of that. Out there, the snow won't be so thick. The wind'll have shifted it.

Of course, Pyotr was correct. After sliding down the steep bank, the snow covering the ice of the lake was only ten or fifteen centimetres deep making walking much easier.

Do you know the story of Andropov and his driver? Pyotr asked out of the blue.

We skirted a twisted tangle of branches protruding from the ice, the remains of a tree caught fast in the shallows after an autumnal storm. Some animal had been nesting or sheltering under it, footprints coming and going in the snow.

I do not, I said, but I'm sure I'm about to.

Remember, Pyotr began, Andropov was head of the KGB before he became ringmaster of the whole circus. One day he was due to leave his office to drive across Moscow and Red Square to the Kremlin. However, when he sat in his car, and told his driver to set off, the man half-fainted. He was ill, some bug or other. Nothing to do with his employer's status, you understand. But it was essential Andropov be on time in the Kremlin so he helped the driver out of the front and into the back of the car. 'Don't you worry,' Andropov said. 'When we get to the Kremlin I'll have a doctor attend to you.' With that, Andropov climbed into the driver's seat and they set off. Driving over the speed limit, Andropov was flagged down by two policemen on traffic duty. One policeman knocked on the driver's window whilst the other checked the rear of the vehicle. The window was wound down. The policeman was about to issue a reprimand when he saw who the driver was. 'Comrade!' he said, snapping to attention and getting off a slick salute. Andropov sped away towards the Kremlin. When he was gone, the policeman asked his partner, 'Who was in the back?' 'Don't know,' the other replied. 'Why do you ask?' 'Because,' the first one said, 'he must have been fucking important because his driver was Andropov.'

I smiled. It was too cold to laugh. When I opened my mouth to inhale, the freezing air stung my teeth.

Of course, Pyotr continued, that's only a joke. In reality, Andropov would never have been so considerate.

He halted, studied the far bank of the lake and the way we had come, kicked a circle of snow from the ice, about three metres across and dropped the knapsack and bag.

This'll do. It's where I usually come, between that little promontory and where we left the car. It's deep here, a hole about twenty metres to the bottom. This is where the big ones hide. Give me the auger.

Within a minute, he had drilled a twenty centimetre diameter hole in the ice. I set to with the saw, enlarging it. Pyotr then placed some of the kindling on the ice, piling it round with lumps of charcoal from the brown paper bag. Together, we set up our lines and hooks, baiting them with bread dough and small pieces of raw gristle and sinewy meat.

It'll take a time for the first bite, Pyotr forecast. They're lazy down there. Cold, too. But once they know what's on offer . . .

We sat on our stools opposite each other across the fishing hole. The water was black, in contrast to the white snow and grey ice. Even though it was low in the sky, the sun was so bright I was thankful for my pilot's sunglasses: Pyotr wore a pair of old-fashioned tinted spectacles in plastic tortoiseshell frames.

We did not speak for some time, huddling up with our hands gripping the line. It was never easy telling when one had a bite for the sensitivity of one's fingers was lost through the thick fur lining and leather of one's heavy gloves.

At length, Pyotr quietly said, Did you know I once went into storage?

I looked up with surprise: to go into storage was his vernacular for being arrested on more than a minor charge.

No, I did not, I said.

Many years ago. In the days of Uncle Joseph. I was just married. Anna was scared witless. I was gone for nineteen days. In the end, as luck would have it, I was released without explanation and without charge. Never knew what it was they believed I had done. Or suggested. Or thought of. Or dreamt of. They were funny days.

Where was this?

Vitebsk.

I did not question him further. It seemed inappropriate. Yet I wondered why he had told me this secret. There was no reason: indeed, it was strange for him to impart such a piece of knowledge for one never spoke of such things, even to the closest of friends in the post-*perestroika* times.

The guards in the cell block were a dozy lot, Pyotr suddenly went on. But one of them was a really thick son of a bitch. A Ukrainian.

He grinned so expansively from beneath the brow of his hat I wondered if what was to follow was another anecdote or a justification for his prejudice.

We had great fun tormenting him. He was a gullible bastard.

He tweaked his line and, taking the stick, stirred the water about in our ice hole. It was beginning to freeze into a mush.

There were nine of us held together. Usual facilities of a couple of buckets and six bunks, open bars on the front. More a sort of cage than a prison cell. Needless to say, the food was atrocious. We were fed stewed cabbage, boiled beans and black bread. Nothing else. That was it, twice a day. But the cuisine gave us the opportunity to get the Ukrainian. He was always nosing round the place, hiding round the corner in the hope of hearing us confess some crime or misdemeanour to the others. As if we would. Anyhow, we found the way to drive him crazy.

Once more, he jiggled his line, pulling a metre or so out of the hole and letting it sink again.

In the cell, our drinking water was provided in bottles, two per person per day. So you know what we did? During the night, we secretly farted into the bottles, each man storing up his gas until he could no longer hold it. The beans and cabbage gave us all terrible wind. He held his gloved fingers to his nose. Then, when we knew the Ukrainian was on the snoop, we ignited a bottle. We were allowed to smoke so we had matches. The gas caused a loud report. He would come running. We all feigned innocence or to be dozing. He would go away and we'd light the next bottle.

Pyotr laughed loudly at the memory as I looked in admiration at him. He had spent nearly three weeks as a guest of the KGB, in conditions which must have been far worse than he admitted to, and he still recollected it in humorous terms. There was no rancour in his voice, no hatred in his heart, no enmity in his character: there was just a joke born of his adversity. Yet every time he told it, he had to remember also the privations, the stink of the cell, the fear and the beatings.

Mind you, Pyotr finished as if reading my mind, the Ukrainian had his fun at our expense too. He was a sadistic sod . . .

My line jerked and went taut.

They don't fight like in the summer, Pyotr said. Just bring him up slowly.

I hauled the fish in, letting it run when it wanted so as not to snap the line. At last, it came to the ice hole and Pyotr gaffed it, dumped it on the ice and stamped on its head with his boot.

They're learning about us, he said with a quiet satisfaction.

For three-quarters of an hour, as the sun disappeared, we caught fish at a steady rate of one every three or four minutes. As darkness fell and the sub-zero temperature dropped even lower, we lit the fire on the ice and remained.

The light'll bring them up, Pyotr whispered, as if they might be listening to him. Shorten your line. We'll stay at it until about seven if that's all right with you. The fire'll keep going until about then.

When night came, the sky was alive with stars. Sure enough, the fish started to rise to the water not far below the ice and we continued to catch them at a steady rate. They were none of them under a kilo in weight.

Can I ask you something? Pyotr enquired.

He threw a few more handfuls of charcoal on to the fire with the last of the kindling. Tiny sparks soared out of the fire like minuscule tracer shells as the new charcoal knocked against the old and started to ignite.

Anything, I said.

And you'll tell the truth?

Of course, I responded, wondering what subject he was going to broach.

How did Vasya really die?

His sudden question and the seriousness in his voice shocked me. He had never ever broached the subject before, accepting as read the explanation I had sent him in my letter from the barracks late on the evening of the auction.

He died of hypothermia, I said. Just as I wrote to you.

Just as I told you the first time we met. On a mountainside in Afghanistan.

You're sure?

Yes, I said, I'm quite sure. I was there with him.

I looked him full in the face. His cheeks and nose, surrounded by the fur lining of his *oushanka*, were tinged with red from the glow of the fire.

You're not lying to save my feelings? Anna's feelings?

No, I answered. I am not. It wouldn't be right.

He seemed satisfied and turned his attention to the ice hole.

Why do you ask me? I ventured. So long afterwards.

Stories, Pyotr replied. They say the war was not lost because we were out-gunned, out-manoeuvred. They say the Mujahaddin won not with guns but with hypodermic needles.

He was right. I thought of all the soldiers and ground crew I had seen become addicted to heroin during the years of the war, the dope supplied by back-street pushers in Kabul, by the Afghani girls the men screwed on their nights off, who railed against Capitalism and Islam and the Americans as they filled the syringes or lit the pipes.

Did you ever . . . ? Pyotr began.

Yes, I interrupted him, I did. So did Vasya. Everyone did. But we kept clear of the white powder merchants. We smoked a little opium from time to time. It calmed our nerves and took us back home. Or at least, it took us out of Afghanistan for a few minutes. Yet we weren't addicted. Opium's not as dangerous as people think. It's psychologically dangerous, perhaps, because one comes to lean on it as an escape but the body does not become physiologically dependent upon it as quickly as it does with heroin.

So many came back hooked, Pyotr said. I was afraid . . . He paused then continued, You won't tell Anna, will you? Ever! This is just our secret.

I agreed and we fished on in silence. The fire gradually died, the fine charcoal ash drifting on a light breeze which had sprung up across the lake.

We'd better pack up, Pyotr suggested. If the breeze strengthens, the wind chill will be bitter.

The fish were dumped in the kindling sack, every one of them frozen stiff as a brick.

Walking back to the car with the aid of a small torch, sharing the load of gear and fish between us, Pyotr suddenly asked, How will you die?

How do I know! I retorted.

I mean, how would you like to die?

I do not expect to have the good fortune to make the choice.

Well, if you had.

I thought about it for a moment as we passed the ice-locked dead tree.

By my own hand, I decided. Not reliant upon an outside source, not held ransom by some disfiguring disease or a gangster with an AK pilfered from the local armoury.

You're a brave man, Pyotr said. To be in the space programme, you must be. But beyond that.

I am not brave, I retorted. You asked me what choice I should make. That would be it. In the event, I shall no doubt be in the same strait as everyone else, having to take what comes.

As we reached the Zil, and were loading the kit, I asked, Do you know what Vasya's best story was?

I do not, Pyotr said, imitating me as best he could, but I'm sure I'm about to.

There was an Aeroflot pilot taking a group of top Party officials on their holidays to Odessa, I recounted. Vasya was the co-pilot of the flight. One of the passengers, sitting just behind the cockpit, was a crusty-faced old biddy who was giving the stewardess a bad time. She complained about the food, the seat, the roughness of the lavatory paper — everything she could. When the aircraft hit a patch of turbulence, she ordered the stewardess to bring the pilot to her seat. The stewardess dared not disobey and the pilot got an earful of complaint. After suffering a severe ticking off from Mrs Politburo, the pilot returned to the flight deck in a fuming rage. For half an hour, he fulminated in a quiet voice then, after a few minutes' silence, he left Vasya to fly the plane and, undoing his overnight flight bag, took out a pair of pyjama trousers, tugging the cord out of the waist. This he unravelled into two long strings. 'You going to hang her?' Vasya asked. 'Next best thing,' said the pilot. He tied the ends of the strings to his seat. 'When you hear me say *piss*,' the pilot ordered, 'bank sharp left, drop a hundred metres or so and bank right.' With that, he left the flight deck, trailing the lines. Vasya heard the conversation through the flight deck door which went like this. 'Madam', said the pilot, 'as you can see I have left the flight deck. Here are two lengths of string.' Vasya imagined him giving her the cords. 'If the plane banks right, pull this one, if left, this one. You, madam, are now flying the plane. I am going for a piss.'

Pyotr slammed the lid of the trunk down and roared with laughter.

Did Vasya obey his orders?

I'm sure he did, I confirmed.

He laughed again, throwing his head back. By the torchlight, I could vaguely see his throat inside the fur trim of his collar.

That's my boy, he guffawed, opening the driver's door. A chip off the old block. I'll bet the old bitch was a Ukrainian.

❧

When a man is worried, or afraid, or feels unloved, or unwanted or alone, he seeks out one of two things — a woman or his god.

It is my belief, *in extremis*, a man only requires either a good fuck or a good pray.

Both of these have the same effect upon him. They calm him, reassure him, offer him solace, make him promises in which he mistakenly places his trust (if only for a while) and lull him into a state of false security.

A prayer is a letter to God. And don't you forget it!

This phrase, or one very much like it, frequently played on the lips of my grandmother, Zina. She used it to scold me when I dismissed her latest visit to the church as an extension of her peasant, superstitious nature or yet another instance of her secret admiration for the young priest in the black cassock and flowing black beard.

It is not inconceivable she could have come across the Siberian Demon, Grigori Efimovich Rasputin. My great-grandfather had worked for the Imperial family until just a few weeks before the revolution in March 1917 by which time my grandmother must have been in her mid-twenties. She had married, on her seventeenth birthday, my grandfather, Boris Ivanovich Miroshnichenko, who was a tailor in St Petersburg, but I know she still visited her father from time to time at Peterhof or in the Winter Palace when he was temporarily transferred to the city.

Musing on her — in my opinion — irrational religiosity, I used to fantasize about her sneaking round a corner below stairs or nipping into a butler's pantry only to come face to face with the Bearded Starets himself, lecturing to the staff or rogering one of the maids over a kitchen table. Perhaps he even gave her a little tickle, squeezed her buttocks through her corset or stroked her tits.

If you ask me, this would account for her illogical devotion to the Russian Orthodox Church for I am utterly convinced she would have fallen under his spell without anything more than a passing smile.

On one occasion, when her mind was growing very vague and her death was not far off, I decided to ask her about Rasputin.

He was a holy man, she said, her eyes closed against the sunlight shining through her bedroom window.

Did you ever meet him? I ventured.

She opened her eyes and stared at me. My heart jumped. The truth was going to come out.

He could heal, you know, she went on, her eyes glazing

over in the way those of old folk do when they return to their histories.

Heal? I prompted.

He could put his hands on your head and cure you of all sorts of things.

She paused. I held my breath. If she admitted to having met him I would, for evermore, have a lever with which to prise at the heavy boulder of her belief, loosen it and one day topple it over the cliff of rationality and into the sea of reason.

He was able to halt the bleeding. The blood in the Tsarevich, in Alexei Nikolaievich. His blood was bad. Even Doctor Fedorov could do nothing.

Did you ever see him cure someone? I enquired gently.

Oh, yes! Often. He had a black bag. Leather. Brass clips. Inside were all sorts of wonders. Small bottles. Syringes. Little cardboard boxes of pills. He was a good doctor.

Not Fedorov, I said patiently. Rasputin.

He cured Nadezhda. She had headaches. Bad ones.

Who cured her?

Father Rasputin.

I decided not to dispute this: I know, as does every good Russian historian, Rasputin was no more a priest than Brezhnev. He was a legally married man with a wife called Proskovia, two daughters called Matriona and Varvara and two sons, one of whom died before his first birthday and both of whom were called Dmitri. He was a notorious drunk with a penchant for pussy and he rode as many ladies as a coachman rode carriages. Perhaps he was distressed, or scared, or lonely like the rest of us.

And you saw this? I enquired. You saw Rasputin do it?

She told me. He touched her and the pain was gone. Never came back.

I was inclined at this juncture to be sarcastic and ask where he touched Nadezhda, on her forehead, or her neck or up her night-dress, but I desisted.

Did you see him?

Who, dear? she asked, her eyes returning to the present and careful not to study the future.

Rasputin.

She looked at me again, not staring this time but with a laughter way back in her eyes, shifting like shadows in an autumn copse. And she said nothing, just slowly tucking her feet up on her bed and sliding under the sheets.

You will remember to fetch the priest, won't you, Misha? When it's time.

Yes, *babushka*, I replied and I kissed her on her forehead and wondered again if Rasputin had stroked the same spot.

Some years ago, I visited the room in which Rasputin had been done for. Or, as truth would have it, nearly done for.

The chamber is in the basement of Yusupov's palace in St Petersburg, a dingy room approached down a narrow staircase leading off one of those trick hallways surrounded by mirrors.

My call on history, in the days before the city was renamed St Petersburg and foreigners were a rarity, was made in the company of a female tour guide, three Muscovite economics students, an elderly retired couple from Kiev and a dozen Ukrainian farmers accompanied by their dumpy wives, visiting the city on their annual vacation.

Pyotr would have revelled in it.

Chivvied through Felix Yusupov's study where the assassination was planned, we were herded down the stairs (*This is the way the murderers went*), past a door leading into the garden (*This is the way Rasputin entered*) and into a room the ceiling of which was supported by several pillars and sturdy masonry arches covered in plaster. Upon a Persian carpet, behind a white rope barrier, stood a circular table at which sat a waxworks mannequin of Rasputin dressed in black baggy trousers and a loose silk shirt.

This dummy, the guide reported in plangent tones, is an exact replica of Rasputin. While it was being made, a number of strange happenings occurred.

She stressed the word *strange*, her voice deep and attempting awesome horror: the effect was to make several of the Ukrainian bumpkins' wives titter nervously. The narrative went on in an equally sonorous manner: we were told how, on 16 December 1916, Rasputin was lured to the room and fed sugared cakes laced with cyanide.

A number of extraneous bits of information were thrown into the narrative from time to time. For example, as the murder was being perpetrated downstairs a phonogram upstairs was, for some bizarre reason, playing *Yankee Doodle*: I like to think it was the first instance of American culture impinging itself upon Russia or, better, it was the first time America was to be used by Russians to cover up for Russian wrong-doings.

The impregnated cakes had no effect. Rasputin called for wine and was served madeira, similarly fortified. This too was a failure. Rasputin requested a cup of tea. Not to be outdone, the conspirators then shot Rasputin but although he screamed and fell on to a bear-skin rug, he still did not die.

On this very spot, the guide said reverentially, pointing to the floor at the foot of a particularly solidly built Ukrainian dowager with expansive, sagging bosoms held in check by a blouse printed with daisies and stretching lewdly at the buttonholes.

The woman uttered a little squeak and stepped back smartly.

From this point, the guide's voice began to quiver, Rasputin attempted to escape. Mortally wounded, he was still not dead and tried to get away, such was his supernatural power.

Several of the other Ukrainians exchanged hurried glances. The Muscovites were seemingly unmoved. We followed the guide up the stairs again (*Rasputin crawled up here*), through the door into the garden (*Rasputin crawled through here, too*) and across to the edge of the garden, now weed strewn.

Here, the guide ended her monologue, Purishkevitch shot Rasputin. His body was bundled into a blue curtain, tied with rope and driven to the Petrovsky Bridge where it was thrown into the river. It cracked the ice and vanished beneath it. When his body was eventually dragged from the river, it was discovered he had half untied the ropes whilst under water . . .

What a strong man! marvelled one of the Ukrainian dames.

What an unlucky bastard! murmured one of the Muscovites.

Tourists go there now, ogle the waxworks dummy and

peer at the floor. Some of them are foreigners visiting Russia with their dollar traveller's cheques, Samsonite suitcases and Japanese cameras: but many are Russians, one-time good communists who are in favour of the restoration of the churches not because they wish to make their devotions in them but because they are a part of the national heritage. They encourage more dollars. The Russians are also as curious as the foreigners but far more superstitious.

Just as the guide was leading us back into the building and up the stairs at the head of which we could hear the next tour party assembling, I turned to see one of my group lingering. He was one of the Ukrainians, a man in his late thirties with a heavily bandaged thumb, his arm held in a cord sling around his neck. When he thought no one was watching, he quickly unhooked his sling and, kneeling on the carpet, pressed his injured hand to the spot where Rasputin had lain. Rising to his feet again, he saw me watching him and grinned sheepishly.

You never know, he said. There might be something in it.

Recalling this presented me with an idea. Rasputin would have approved of it and every charlatan who has ever sold pigs' bones claiming them to be the fingers of St Paul with which he held the pen when he wrote to the Ephesians, or squares of rotting canvas claiming them to be fragments of the sail of St Peter's fishing boat, will envy me this sublime opportunity.

Pyotr would fall off his chair at it.

For two orbits, I sat at the table and wrote out a short screed in English, checking my grammar and making sure I could pronounce it, drawing my facts from the book collection in the IFEAL. This done, I rehearsed it a few times, reading it aloud, timing my delivery and attempting to make my accent a little less Russian, cutting down on the stressing of my *W*s, taking care of my *A*s and suppressing the length of my *R*s.

Shifting over to the seat in front of the flight command controls, I waited until I was on the next track in the northern hemisphere, over the mid-Atlantic. Re-tuning the most powerful of the on-board VHF radios, I selected the most appropriate waveband I could think of.

On the hour, an announcer came on.

This is the World Service of the BBC.

There followed sixteen bars of *Lily Bolero*.

I waited, calm and composed.

The time is eighteen hundred hours, Greenwich Mean Time. Here is the news read by . . .

I pressed a switch. The signal was jammed. The microphone was on. I studied my sheet of paper, started the digital stopwatch on the flight control console and began.

Planet Earth, I read, *this is a message from your Creator whom you may call God, Jehovah, Allah, Krishna or any of a number of alternative names. Listen unto me for I speak the Truth unto you in your most universal language.*

I paused, giving time for the words to sink in and imagining the fury in London at such an infiltration turning to astonishment, then wonder and finally apprehension as the direction-finding equipment actually proved the signal came from space and not a maniac's transmitter somewhere in North America.

Your world, which I toiled six days to create only resting on the seventh, and you whom I fashioned out of the mud of the earth and the water of the seas, are doomed to destruction. This is not of my divine making, nor is it the work of that which you call Satan, Lucifer, Shaitan, Abaddon, Belial and Beelzebub, to mention but a few metaphors by which you name the cruelty in your hearts. It is of your own making for it is you who have created wars and famines, who have corrupted the soil, poisoned the waters and debased the air, annihilated more species than remain alive and invented weapons of mass self-destruction and ingenious death.

For is it not written in the Christian bible

Nation shall rise against nation, and kingdom against kingdom: and there shall be earthquakes in diverse places and there shall be famines and troubles: these are the beginnings of sorrow.

And does it not warn

The sun shall be darkened, and the moon shall not give her light, and the stars of heaven shall fall, and the powers that are in heaven shall be shaken.

In the Koran, which is of my teaching, is it not written

Would that you knew what the Disaster is! On that day, men shall become as scattered moths and mountains shall be as tufts of carded wool. Then shall he whose scales are heavy dwell in bliss: yet he whose scales are light shall dwell in the Abyss which shall be his home. Would that you knew what this is like! It is a scorching fire.

Take heed, Planet Earth! Your time comes, your fate is in your hands and none can help you, not even I, the Creator, the Grand Architect of the Universe, the One and Only One. Only you may save yourselves.

With that, I switched off. The digital clock read 00:02:22. I was certain there was insufficient time for them to get a positive identification or reliable fix.

I would wager, throughout the transistor radio-, television-owning world tonight, there will be a lot of men fucking and, come Sunday, a fair number of churches, mosques, synagogues and temples will be a sight more crowded and the mullahs, priests, vicars and rabbis a damn sight busier than usual.

❧

I have again made use of the IR2. Indeed, I have been at the controls throughout the daylight sectors of the last sixteen orbit tracks.

At first, it was curiosity that had me switch it on: I had found, going through the memory bank on the main in-flight computer, the co-ordinates Vladislav had been instructed to enter on +4, when we saw the silo. As I was at the time approaching the mid-west of America, I tapped the figures out and let the IR2 go to auto. Within a few minutes, *Mir* had entered the correct range and locked on. The monitor screen cleared and, as before, I saw the low, oblong building, the pair of bushes and the tree which was now casting a longer shadow over what was still sun-scorched but obviously taller grass. Where there had been the cars there now stood one small van. The flagpole, however, was missing which puzzled me.

Manipulating the camera angle shift control, I moved the image in the direction Vladislav had panned. The pathway came into view, the bushes growing at its side encroaching upon the concrete, the tree now much thicker with leaves. The trench and steps were surrounded, and even filled, with a thick tangle of barbed wire. A notice hung on a leaning pole, the writing red but indefinable. Beyond this was a circle of more barbed wire at least two metres thick surrounding the silo entrance: but this was open, the semi-circular plates of the doors missing, the silo now a dark, black hole in the ground looking for all the world like a derelict mine shaft. Of a missile there was no evidence whatsoever.

Freezing the image, I tinkered about with the contrast, trying to see into the hole. It was definitely empty. The camera lost its fix and the screen deteriorated to white static.

I took heart at this scene. As a semi-god, it amused me to see some sanity exercising itself.

After this, I thought to play a game. On the next sweep over the USA, I punched in random sets of co-ordinates and let the IR2 do what it would. There is an automatic focusing device built in to the equipment. Unless otherwise ordered, the camera focuses on the sharpest object it sees: in other words, if a rock and a bush come in view, it will focus on the rock, but if there is nothing sharp, or there are too many objects alike — say a valley of equal-sized rocks — it will zoom out until the rocks form a pattern of solidity which is recognized as a whole and used as a focusing point.

The first image to appear initially puzzled me. It was almost an abstract composed of unevenly smooth objects which, according to the scale read-out, were between two and four metres in diameter. I shifted the image. The focus was lost and searching again, zooming out. Suddenly, I was confronted with a view down into a deep chasm. At the base ran a river, tumbling over boulders with dark, dense trees growing on the banks. There was not a sign of any human habitation. I could have been peering into the primeval past.

Pushing myself to the window, I stared at the planet below me. Somewhere down there was the place I had in fine shot on the monitor.

I was orbiting over the Rocky Mountains. Wisps of cloud hung in streaks along some of the ranges but the rest of the panorama was bathed in direct sunlight. It was near noon so the shadows were short.

Returning to the monitor, I panned around, from the bottom of the canyon to the rim where, I now saw, the confusing objects were wind-blasted boulders. There was still nothing to signal the presence of humans and so it remained until the picture collapsed.

After such a sight of pristine Earth, I was loathe to view any areas of the eastern seaboard of the USA and, as there was little point in operating the IR2 over the Atlantic, and I was hungry, I did not flick the switch again until I had eaten, dozed through the nocturnal sections of several orbits and was passing over eastern Africa.

Using the map positioning programme in the computer to ensure I was not likely to feed in co-ordinates for a slum suburb of Nairobi or some such, I set up another viewing.

On this occasion, the camera had to pull back for nearly ten seconds before it found something upon which to gain a fix. I had chosen grassland and the IR2 was searching for an object. At last, it discovered what it required and moved in on it. I found myself staring at a large antelope. It was standing, statue-still, on what appeared to be a low mound of beaten earth surrounded by waving grass I estimated was a metre high. The animal's curved horns cut twin shadows across its shoulder and on to the earth — the sun was an hour past the meridian — but what entranced me was the colour of the beast's pelt. It was a dark russet brown but it bore a metallic sheen to it, so rich it might have been polished and cast of bronze.

Eager to see if there were others like it around, I altered the setting and zoomed back. There were no others near by but, some fifty metres off, there was a patch of thick scrub and I guessed the remainder of the herd were in the shade and what I had seen was the sentry on the lookout for lions with their claws extended and men with spears or worse.

I longed to know what the animal was, felt frustrated I had discovered it, as if I was the first man ever to set eyes on its species, and was in ignorance. I wanted to understand it, know what it ate, what its courtship rituals were, how long it lived, what habitat it preferred and what its name was.

As the transitory image vanished, I realized I should never know any of this and would never again be able to see this fabulous creature. By the time I was next over its territory, it would have moved.

It occurred to me whatever I saw through the IR2 I would remain in ignorance of forever for there would never be a chance for me to learn more. I would never have the opportunity of returning and visiting the mound of soil, stand on it, look up and think, once, I was far out there and saw a marvel.

For hours thereafter, I wandered over the Earth, looking down through my tiny, temporary electronic eye-hole in space. Often, I saw nothing of interest to me — a road with vehicles upon it, a farmstead, an isolated factory or just countryside. They contained nothing to capture my imagination.

Yet the last two views remain with me.

Out of perversity, I set the IR2 to scan the eastern quadrant of the Indian Ocean with focusing parameters requiring it to only lock on to objects greater than ten metres across. Had I not done this, the sensors would have been grabbing on to every wave head. In addition, I gave a wide range of co-ordinates in which to search, covering a strip of the ocean a mere few kilometres wide but about 750 kilometres long. For some minutes, nothing happened. The monitor remained distorted with static and the focusing lock light stayed off. I was about to give up and wait for the orbit to reach Thailand when the lock light illuminated and on to the screen appeared a tropical isle in what, by IR2 standards, was long shot. I could see the whole island and, using a vernier scale superimposed over the picture, assessed it was three kilometres long and 600 metres wide at the widest point.

It was paradisaical. In shape, the island resembled an elongated crescent, one end a little fatter than the other. The peripheral edges were lined with palm trees interspersed with areas of dense undergrowth whilst the centre of the island was patchily vegetated. The beaches were starkly white, the shallows a light aquamarine blue graduating to azure then the dark, rich blue of deep tropical seas. Across the concave side of the island, from one tip to the other in a slight curve, a coral reef ran just beneath the surface, breached in two places to give access to a lagoon.

I could see no human settlement and, with the focus short, was able to pan to and fro across the island. A flock of white birds took to flight from a sandy outcrop, their wings drifting like animated commas over the sea. Following them, I caught sight of a dark object in the lagoon. Although it was stationary, I wondered if it might be a huge shark basking in the safety of the still waters or a whale at rest.

Working the controls, I moved in on it.

The refraction of the water and gentle ripple on the surface kept the outline vague so I engaged the image analyser, in fact a software programme capable of studying a picture and reassessing it, erasing any distortions and imperfections to arrive at a conclusive, if still not sharp, reinterpretation of the subject matter.

It was neither a shark, nor a whale. Nor was it, as I

men were dancing, twirling and pirouetting, passing from one to the other.

My eyes followed them. This was no reckless, disorientated modern jive with thrusting hips and grotesquely exaggerated motions. These couples were dancing to a pattern of music centuries old. Every one of their actions fitted into a designed and graceful plan passed on from generation to generation on just such a day as this. Some of the onlookers clapped in time to the music the main instigator of which seemed to be a man with an accordion who had stepped to the front of the band to squeeze and pull his instrument, his body swaying in time, as if in sympathy, with the revellers before him.

The image faded and I was moved on through space.

With the monitor blank, I felt a terrible longing to hear the music they were playing, to join in the dancing with the prettiest girls in the village, to help myself to the banquet and lean against one of the trees to talk to the old men with glasses of wine in their hands.

Enough!

It was the first time I had spoken out loud to myself since the others descended to Earth and left me here. I was almost shocked to hear my own voice.

No more would I be tempted, teased, tantalized.

With a jerk of my index finger, I closed the IR2 down. It had served its purpose, had afforded me a select glance or two downwards as if on all my creations, given me a feeling of omnipotence, made me both proud and ashamed to know I come from that blue planet above which I now hover, like a god, watching over it.

The greatest disappointment is I cannot intervene: but

then gods never interfere. They remain aloof, remote and detached. Like admirers in an art gallery.

❦

Pyotr and Anna had gone to bed.

We had stayed up talking until about ten o'clock when Anna started to yawn capaciously. Pyotr tried to stifle her yawning at first with sharp looks, finally recoursing to sarcasm.

We're not keeping you up, are we? he muttered.

Yes, you are, she replied bluntly, and I'm going to bed.

Pyotr, determined not to be outdone, ironically continued, I trust we haven't bored you?

No, you haven't, Anna said sharply. I listen with interest to everything you two say even if I don't understand it all. Boredom is nothing to do with it. I'm tired.

We are all tired, Pyotr remonstrated. It's what comes of living in Russia. Tired of price rises, tired of crooks, tired of politicians which amounts to the same thing, tired of rooting about like pigs in the swill of history.

Nothing else? I enquired.

He glowered at me.

What do you mean?

I shrugged and said, I thought . . .

That, too! Tired of damn Ukrainians! he snapped.

Well, I'm just tired of Wednesday, Anna declared, and I'm off to my bed. You two boys can talk the snow off the roof in my absence.

Pyotr waved his hand dismissively at her but, within five minutes, he was gone, too. I could hear them shifting about as they got comfortable under the blankets over my head. The last noise I heard before I opened the door was the commencement of Pyotr's snoring and Anna's drowsy complaint.

Outside, the air temperature was in the minus twenties, my breath smoking and disseminating in the still air. There was a low moon rising over the firs, the whole world black with shadow and grey with moonlit snow. Under the woodpile at the end of the porch, Bujan was curled up tight, three sides of his sleeping quarters made from compacted snow upon which had formed a glazing of ice where his body heat, in the early weeks of winter, had melted the surface. Like his master, he was snoring.

The air was utterly still and silent, bar Bujan's soft and intermittent wheezing. It was as if the snow had not only pressed the ground flat but had suborned all sound.

Huddling my collar around my neck and pulling down the ear flaps on my hat, I was about to set off along the path when I spied a shadow stirring on the edge of the forest. With reflexes born of seeing action, I squatted down, lowering myself slowly so as not to be conspicuous by a quick movement, breaking up my silhouette. My position was in the open but this was immaterial. In the false light of a midwinter's moon I would look as much like a pile of wood as a hunched man.

The shadow stopped for a moment then started again, a blackness moving against the blacker backdrop of the trees. It reached a point where the stand of firs cut it from my view. Taking advantage of this, I rose slightly and ran at a half-crouch towards the firs, halting at a snow-covered compost heap thrown up by a neighbour on the edge of Anikushin's plot. Squatting down again, using the heap for cover, I waited.

Not a fortnight before, gangsters had attacked the village of Vokhtoga about fifty kilometres away. They had come in the night, surrounded the houses and systematically robbed the inhabitants of their money, jewellery and watches, television sets, cars and, curiously, an electric cooker. Their intention was to take the spoils of their raid to Moscow or St Petersburg to sell in the street flea markets.

I regretted not carrying a side-arm. Had I still been on active service and not a cosmonaut, I would have been in possession of my service issue PSM: it might have been a low-powered weapon but it was reliable over short distances and I was accurate with it. The muzzle flash would have given me away in such a monochromatic landscape but the first shot would be all that was needed to rouse the village. Every man who had one slept with his gun by the bed.

It was at least a minute before the mobile shadow appeared again. To my horror, it was no longer on the forest edge but by the firs, not thirty metres from my hiding place. It came round the rim of the trees and halted. I heard a snuffling sound, like a man with a bad cold wiping his nose with a sodden handkerchief.

The shadow was a bear. It came into view, the moonlight catching its light brown snout, the damp bulb of its black nose and, momentarily, its keen eyes.

It was, I guessed from its size, a male. His long, coarse

coat was spattered with snow where he had brushed against low branches, dislodging a fine white powder. Moving on all fours, he set off again, keeping to the periphery of the firs, his massive shoulders swaying at each measured step.

Hoping he would pass on by, I kept quite still. Suddenly, he stopped again and rose on to his hind legs. At about two metres in height, he was a daunting sight. He sniffed the air again but not with a snuffle. This was a more concerted, attentive sniff, a gentle drawing in of the air in three or four little gasps. I wondered if he was on to my scent or that of Bujan. He could take the dog if he plucked up enough courage to approach the building and was quick in demolishing the woodpile. Yet I knew Bujan was safe. He was no fool and, besides, at the first log tumbling off the stack, Pyotr would be out of bed and into his fur coat and boots, heading down the stairs and grabbing his antiquated gun as he went. As soon as the door opened, the bear would be off, Pyotr aiming at his rump.

Lowering himself to all fours again, the bear set off through the snow, his every step kicking up a little plume of dry flakes. He passed along the far side of Anikushin's wild plot, paused then started up the side of widow Kuteeva's parcel of land. In the centre of it, the bear halted once more and, after shoving his snout into the snow, commenced digging, his breath coming in bouts of exertion as he clawed at the frozen soil.

I shifted my position so I might get a better view of him, but still kept myself behind the compost pile. If the worst came to the worst, I was doomed. I could not out-run a bear over a football field never mind snow-covered farmland. Nor could I, I now realized, retreat, for to do so would be to step into full view of the creature. Until his business was over, I was in essence pinned down.

For five minutes, I watched as the bear tore at the hard earth, flicking the spoil out to his side, grunting with the effort.

Something lightly touched me on the shoulder. I went to let out a squeak of terror but it was suffocated instantly by a hand over my mouth.

Pyotr put two fingers to his lips and let me go. He was fully dressed in his fur coat and hat, his gun in his hand.

We watched the bear for a few minutes.

What's he digging for? I mouthed at Pyotr.

He put his lips close to my ear.

He's digging for potatoes.

Widow Kuteeva had harvested her field but, no doubt, she had missed some: her eyesight had been failing for several years but she refused to wear spectacles except to read. What she had overlooked, the bear was after.

Pyotr signalled to me by pointing upwards. Very gradually, we stood up until we were erect behind the compost heap. The bear seemed not to have seen us, so intent was he on his foraging in the snow.

Signalling once more, Pyotr and I stepped very slowly out of our cover and moved forwards towards the bear. I stepped cautiously, not wanting to take my eyes from him. Pyotr had his gun ready to throw to his shoulder, his thumb on the safety catch. I heard it click.

Step by step, we drew closer to the bear until not ten metres divided us from him. He paid us little heed although it was obvious now he had knowledge of our presence.

Twice, he left off his digging to look straight at us and I was certain he recognized us for what we were, his only natural enemies, yet he chose to ignore us.

Close up, we could see he was not in his prime. His coat looked out of condition and one of his ears was torn and matted with blood. I was reminded of the black and white dog with the ripped ear.

At last, he found a potato, sat back on his haunches and chewed on it, his lips drawn back in a semi-grimace. Perhaps it was not only frozen but half rotten. He ate slowly, as if he was exhausted not with his digging but with the whole winter, the whole burden of being an old Russian bear in a harsh world.

He's very hungry, Pyotr said quietly.

The bear stopped his chewing as if listening to the words. When Pyotr fell silent, he chewed again.

He's been driven from hibernation by hunger, Pyotr went on. There was not enough for him in the summer. To build up his fat.

This time, the bear did not stop chewing. Instead, he desultorily pawed the earth in the expectation of finding another potato. There was none.

Are you going to shoot him? I asked, not bothering to keep my voice down but not raising it so far as to alarm or antagonize the bear.

Why? If he dies, he dies. I'll not kill him. Let nature have him. He's seen enough anguish in his ursine life. Like all of us, he added.

Just then, the bear rose on all fours and, at his steady pace, turned and moved away, between us and the firs, making off in the direction of the village dump.

He'll be lucky, Pyotr commented, slipping the safety catch on. They burned all the garbage last Thursday.

I thought he was a gangster, I admitted as we returned to Pyotr's place.

In a way, isn't he? Pyotr said. Aren't we all when the going gets rough?

Bujan dragged himself out from under the woodpile, his head hung low from cold.

The brave hunter! Pyotr said. Look at him. I should shoot Bujan, not the bear.

At the sound of its name, the dog half-heartedly wagged its tail.

All right, you flea-ridden cur! Pyotr muttered, opening the door, in you come. Turning to me he added, You coming in? A hot glass of tea? I can't sleep. It's Anna's snoring. Like being in bed with an owl.

I declined his invitation and set off through the village towards the cabin I rented periodically from Zoya Kuteeva, the moon's grey shadows still over everything, my boots crunching on the fresh, hard snow.

Thinking back now, I realize how much like Russia the bear was, getting along as best he could against the odds, picking up the scraps and pretending it was a banquet fit for a tsar or a commissar. Digging in the snow, he was waiting with an infinite patience for a summer he felt had to come one day. Inured to winter, he fed not only on the occasional potato and garbage yet to be thrown into the incinerator but also on his dream of the good times to return when the bushes would be laden with berries, the forest clearings alert with small rodents and the rivers silvered by spawning trout and running salmon.

Just as Russians put about themselves coats and *oushankas* of bear-skin so do Russian bears bedeck themselves in the optimism of humans.

❧

+261:01:21:45.

I was woken by a loud thump and the raucous grating klaxon of a Major Damage Event alarm. Ripping open the sleeping restraints, I thrust myself up towards the nearest window in time to see the outer half of one of the solar panels drifting off on the right beam.

Closing down the alarm, I quickly went through the MDE procedure, shutting off compromised circuits, checking the computer had gone through its damage limitation programme, assessing the situation.

It was not good. Apart from directly losing about fifteen per cent of my solar cell surface, the sheared solar panel seemed to have affected other aspects of the craft's power recharging capability. Running a check scan over the system, two of the three remaining units was operating under par. It would not be long before the batteries were seriously low, jeopardizing the functioning of the whole spacecraft.

There was nothing for it. If a repair was to be effected, I would have to go on EVA — Extra-Vehicular Activity — assess the damage and fix it, if I could.

One of the most basic rules of scuba-diving and walking in space is this: never do it alone.

I had no choice.

The EVAMU — the EVA Mobility Unit — is more than just a spacesuit such as a diver might wear. It comprises the outer primary pressure garment (PPG), the secondary inner cooling garment (SICG), the pressure helmet unit (PHU) with attached anti-radiation visor (ARV), the pressure gloves and boots (PG and PB) and the cosmonaut life support system (CLSS). The PPG provides an oxygen environment, ventilation and pressurisation, and carries an internal EVAMU/*Mir* communications link. The SICG resembles a pair of long johns criss-crossed with fine water-bearing pipes attached to a circulating pump and automatically controlled heater/cooler unit. More than just a helmet, the PHU is a detachable, spherical transparent orb to which is attached the ARV affording not only radiation and solar glare but also thermal and micro-meteoroidal protection, as do the gloves which reach up to the elbow and the boots which encase the ankles. Finally the CLSS, the control panel for which is worn on a belt round the waist, governs the oxygen and coolant flows. As well as providing connections for power and communications cabling, the belt bears an attachment for the Umbilical Safety and Retention Line (USRL) connecting the PPG harness with self-locking anchor links on the outer casing of the spacecraft. The USRL is twenty metres long and marked in two-metre lengths: it not only acts as an anchor chain but carries all the pipes and such like to the CLSS.

Donning all this equipment is time consuming and requires many checks along the way. I worked at it as quickly as possible, stripping off all my clothing to pull on the slightly elasticated SICG. Normally, a complete kitting out takes upwards of forty-five minutes: I managed it in twenty.

Checking the status of the Environmental Control System (ECS), I entered the airlock and, with difficulty, succeeded in turning round and closing the circular inner door. The EVAMU does not allow for very flexible body movements in the long axis and, in usual circumstances, a second crew member would fill the role of doorman. Once the seal check light illuminated, I evacuated the airlock, waited for the pressure/vacuum lights to show me I was in condition blue and operated the release mechanism on the EVA hatch. It swung slowly open and I gazed out as if from my front door on to southern Africa.

The coastal skies were clear and I could see quite distinctly the Atlantic and southern shores of Cape Province. Table Mountain was visible inland from the sprawl of Capetown with the little hook of hills which runs down to the Cape of Good Hope. It seemed an auspicious omen.

Attaching the USRL retaining clip to the anchor link by the door, and ensuring the connections were firm, I let myself drift out of the hatch.

An immense sense of freedom overwhelmed me. After more than two hundred and sixty days cooped up in my interplanetary hutch, I was elated to be able to move without being hemmed in by walls and bulkheads, lockers and control panels, computers and technological wonders. Of course, I was still tethered like a dog chained to its kennel but at least I had the run of my line.

Drifting to the fullest extent of the USRL, I turned my back on *Mir* and looked down beneath my feet. The Drakensberg range slipped gradually by between my toes, the farmlands of the Transvaal coming up on my left ankle.

I remained at the end of my line for another ten minutes as the lush greenery of South Africa gave way to the parched grasslands and scrub of Zimbabwe and western Mozambique. Not until I was overhead Harare did I work my way round and retrace my spatial steps towards *Mir IV*.

The damage was extensive. Not only was half one solar panel missing but, in breaking off, it had knocked the one next to it awry, smashing many of the solar cells and buckling the mounting beyond repair. Worse, the telemetry and command antennae were snapped from their bases, the cowling around the Sun Acquisition Sensor Assembly (SASA) was dented and the support for the third solar wing was bent. In other words, only one cell array was unaffected.

Even were I sufficiently competent to carry out repairs, I dared do nothing. Here and there, bare wires stuck out through gaps where there had been solar cells. There were no live cables sparking — everything had been shut down by the damage limitation programme — but there were angles of sharp metal projecting into space of which I had to be very cautious. One snag on a jag-toothed bracket and the PPG would be ruptured. My body would then instantaneously explode.

Accepting there was nothing I was able to do to rectify the situation, I allotted myself two tasks. First, I wanted to find out, if I could, what had caused the catastrophe and, second, I needed to reassure myself there was no other damage.

I let myself move over the entire surface of *Mir*, shifting from place to place by using the hand-holds provided, keeping an eye all the while on the USRL, ensuring it did not catch on anything or become tangled in the mess of snapped spars and bars. As the track of the orbit took me over the night side of Earth, I switched on the EVA spotlamps mounted either side of the collar of my PHU and raised the ARV. To my relief, there seemed to be no other damage and the pressure hull was neither breached nor dented.

Discovering the cause of the impact was not such a simple task. I studied the region of the solar wings in close detail, panning my eyes up and down over an imaginary grid, watching for anything which looked out of the ordinary. *Mir* entered daylight once more and I closed down the ARV again, extinguishing the spotlamps. It was not until I was well over India on the second orbit I found what I was looking for. Wedged under the frame of one of the Battery Charging Regulation Units was a length of metal, shinier than any other in the immediate vicinity. At one end it was sheered off whilst, at the other, there was a round bolt attachment.

With considerable regard for the surrounding damage, I edged myself in to grab hold of it. It was jammed firmly in place and I could not shift it but I was quite certain it was not a part of *Mir*. Moving forward again, getting in closer, I noticed some kind of what I took to be hieroglyphic writing on it. With the visor of my PHU close to it, I tried to work it out, running the finger of my glove over it in the hope that physical contact might aid my deliberation.

ՍՍ ＧＥＭＩＮＩ ＤＤ０

Yet it made no sense. Swivelling myself round, I tried to read it from another angle but was still baffled until it occurred to me I was looking at only half the message: there was a scorch mark running along from the break.

After some minutes of puzzling, I suddenly figured it out. It spelt out *US GEMINI PRO*. I had been hit by a piece of space garbage, a fragment of an old NASA spacecraft.

Once back inside *Mir*, I sat at the food table and calmly assessed my situation. It was quite obviously terminal. The surviving solar panel would only provide me with twenty-five per cent of the power I required to charge all the batteries. This might be sufficient to maintain the ACS and other essential life-support requirements but little else. I would have to cut down on internal lighting, close down all but the most essential computer systems and avoid heating water and the like. Although the SASA was still operative — had it not been, the spacecraft would not have adjusted its angle at the last orbit and I should have been baked alive by now — I was living by the skin of my teeth, flying, as Vasya would have said, by the seat of my pants, an American expression for which he had a fondness after hearing it in a movie.

Certainly, I should no longer be able to operate the IR2 or any of the other equipment which would drain the batteries.

It is only a matter of time now before the end. I know that.

Yet this has always been the case. We have an allotment of years, or months, or days in which to sing or cry and, when the quota is expended, that's it. I need not be a cosmonaut to face such a reality: every man who has ever lived has worn these shoes of mortality.

❧

+286:14:56:00.

With so much of the power closed down, *Mir IV* is running almost silently. There is hardly a vestige left of the hum to which I had grown so accustomed I no longer heard it. I keep only one light switched on during the nocturnal portion of each orbit and switch it off when I enter daylight. This means, of course, my biological clock has adapted over the last three weeks to letting me sleep for about forty minutes then wake for the same length of time.

During the short nights, the temperature drops to near or just below zero and I have to bundle myself up in my sleeping restraint which I have adapted by sewing round it a few layers of my clothing plus the three blankets from the unused restraints. In contrast, and because I am using less power in the cooling system pumps, during the short days the spacecraft heats up to a cabin temperature approaching 40°C. To keep comfortable, I remove all my clothes and drift about, checking systems and watching for malfunctions, bollock-naked.

The atmosphere is getting stale. I dare only run the filtration system once every three orbits, having switched it to manual. Towards the end of the third orbit, I find it hard to breathe and am obliged to slow my body activity down considerably so as to conserve air. This is not easy for although the CMGs are working in more or less accord with the Sun Acquisition Sensor, the Fine Sun Sensor, the

Rate Gyro Processors and the Star Track Sensor, there are occasional glitches when I have to take over to revolve *Mir* myself. The stress of paying attention to the controls speeds up my heart-rate and, therefore, my respiration.

Other malfunctions do not help. The ACMS filter has become clogged again with another fuliginous sludge of damp dust, no doubt contributing to the taste of the air, and the iodine pills have run out so I can no longer fight any microbial build-up in the water. An increasing number of screws, nuts, bolts and washers seem to be appearing, floating in the cabin to greet me when I wake.

Worst of all is the failure of the power supply to the waste management airlock. Presumably, the section of solar panel which broke off has somehow affected the wiring circuits or snapped a connection between the existing panel and the batteries controlling the airlock mechanism. Whatever is the case, I cannot open the airlock to void into space the garbage created by my being alive.

As an alternative, I have tried putting the bags of trash in the main airlock and voiding it but the bags do not exit the spacecraft: the external EVA door is too small. All they do is lose their water content and become somewhat shrivelled. Consequently, I create as little rubbish as I can and store it as hygienically as possible. To this end, I am gradually filling up all the spare crew lockers with bundles of refuse. At least I can be thankful the system which removes my body wastes has yet to malfunction and does successfully dump my shit out into space.

The circumstance in which I find myself is, I have to admit, ironically amusing in a twisted sort of a way. Here am I, in the vast sterility of pristine space travelling along in a filth-bucket which is, in so many respects, a microcosm of the planet below. It does not escape me that, were it not for me, *Mir* would be a spotlessly clean technological marvel. Yet, as in so many instances, the presence of a man ruins it all.

Just an hour ago, I found the spider dead. It was in its surgical equipment box, drifting in the middle by the transparent lid, its eight legs curled up like the wizened hand of a crone. As I unzipped the lid to remove it, I recalled Anna's words.

If you wish to smile and thrive, leave the spider running live.

Yet I had nothing to worry about. I had not killed it. At least, not directly. It had died as a result of my manipulation of the world, of the artifice of my kind, but I had not personally been the agent of its demise.

Watching its little corpse hang in the centre of the cabin, I felt a pang of loneliness and sadness. Now, bar microbes, I was alone and just as inadequate as the spider. It was unable to weave a competent web and I am incapable of repairing my own habitation.

Both of us are fate's eunuchs.

My present situation cannot be sustained much longer and, assessing how things stand with a logical coolness I have, as I see it, three options.

The first is to simply ignore the machinery around me. Without my intervention, it would not be long before the air became so stale and devoid of oxygen I would pass into unconsciousness, never to wake.

My second alternative is to stop the main computer, the only one I have left in operation, from maintaining my orbital altitude. Without the regular trimburn, the orbit will progressively decay as the minute amount of atmosphere outside slows me down by friction and the gravitational pull of the planet below exerts a stronger influence. After a time, not in excess of forty-four days according to my calculations, *Mir* would start to enter the upper atmosphere, slow further, start to spin and quickly heat up. Within an orbit or two, the whole spacecraft would burn up.

Finally, I have the option of gaining some kind of immortality for, if I allow the orbit to deteriorate but, by using the trimburn thrusters, liquid fuel booster system and main rocket engine maintain a gentle angle of attack on Earth's atmosphere, I may be able to use it to bounce off into space. The momentum of my orbit plus any fuel I may have remaining after the manoeuvre will give me sufficient velocity to escape the gravitation field.

Considering each choice, I disregard the first as passive and weak, a surrender of sorts.

Where the second is concerned, I would return to Earth in a glory of fire. Men watching the skies would see my death as a meteor cutting its brief infernal signature across their heavens. This is the way a god might die, in a blaze of cosmic flame.

Who am I fooling? I am no god. Gods are creatures of governance and I am in control of nothing. *Mir* gradually edges towards what the Baikonur boys call terminal redundancy whilst I head towards what another bit of official terminology refers to, quite coolly, as a non-viable life sustenance situation. Over both of these I hold absolutely no sway: Newton's invincible cannon-ball is dipping and Kelvin's law is coming home to roost.

Furthermore, I have faced my own reality and am no longer deluded by grandeur. I am not, nor have I ever been, any of those people I imagined: no one's lived in this box of bones and blood save me. No one has been trundled off in a cattle truck to a lung full of Zyklon B on my account, no babies served up on a platter, no firing squads called to attention: true, I have helped a few of my fellow creatures along the highway to Hades but then, I ask you, in one way or another, has not every man alive?

Within each of us there dwells a Napoleon, a Raskolnikov, a Tsiolkovsky, harsh facets of ourselves with grandiose ambitions, inhumanity, cruelty and touches of genius all waiting for the right moment to manifest themselves. There is not one of us, of you, who cannot say they have never wanted to govern the dolts and buffoons who govern us, to kill the old Trotskyite down the lane whose scrofulous dog keeps crapping on the doorstep or, lying in a hotel bath in Kiev, to have devised a plug which will never let the water overflow or a light bulb to last a hundred years. Every man lives in every one of us and we are nothing more than ants in a vast colony, each burdened with the other, interconnected by our truculent genes.

What is more, gods are dispassionate whereas, contrary to my previous behaviour and statements, I am not. I cannot divorce myself from what I am, cannot accept the responsibility I may have of guiding my own kind, like some sort of space age Moses, towards new goals in the firmament. It is beyond me, beyond my morality, to toy with them as a god may do. All those thoughts of being divine, of being what I am not and could never be, have deserted me for the void of all egos. In their place is the plain truth. I am a mere man, hamstrung by circumstance, my end hastened not by a speeding train or a creeping disease but by a lump of trash I have left, by proxy, circling the planet of my birth.

For the remainder of time, so long as I shall exist in flesh or spirit, I shall always be a Russian, Pyotr's loyal friend, holder of a passport with the old Party badge embossed upon it with those four Sisyphean letters — CCCP: I shall stay fond of good vodka, pliant and stoical in the face of breviloquent officialdom, stubborn and ticklish as the man with gold epaulettes and white gloves on feels up my inside leg with his inquisitive hands to see what I might be smuggling through the customs post.

Perhaps it is time to pray. *Babushka* would say so.

Get down on your knees, Misha, I can hear her calling from somewhere in the night lingering at the back of my mind. It's only a way of calling for help, Misha. Keep it up and God will hear you.

And so he may, but he will not help me. Not now.

At the final count, I have to accept I am frail and stupid, a confidence trickster of the first order who has perpetrated the ultimate sting on myself. I fell for all the bullshit of my own arrogance and that of my species. Now the time has come to pay the price.

Or perhaps not.

For the last alternative is the one I shall go for. It will not be easy. I will have to evaluate the mathematical aspects very carefully for even the slightest error in my computations will spell disaster.

Yet what an opportunity I will have presented to me

if I succeed! I shall travel on forever through space, an ambassador for my own kind, albeit a dead one.

Should I be discovered by some other living entity, perhaps they will gain knowledge from me. I would hope so. I would hope they have the technology to tap into my dead brain and see what an arrogant, ignorant, good-for-nothing, blind fool I was and from that assume all my fellow beings are alike to me, for such is the truth. They would then be able to avoid making the same mistakes on their world.

I accept the chance of my cadaver meeting with such a fate is thin in the extreme. I am more likely to burn up on entering another atmosphere or crash on to the surface of some rocky knoll in space where all the lessons I carry in my head will go to waste and I will either disintegrate into dust or become a rather delectable gourmet meal for small life entities as yet to organize a basic language of grunts never mind a brain-scanning interpretation machine.

What an irony that would be! The waster of one world wasted on another.

Now it is time for me to start my appraisal of numbers. I have some hours of complex mathematics ahead of me. It will be a race against time. I have only enough fuel left for one attempt at the bounce and every minute I am edging a metre or two towards the point of action. Miss it and there is no alternative: I burn up like a spark arcing out of Pyotr's charcoal fire on the ice of a winter lake.

Then, Shura, I shall assuredly be sailing without a sextant in your ocean of mercy.

I regret I shall never again see the firs.

When next they run with liquid gold, if things don't go well and my mathematics is flawed, I may well join them, a speck of dusk kicked up by Anikushin's hoe as he prepares the ground for his harvest of weeds or Minarsky's plough turning over the shining sods. Perhaps I shall be their very gold, the glow of the sun cutting through the dusty air of a harvest-tide evening, daubing the trunks as Pyotr downs another vodka in the encroaching twilight and possibly thinks of me as Bujan twitches in a dream of catching wild piglets in the forest.

If, on the other hand, my calculations are accurate, I shall instead be an anonymous star to which the pinnacles of the firs will point until Pyotr finally stretches his legs, puts down his borrowed third of a book, gets out of his chair, takes up his axe and, in the warm light of a summer day, fells them one by one.

And maybe — just maybe — they will bestow me with a name.